Things That Go Bump Into Each Other

Kylie Casino

Kylie Casino

ISBN-13: 979-8-9930432-0-3

Cover design by: Kimberley Ayers
Editing by: Lauren Reybould
Library of Congress Control Number: 2018675309
Printed in the United States of America

To all the introverts who are searching for a himbo of their own.

Chapter 1

Slate-blue shingles topped a rainbow-arched roof as Sephie Blake trekked down the road. Normally, she'd have driven the three minutes to her next job, but her therapist insisted she needed more fresh air. And since good ole Dr. Alias had a pesky habit of always being right (though she'd never admit it), Sephie begrudgingly decided to walk. It saved gas money anyway.

Grey clouds loitered across the sky, refusing to do anything useful.

Rain or shine, just pick one, already.

As if trying to make amends for their indecisive nature, a single shaft of sunlight broke through, spotlighting the mansion ahead. It was dramatic, yet effective. It was a stunning building. Brick and stone laid with meticulous care, regal and quietly imposing. The kind of house that looked like it had been plucked from the 18th century and dropped into the middle of modern-day Maryland. No renovations or modern touches—it had stood unchanged and empty for decades.

Until today.

Sephie kept working in paranormal research for as long as she had, not because she believed in ghosts (she didn't), but because she loved architecture. Houses with creepy sounds and plasma leaking from the walls tended to have character. Sephie loved exploring old buildings almost as much as helping the historical preservation specialists she had to call in. Yes, the landlords could be a pain to deal with, but usually, her job was enjoyable.

She jumped as an all-too-familiar '80s theme blasted from her pocket. Sighing, she pulled out her phone, which was the culprit of the offending music, and frowned at the caller ID. "Would you quit changing my ringtone to *Ghostbusters*?" she grumbled. The familiar, annoying giggle on the other end confirmed who was responsible.

"Oh, come on, it's funny!" her younger sister, Thalia, insisted.

"It really isn't. I need to change my PIN. Now, what do you want? I'm about to go into work."

"So it *is* true?"

"Is what true?"

"You're working with *Dead Serious*?"

Dammit, who let it slip?

"They haven't made me sign an NDA or anything. So, yeah."

The giggle turned into a full-blown cackle.

"What's got you so tickled?"

"You hate that show! All you do is criticize the Ghostie Boys when I watch it. Why are you working with them? And why didn't you bring me?!"

She held her phone away from her ear as Thalia's voice became shrill. That was exactly why she hadn't brought her.

"Because you don't give a crap about the paranormal?"

"Do too!"

"The Ghostie Boys' abs are not paranormal."

Thalia grumbled on the other end. "I never get to have any fun."

"My job isn't fun, Thalia. Most of the time, I'm dealing with structural problems. You know what a nightmare zoning laws are?"

"But you're gonna be on TV!" Thalia squealed. "Oh my god, what if they give you your own show?"

"I would shut that down immediately," Sephie grumbled. "You sound like Gran."

Thalia fell silent. Their grandmother always wanted the best for both her granddaughters, but there was no doubt Sephie was the favorite. Before she passed, she was always pushing Sephie out of her comfort zone, often recruiting the far more extroverted Thalia to drag her to clubs. Sephie didn't care about being seen. Being invisible was usually easier. Her sister's voice reappeared, breaking the awkward silence with a gentler tone.

"I'm sure Gran would be thrilled for you."

Sephie huffed. "She'd be more thrilled if it were a dating show." She could just picture Gran trying to set her up with some dearly departed duke. Granted, she probably had a better chance with a ghost than a living person, seeing that ghosts weren't real.

"… Are you okay to go back to work?"

"The paycheck covers my rent for the rest of the year, that's literally the only reason I accepted."

"WHAT?!"

"Mother of God, Thalia, take it down a notch!"

"Sorry. But Seph, you can't quit after this! Spooky people make bank, why leave it?"

"I told you, it's not all fun. Paying my bills is the only reason I got into this, I can just get a normal people job to do that."

"You are insane. Maybe I should get into ghost hunting."

Sephie pictured her perfectly manicured sister trembling through a decrepit house, flashlight flickering like a rave strobe, and couldn't help but laugh.

"And what's so funny?"

"Nothing. Now, did you have anything of substance to tell me, or did you just want to confirm my next job?"

"I hate you. Please get an autograph from Jace for me."

"I will not." With that, she hung up.

Jace Eter was the douchebag of a host for *Dead Serious*. How the former frat bro had landed a TV deal, she'd never understood. And how the show ended up being a huge hit was even more baffling. Probably just dumb luck. The first season aired right when true crime and all things spooky became popular. Mixing Jace and three other conventionally attractive men with ghost hunting did it for the creepy girlies.

Sephie was not a creepy girly.

Dead Serious was complete crap, but nobody cared. Jace and his team were given unbelievable opportunities to explore gorgeous historic buildings, and they spent most of their time yelling at flickering lights and getting "possessed." They had been to at least three of her dream locations and it pissed her off every time.

Her initial response was a resounding "hell no" when Jessica Hills, Jace's agent, reached out about appearing on the show. But the woman was relentless. First, she had tripled the initial offer. Then she insisted Sephie would have minimal contact with the *Dead Serious* crew. It wasn't until Jessica revealed that *Dead Serious* would be exploring Ashland Manor that Sephie had finally caved.

The manor had been a local legend for as long as Sephie could remember. Little was known of the family who last owned the manor; any trace of the Ashland family had disappeared. Closed off from public access, the house simply stood, just begging to be explored. The hope of one day getting inside was the only thing that ever kept Sephie in her Maryland hometown. It was the kind of bucket list location she never thought she'd check off, especially with the city constantly insisting it would stay sealed.

How *Dead Serious* had scored access, she didn't know. But she knew this would be her only chance to explore it. She could handle Jace, useless ghost equipment, and a camera crew following her, as long as she could get in that house.

Walking up the long, winding cobblestone path to Ashland Manor, Sephie spotted a cop car next to the building, and scowled at the officers. They were always screwing things up and touching antique objects they shouldn't. Sephie didn't have the best opinion of them. Something was off with the manor, but nobody knew exactly what it was. As far as she knew, not a single human had set foot on the property in decades. And there was no documentation of the place; no articles, no records, and nothing accessible to the public. Just whispers, rumors, and a lot of security.

A cop held up a hand as she approached.

"Sorry, Miss. Only those with clearance are allowed past this point."

She rolled her eyes and flipped the ID badge hanging on her lanyard—a glow-in-the-dark, ghost-shaped pass she'd kept hidden under her sweatshirt. The cop nodded and pointed her toward the massive front porch.

"Hey," he called after her. "Be careful."

"No offense, officer, but I've been doing this a while."

Her foot plunged through the first step. Rotten wood splintered under her, swallowing her ankle whole. She could definitely hear the cop hold back a chuckle.

Great. Just great. Welcome back to the workforce.

Chapter 2

"Ah, Ms. Blake! Glad you got here!"

Sephie gave a quick once-over of the woman she assumed was Jessica. She looked exactly as her voice conveyed over the phone: tall, tan, with shiny brown hair swept up into a tight ponytail. Sephie figured she'd be leaving as soon as she finalized all business matters, and was wearing a stark white power suit. She offered her hand, smiling with teeth so bright, Sephie swore she heard a ding.

"I already have your contract and media release signed, I just wanted to greet you in person. Daniel will handle everything else from here."

She gestured to a man in a ball cap, who Sephie learned was the showrunner beforehand. He offered a limp wave. Not exactly enthusiastic, which was a shame; Sephie would have killed for a position like his. She would fully appreciate the job and could use her position to make things right and prove ghost hunting was a farce, and show how actual knowledge could solve paranormal "problems".
Funny how reality TV wasn't real in the slightest.

She'd only made it into the foyer of the mansion and was already left speechless. Given nobody had been in the building for Lord knows how long, it was in incredible shape. Well, aside from the porch trying to eat her, but that was expected given the torrential Maryland rain.

The entryway was a large, open area with a beautiful chandelier, its crystals glittering off the marble flooring. A few steps away from it stood a grand staircase; Sephie had to resist the urge to run up it.

Everything was structurally sound, frozen in time. The lack of human contact had left the hallway fairly pristine. A thick layer of dust covered everything in sight, and there was obviously no working electricity, but nothing seemed on the verge of collapsing or falling apart. A few of the grand windows had been thrown open to let in some natural light, which she wasn't too happy about. Exposing potentially fragile furniture or infrastructure to the elements wasn't a good idea.

She turned to Daniel. "Hey, the windows shouldn't be open."

He ignored her, completely absorbed in his phone.

Yeah, no. That wouldn't do.

She marched over and ripped it from his hands.

"What the hell?" he gasped.

She scowled. "You're the showrunner, so I assume you've worked with historical experts before?"

He just blinked at her. That was a no.

"Close the windows. Any sudden environmental shock can cause serious damage."

"It's not a big deal. We try to avoid filming lights because they take up too much space."

Her hands clenched into fists. This guy didn't care about his job, meaning he didn't care about Ashland Manor.

"Close them. I'm sure your budget can cover flashlights and a decent night camera."

"What? Nobody wants to watch that."

"Jessica?" Sephie called over her shoulder. "Isn't there a clause in my contract about taking preservation concerns seriously?"

"One sec," Jessica covered her phone. "That's correct," she confirmed. "Daniel, we went over this already, close the damn windows. Polls show night vision gets good engagement, anyway."

Daniel snatched his phone back from Sephie. "Fine. But why the hell is this chick even here?"

"She's the expert, now do your job and listen to her. Besides, you're the one who wanted to attract more male viewers. Cute chicks help." She went back to her phone conversation, muttering about ghost goo cleanup.

Sephie tensed; she was not going to be the "hot ghostie girl." No way, no how.

Daniel stomped off, mumbling something about women and witches. Probably bitches. She didn't give him the satisfaction of a reaction.

"Now," Jessica chirped, "I know I said you'd have minimal contact with the boys, but I do have to introduce you. Want to get that over with?"

"Must I?" Sephie sighed, even though she knew the answer.

Jessica smirked. "They're not that bad. And you're gonna have to work with them eventually."

"Not that bad means they're at least a little awful."

"But they make good TV. Come on, they should be in hair and makeup by now." Her eyebrows shot up. "Makeup?!"

"Don't be shocked. Everyone wants to look their best on camera. They'll probably powder you a little, you've got a bit of a shine on your forehead."

Jessica motioned to Sephie to come with her as she headed outside. Sephie grumbled but still followed. They walked around the mansion to the gardens, the latter being one element of the manor officials hadn't been able to hide from the public; the flowers and greenery still flourished, even without any care. They walked through a glorious arch of wisteria to a tent set up next to a large water fountain. At least they had the decency not to park a trailer back there.

Inside, Jace was being pampered in the makeup artist's chair. His eyes were closed as the artist applied eyeliner. A pretty blonde massaged his neck from behind. Jessica cleared her throat, loudly.

"Jace, I told you, no more girls on set without permission."

The blonde pouted. "I'm his… massage therapist?"

Jessica grabbed her firmly by the shoulder and hauled her out, glaring at Jace. He didn't seem to care. Everyone knew that although he had a long-term girlfriend, he'd still have a new model on his arm every month. Either the girlfriend was oblivious, or totally fine with it. Paparazzi loved the drama.

"Hey, pretty boy, I told you to quit with the eyeliner. Gerard Way, you are not."

Jace raised a perfectly groomed eyebrow. "It makes my eyes pop."

"That Cali girl who told you that was a liar." She glanced at the makeup artist. "Take it off."

The artist muttered under her breath as she reached for remover. Clearly it wasn't the first time she'd had this argument with him.

Jessica went to touch Sephie's shoulder, causing her to flinch.

"I'm so sorry," she said quickly. "It's not you…"

"-No, no, I'm sorry I didn't know. I'll make sure you're not to be touched by anyone."

Thankfully, Jessica seemed to understand immediately. Sephie hated explaining the details. It always brought the memories back too vividly.

Jessica instead gestured her over to an empty makeup chair. Sephie gave a pout of her own.

"Don't act like that. You'll look exactly the same, we just need to make sure you don't get washed out on camera. Oh, Jace," she turned back to him, "This is the investigator I told you about, Sephie. Listen to everything she says, okay?"

He rolled his eyes. "Whatever."

Sephie's eyes narrowed. He was quite different from his on-camera persona. Perhaps this would be easier than she originally thought. Jessica gave one last grin before leaving the tent. She turned to face Jace, who was now looking at her like a piece of meat.

Ah. He just hadn't gotten a good look at her before.

All things considered, Sephie knew she was cute. Pale as death, sure, but the freckles softened the look. Her thick, dark brown curls were cut into a '70s shag that framed her sharp face. Years of crawling through decaying basements had added wiry muscle to her small frame. At 5'2", she liked to think of herself as an imp.

An imp who was apparently Jace's type.

He leaned over the arm of his chair, the aggressive scent of Axe Body Spray forcing its way into her nose. She held back from gagging, barely.

"Persephone, right? Great name for a goddess like you."

Ew.

"Call me Sephie, please."

She hated her full name. Her parents thought naming their daughters after Greek goddesses was so original. Thalia had lucked out with a somewhat normal name. Sephie hadn't been so fortunate.

"Cute nickname."

Sephie didn't reply. She wasn't going to acknowledge his apparent need for eye candy. He didn't take the hint.

"Jessica said you're pretty well known around here. We're glad to have you guest on this episode, you and Luke should work well together."

She blinked. "Luke?"

"Luke Mavros? The medium?"

Crap.

Chapter 3

Luke double-checked—okay, triple-checked—the restaurant door again. Business was slow these days. Not many people knew about his little hole-in-the-wall business, despite his best efforts to market it..

Which is why he said yes to appearing on the show. He didn't even want to go on this wild ghost chase for some cheesy reality show. Running around with a bunch of asshole wannabe investigators wasn't exactly his idea of a fun night, but rent was due and customers don't show up out of nowhere.

His food was good. He knew it was good. He just didn't know how to get other people to come in, try it and realize it was damn good.

Sure, he could've made money off his gift—charged for medium sessions like some psychic-for-hire. But that always felt... wrong. His ability wasn't a party trick, and he'd always been dead-set (pun maybe intended) on keeping it in the family. That plan lasted right up until his big-mouthed uncle downed three too many drinks and let it slip at the local bar. The next morning, Luke's apartment was swarmed with drunk patrons begging to talk to their dead grandparents. Someone even asked about their parrot.

He'd managed to scare off most of them with a few vague, spooky warnings. But then he noticed a young woman hanging around, hiding in a large sweatshirt. Luke figured he could scare her off too if he needed to. But she hadn't been annoying or drunk, so he listened.

The woman had recently lost her grandmother and inherited her house. While honored, she was wary about moving in, fearing she'd mess something up. She couldn't understand why, of the dozens of grandkids in the family, she was the one the estate had been left to. While Luke hadn't managed to connect with her grandma, a random second cousin had come barreling through to talk.

Apparently, the rest of the family would've auctioned the place off in a heartbeat, along with the priceless items inside it. The only reason the house hadn't ended up on the market already was because Grandma had outlived all the greedy members of the family, himself included, the cousin admitted. The girl at Luke's doorstep was the only one in the family without ulterior motives.

After assuring her that her grandmother had most definitely left the house to the right person, Luke sent the young woman on her way. It hadn't seemed like a big deal to him, but as he watched her walk away, it seemed like a giant weight had been lifted from her. She'd seemed far more sure of herself, and it made Luke feel satisfied. That feeling was the only payment he ever wanted for using his gift, which was probably why he now owned a struggling "real" business in honor of his own family member, who was actually dead.

A figure leaning against his car pulled him away from the thoughts of his failing restaurant and how disappointed his cousin would have been. As he walked closer and realized who it was, a scowl settled on his face.

"Connie, I told you. I can't do anything else for you."

She was wringing the same damn embroidered handkerchief like it was a lifeline. More like a grown-up version of a security blanket.

"Please, I'm willing to pay you."

Luke dragged a hand down his face. Connie's husband was, unfortunately, beyond the reach of his abilities. He couldn't talk to the dead if they weren't really there. The man's energy still lingered, sure, but the soul was long gone. Either Connie didn't understand or just didn't want to. Luke assumed the latter.

"Just let the man visit the stable. He's not hurting anyone."

"It's hurting me!" Connie dabbed the nonexistent tears from her eyes. "I can't bear to see him anymore!"

Luke groaned. She was standing right up against his car door. He could have shoved her aside, but he wouldn't. He just had to use his words.

"You hardly cared for him when he was alive, Connie. I think you're just worried his ghost is going to watch you and that side piece of yours getting frisky behind closed doors."

Connie's whimpering quieted immediately. She just stared at Luke, mouth slightly agape.

"How did you—"

"You're not exactly discreet. Your husband knew, by the way, which is why he started focusing more on the horses. That, and it was easier than getting a divorce. He didn't linger because of you—he stuck around to make sure the horses were still well cared for. I told you, his energy's still there because he spent so much time at the stables. It's not really him anymore. It's just a memory."

He gently nudged her away from the car.

"If you don't mind, I have places to be."

Connie's face turned deep red, but she turned and clacked down the sidewalk. Luke hated pulling out the dirt he'd picked up during readings, but she had refused to back off.

Groaning, he climbed into his car, his knees popping in protest. He really needed something bigger. As reliable as his Toyota Camry was, he could only smack his head on the ceiling so many times. Buying a new car took money: something he was currently lacking.

As he drove toward Ashland Manor, he fantasized about all the things he'd fix at the restaurant once the show's paycheck cleared. Aside from rent, he might be able to hire a real staff, maybe even a marketing manager. And once this ghost-hunting nonsense was over, he could retreat into the kitchen where he belonged. He was good at the cooking part. It was the business side where he fell flat.

Before he knew it, he was parked outside the manor gates. What caught him off guard was the sheer number of vehicles already there. Cars, vans, and a police car even, were all parked on the lawn. That was going to be a problem and Jessica needed to hear about it. You don't stomp all over sacred ground like that, not if you wanted to avoid spiritual consequences. He didn't want to find out what any possible ghosts might do in retaliation.

A cop came into view as Luke made his way up the cobblestone path. The man's eyes widened as he approached; Luke knew his height was intimidating. He offered a gentle smile and whipped out the idiotic, ghost-shaped lanyard he'd been given. The cop simply nodded and waved him along. Stepping over an odd hole in the porch step, he heard loud voices arguing from inside.

"Did you get a permit to update the electrical system?"

"Ms. Blake cut me some slack. We'd be doing the city a favor—"

"What, by causing a house fire? No one—and I mean no one—changes anything about this house."

The first voice was a sleepy-sounding guy. The second—sharp, no-nonsense, and female—probably belonged to Persephone, the investigator Jessica warned him about. Luke had Googled her, but all he found was her business website.

"This is why I don't like working with women…"

Oh hell no.

Luke knew better than to piss off a woman, especially one who sounded fiery. He quickened his pace and flung open the front door. Inside stood an unbelievably short woman radiating fury at Daniel, the showrunner Jessica introduced him to when he'd signed the contract. Luke had been shocked that someone so disinterested could helm a successful show. He wasn't helping his image now, arguing with what appeared to be a tiny demon in human form.

Luke gave the woman—who he was now positive was Persephone—a once-over. Black jeans, a sweatshirt, and combat boots on a petite frame, with wild dark curls framing an angular face. If not for the anger in her eyes, he might've thought she was harmless. But there was no doubt in his mind she could tear Daniel limb from limb.

Unfortunately, one of the most effective ways to shut up a chauvinist was with a bigger man.

Luke stomped into the room, deliberately making his steps loud.

"Did I hear something about electricity?"

Chapter 4

Sephie ran back down the cobblestone path, chasing after the SUV Jessica climbed into. Thankfully, it slowed as she waved her arms wildly. She jogged up to the driver's side as the window rolled down.

"Something wrong, Sephie?"

"Is there a reason you didn't tell me you hired a quack?!"

Jessica looked sheepish. "Because I knew you'd react like this." She turned off the ignition and stepped out of the car. "Look, the producers wanted a local expert and your clients do nothing but sing your praises. Jace wanted drama, so hiring a medium was the easiest way to keep him happy."

Sephie crossed her arms. "Here I was thinking you wanted to broadcast something honest. Mediums are just grifters, he'll make a mockery of the investigation."

Jessica cocked a hip. "Luke is legit."

"See? He already got to you!" Sephie groaned.

There was no such thing as a legit medium. They were all the same; smarmy, money-hungry people who were far too intelligent for their own good. Instead of using their intelligence to actually help people, they preyed on the vulnerable. Widows aching for one last "I love you," parents grieving children, caretakers wracked with guilt over a death they couldn't prevent.

Sephie would have nothing to do with any of it. Not again.

"Come on," Jessica was pleading now, "The Conjuring franchise was a big hit —"

"Do not get me started on those predators." Sephie's tone darkened .

Jessica bit her bottom lip between her teeth and blinked. Sephie sighed.

"I'm sorry. I have a lot of strong feelings on the topic, but that's not your fault. I just wish you would have told me..."

"I'm sorry too," Jessica replied, "if you'll just hear me out though."

Sephie dropped her arms to her sides and slumped. Despite the Hollywood veneer, Jessica seemed genuine. She didn't tolerate Jace's nonsense and pushed for the right things since the start. With a resigned wave, Sephie gestured for her to continue.

"I heard you were a skeptic, and I took it seriously when I picked Luke," Jessica said. "He doesn't charge for his services. He turns down way more people than he helps. Doesn't even market himself. I only found him because an anonymous client insisted he deserved recognition."

Sephie exhaled sharply. She had to admit, she hadn't heard of Luke, which said a lot as she tried to keep tabs on the con artists.

Jessica rubbed the back of her neck. "He's flat out said this won't change anything. He'll do the guest spot, take the check, and go back to his independent business."

Not doing this full-time? That was a good sign.

"What's his 'real' job?" Sephie asked.

Jessica shook her head. "He refuses to tell us. He doesn't want word getting out because he's terrified he'll get bombarded with ghost requests."

Sephie grumbled. "… Okay."

Jessica's eyes lit up. "Wonderful. You have my cell, reach out if anything makes you uncomfortable, alright?"

Sephie nodded. Jessica gave her a quick grin before climbing back into her car. "I'm in your corner, yeah?" she assured as she buckled her seatbelt.

Sephie watched the SUV until it disappeared from view. She resisted stomping back up the pathway to the house, using the long walk to regulate her breathing. *You can do this. You can totally do this.*

The last experience she'd had with a so-called "medium" was on a girls' trip to Louisiana with Thalia and their Mom, Crystal. After a few drinks and a long stroll down Bourbon Street, they'd ended up at Mama Anriette's Voodoo Shop. Even tipsy, Sephie tried to drag them away. Voodoo was sacred, and whatever this woman was peddling definitely wasn't that.

She held her tongue as the woman spouted nonsense, letting her family have their fun. Her mood changed completely when her Mom insisted on performing a séance. Anriette sat them around the typical round table with what looked like a clay animal skull in the center. The ghosts cutting the lights out (it was a timer), and the objects floating (fishing wire rig) were entertaining enough.

When Anriette pulled the "I sense a recently departed female spirit in the room" line, Sephie nearly snapped. She'd managed to excuse herself from the room before ripping the woman a new one but made sure to "accidentally" tangle one of the floating props on her way out.

Sephie stepped over the hole in the step she'd made earlier and re-entered the house. She didn't have time to dwell on frauds. She had a job to do.

Unfortunately, a mystery toolbox now sat in the middle of the foyer.

"Daniel?"

The showrunner appeared from the next room clutching an energy drink like a lifeline. He had the audacity to look at Sephie and roll his eyes.

"Yes, Ms. Blake?"

She pointed. "What's this?"

"Electrician's toolbox," he said flatly. "We need light if you won't let us open the windows."

This man was testing her patience.

"Did you get a permit to update the electrical system?"

"Ms. Blake cut me some slack. We'd be doing the city a favor—"

"What, by causing a house fire? No one—and I mean no one—changes anything about this house."

Daniel's face turned a deep purple as he barely held in his rage.

"This is why I don't like working with women..."

Oh, he was a misogynist as well. Lovely. Sephie felt a satisfying rant bubbling up in her stomach, but the sound of approaching heavy footsteps distracted her.

She turned to find what could only be a lumberjack standing in the doorway. He had to be at least 6'2", built like a tank, had wild brown hair, and a thick, well-groomed beard. He raised his eyebrows at Daniel.

"Did I hear something about electricity? So not only are you trying to break housing codes, you're disrespecting the spirits."

This was Luke?

Daniel's scowl deepened. "Mr. Mavros, we can't see anything in here. It's a necessity."

Luke strode over and placed a meaty hand on Daniel's shoulder. He could've snapped the man like a twig.

"Like the lady said, nobody changes anything about this house. That clause is in my contract as well, and for good reason. If anything happens here that could negatively impact future restoration, you'll be dealing with me. Got it?"

Daniel could only nod.

"Perfect." Luke let go and his face instantly softened. "Now go find that electrician and let him know he's no longer needed."

Daniel practically sprinted out of the room.

Luke chuckled and turned to Sephie with a grin. "You're tiny."

What the hell?

"You just met me and that's what you say?"

He laughed. "It was the first thing I noticed. You're tiny and cute—like a fairy."

Okay... that was almost a compliment. Maybe he wasn't completely awful.

He extended a hand. "Persephone?"

She stared at it, jaw clenched. "Please don't call me that. It's Sephie. Or Ms. Blake."

His smile dropped. "I don't recall you being my superior, so Sephie it is. I'm

Luke."

Sephie put her hands on her hips. "While I appreciate you shutting Daniel down, I'll be upfront—I'm not comfortable working with you. It's probably best if we keep our distance."

His eyebrows shot up. "Wait, what?"

She ignored him, spun on her heel, and started up the stairs.

She heard his footsteps first, then felt his hand gently land on her shoulder. She froze. Her vision went black. Her body reacted before her brain did. She covered her face, grabbed his wrist, turned, and stomped hard on his foot.

"Ow!" He backed off, limping slightly.

...Oops.

She hadn't meant to hurt him. But she was already so on edge, and grabbing her was the final straw.

Muttering something that might have been an apology, Sephie turned and ran.

Chapter 5

"Mary had a little lamb, with fleece as white as snow."

Sephie felt ridiculous reciting the nursery rhyme, but the sound guy, Rob, needed consistent audio to get his levels right. They were starting off in the incredible library the crew had found on the third floor. Sephie wanted nothing more than to sort through the hundreds of books lining the shelves, but the layer of dust on them was especially thick.

"And everywhere that Mary went—do I seriously need to keep going?"

"Sorry, Ms. Blake, but yes," Rob replied, not looking up from his soundboard.

"Blah blah blah, yada yada yada, I don't want to be here."

Rob chuckled. "Perfect, you're good. And don't worry, the crew will protect you from Jace, we can't stand the guy either."

"She doesn't need protecting," Luke interjected. He held up his wrist, showing off the friction burn she'd left behind. "And I think you broke my toe, so thanks for that."

Sephie sniffed. "How about you don't grab people from behind?"

"Well excuse me, I was just trying to get your attention."

"Attention from someone who just got told to leave her alone."

"Jeez," Rob said, throwing his hands up. "Did you two date or something?"

"NO!" they answered in unison.

Rob gave them a skeptical look. "Are you sure?"

Sephie crossed her arms. "I would never stoop to the level of dating someone who pretends to talk to ghosts."

"You're as bad as a chihuahua. Tiny and loud."

"You said I was cute."

"A man can change his mind."

Rob stood. "Okay, this is just weird. You're both mic'd, try not to mess with them." He walked off, clearly eager to find someone else to talk to.

Luke glared. "I was just trying to be nice."

Sephie huffed. "Again, randomly grabbing people isn't nice."

"What the heck is your problem?"

Sephie felt a rant building up again, but Luke was spared when the director,

Samantha, walked over.

"Hey you two," Samantha said. "Need your attention for just a sec."

They both looked at her, scowls still present.

She offered a weak smile. "So, due to some… issues we had with Daniel, he won't be on set for the remainder of this episode. I'll be taking over his usual duties."

Thank goodness for that.

"We're going to get your initial interviews first. Just introduce yourselves and your job titles, and then I'll ask you some questions. No wrong answers, just be yourselves. You wouldn't believe how many people turn into a character as soon as you yell action." She glanced not-so-subtly in Jace's direction.

"Easy enough," Luke replied.

Sephie nodded in agreement.

"Great. I need to double-check with the cameraman, then we'll get going."

As soon as Samantha turned her back, they went right back to glaring at each other.

"You stick to what you know during this, okay?" Luke growled.

"Just as long as you do the same," Sephie muttered.

This was ridiculous. Sephie had met some unlikable people in her lifetime, but never had she experienced such immediate disdain for someone. She'd known Luke for barely two hours, and he'd already pushed every single one of her buttons.

"Sephie, are you okay?"

She looked up. Samantha had taken a seat across from them, the cameraman at his position.

"I'm fine."

Samantha raised a brow but decided to ignore the obvious tension in the room. A crew member stepped forward with a slate.

"*Dead Serious*, Season Six, Persephone and Luke, take one."

Sephie cringed at her full name. The cameraman counted down as she plastered a smile on her face.

"I'm Sephie Blake, and I'm a paranormal investigator."

"And I'm Luke Mavros, I'm a medium."

Easy enough, just like he'd said.

"So, Sephie, I'll start with you," Samantha said. "What got you into paranormal investigation?"

"Honestly? I was a teenager and wanted some money."

Luke snorted. She ignored him.

"It ended up being a steady job. People always think they're haunted. But when it comes down to it, my job's about helping people. The fact that I get to explore historic buildings for a living is a plus."

"You say 'haunting' almost jokingly. Do you not believe in ghosts?"

"No, I don't."

"One would think, given your profession, you'd be a believer."

"It's the exact opposite. I use research and exploration to give reasoning for what people perceive as spirits. It's what my clients like about me, it puts them at ease quicker."

Samantha nodded. "Interesting. Luke, being a medium, what's your stance on that?"

"I obviously can't speak to Ms. Blake's experiences, but I can confirm connecting with the dead is very real. I know you can't convince a skeptic, but I know it's possible. That's all that matters."

"And when did you first discover your gift?"

Sephie couldn't resist rolling her eyes. Samantha didn't call cut, so either it'd get edited out, or maybe they'd keep it for drama.   Luke took a breath. "My cousin passed away unexpectedly when I was twelve and it hit me pretty hard. Before his funeral, he came to me with a final request."

Samantha leaned in, eyes bright with anticipation. "What was the request?"

Luke smirked. "He gave me his computer password and told me to use a specific playlist. He'd compiled silly, stupid, fun songs—the complete opposite of what my aunt was planning. But it turned the whole thing into a celebration of his life instead of a day of sorrow."

"So that led to you offering your services?"

"Not exactly. Information about my services is spread purely by word of mouth. I don't do séances. I don't do bachelorette parties. It's not for fun. I'll only help someone connect with a departed loved one if there's good reason. And if the departed wants to be spoken with."

Samantha smiled. "Now, we've been given the opportunity to explore the Ashland Manor in Maryland this episode. What's your knowledge of this mysterious location? Sephie?"

Sephie clasped her hands in her lap. "What is so alluring about the Ashland Manor is nobody really knows anything about it. I'm a local, and all I've ever known is that it's been closed off to the public for as long as I've been alive. I'm really grateful to be here, I've been wanting to get my hands on this house forever, so thank you all for that."

Luke groaned, and Sephie narrowed her eyes.

"Do you have something to add, Mr. Mavros?"

He leaned back in his chair. "I'm just guessing the city has kept it closed off for good reason. It's a giant Gothic mansion, gotta be some spirits in here who just want to be left alone."

"Oh please," Sephie huffed, "I thought you were all about helping ghosts 'move on?'"

Luke glared harder. "You'd think a paranormal investigator like yourself would know some spirits are attached to objects. That's most likely what's happening here, Stone Tape theory and all that."

"Theories are plausible or scientifically acceptable, none of your crap is."

"Excuse me?"

"Okay, cut." Samantha stood from her own seat. "While I like the playful banter, people don't like straight hatred on this show. Can we tone it down a bit?"

"It's not playful banter," Sephie snapped. "I don't like him."

"I'm not the biggest fan of her either," Luke muttered.

Samantha bit her lip. "I thought you two knew each other and it was a bit?"

They both just stared at her, mouths agape.

"… Okay, guess not," she mumbled, "just be nicer to each other for the sake of the episode?"

"Fine," Sephie muttered.

Luke made some sort of grunting sound.

The crew member reappeared with the slate.

"*Dead Serious*, Season Six, Persephone and Luke, take two."

"What are you two hoping to accomplish during this investigation?"

Luke perked back up. "I'd really love to identify anyone who might still be connected to the mansion. Depending on their background, we'll see if they need to move on or not."

"Ugh," Sephie moaned. "What's going to happen is I'll determine if there are any issues with the architecture and hopefully bring in some preservationists."

"We need to see what we're allowed to touch first."

"The owner's dead."

"Exactly, we need to respect their wishes."

"They. Are. Dead."

"Do you realize how awful you're being?"

"Cut!" Samantha stood again and walked between them with her hands on her hips like a mom dealing with misbehaving children. "How about we conduct the rest of your interviews separately, okay?"

"Please," they once again said in unison.

Rob snorted behind the camera, barely holding back laughter.

"Just kiss already."

Chapter 6

"We're in the famous Ashland Manor, the most well-known haunted mansion in Maryland."

Jace was back to his Ghostie Boy persona the second Samantha called action. Sephie had to hand it to him, he was able to go from indifferent to oozing charisma in seconds.

"As usual, we've got our resident nerd, Isiah, to tell us all about this location."

Isiah was basically the team punching bag on *Dead Serious*. If there was anyone Sephie might vibe with, it would be him. The guy held two degrees in political science and religious studies. How he ended up ghost hunting with three other bros, nobody knew. All things considered, he was solid with research and acquiring data for the show. And he didn't complain about being constantly ragged on.

He had to be getting paid a lot.

With an eye roll, he nudged Jace out of frame and stepped in. "So, as our local expert Sephie said, it was pretty much impossible to find any information on Ashland Manor. I tried. I failed."

"Cut!"

Isiah blinked at Samantha as she stalked up.

"Isiah, you can't say you failed."

"But I did."

She pinched the bridge of her nose. "Nobody wants to hear that. You gotta come up with something."

"Sam, you know I can't just riff. That's what this bozo's here for." He thumbed at Jace, who looked mildly offended.

"I'm not some clown."

"Dance, monkey."

"What?"

Samantha put her face in her hands. "Boys…"

Sephie took that as her cue to slowly back away from set. This was getting incredibly uncomfortable and she didn't feel like experiencing secondhand embarrassment. Plus, her stomach was grumbling and she wanted to hit the free buffet table.

Unfortunately, the frown she'd been wearing most of the morning made a comeback the moment she found Luke already there, loading up a flimsy paper plate with lunch meat, cheese, and chips. The plate looked like it'd cave in any second under the weight of his personal charcuterie board.

"Save some for the rest of us."

He put his hand over his eyes, squinted, and peered around. "Hm? Did somebody say something?"

Rude. It didn't help their height difference was so ridiculous she wasn't even in his natural line of sight. She tapped her foot impatiently until he glanced down.

"Oh look, it's Scooby-Doo."

"What?!"

He chuckled and popped a cheese cube into his mouth. "You're a little mystery solver."

She would have stomped her foot in protest, but it'd be another thing for him to make fun of.

"I'm a Velma if anything."

"You yap like a dog, sooo…"

"Scooby-Doo's a Great Dane, you moron."

"I'll have you know I'm very well educated."

She grabbed her own plate and helped herself to the food. "Then you should know the difference between a chihuahua and a Great Dane."

He glanced at her plate. "Well, you certainly eat like a Great Dane."

She spun around, nearly spilling her popcorn. "Look who's talking!"

"I'm quadruple your size! I could eat you!"

"You should go right ahead and do that," Rob interrupted. "There's plenty of bedrooms here, go work off some tension."

Sephie needed to work off some tension alright, but she was thinking something more along the lines of a baseball bat and Luke's skull…

"Sephie, we need you back on set," Rob added.

"What? Why?"

"Isiah's being difficult, we need some kind of expert to give us something."

Sephie grumbled before shoving an entire slider into her mouth. "Jessica said I wouldn't have to interact with Jace."

Luke held up a finger. "Uh, uh, uh, she said minimal contact."

"Shut up, Flexorcist."

Rob let out a hearty laugh as he led Sephie back to set. "I'm serious, you two act like an old married couple."

"He's an idiot."

She ran her tongue over her teeth before stepping in front of the camera again. Thankfully, they had a boom mic for these shots, so she wouldn't have to recite any more nursery rhymes.

Samantha walked up to her, looking frazzled. "Okay, we need some sort of hook. Isiah's being too technical, and since he didn't find anything on Ashland Manor, he just stopped. Please tell me you can spout some BS?"

Sephie wrinkled her nose. "I mean, there isn't anything on Ashland Manor—"

"Something! Gimme something! Go personal, I don't know!" Samantha threw up her hands and marched back to her chair. "Sorry, usually it's not this hard to film idiots running around an abandoned house."

The slate clacked in front of Sephie's face again.

"*Dead Serious*, Season 6, Persephone on Ashland Manor, take one."

How hard was it to call her Sephie?

"Okay Sephie," Samantha started after the countdown, "What can you tell us about Ashland Manor?"

"Like I said, there's absolutely no information available to the public."

Samantha ran a hand through her hair, but Sephie continued on.

"But I also said that's exactly what makes it so alluring. The manor's been a mystery to locals for decades. Something's always felt off about it, but no one can quite put their finger on why. And yet, look at it, whoever lived here must've cared deeply. The only real structural issue I found was the rotten wood on the front porch." She grimaced. "Don't recommend stepping there, by the way."

She shifted her weight slightly and softened her voice. "The mansion is a Gothic gem. It's stunning. And the gardens? They look like someone's still taking care of them. We know they're not. But it's like time just… stopped. We admire the outside, sure. But we need to learn more about what's inside if we want to truly understand what Ashland Manor is hiding."

"Cut."

Sephie exhaled. Hopefully, that had been enough. She wasn't used to talking so much.

Samantha beamed. "That was absolutely perfect. Take a break, you can explore the house on your own for a little bit, we're gonna film with the main cast for a while."

Sephie spun on her heel and booked it back to the buffet, silently praying Luke hadn't eaten the last of the fruit salad.

Chapter 7

"Shut up, Flexorcist."

Sephie's curls bounced as she sharply turned and stomped after Rob back to set. Luke rolled his eyes and went back to his plate. He had to admit, Flexorcist was pretty clever.

She was pretty clever.

He shook the thought out of his head and spooned more fruit salad onto his already overloaded plate. Maybe he should've layered the food better; the middle was bowing like a badly built bridge. Not his fault he was apparently part giant.

"We got enough food for you, hungry man?"

Luke looked up to find one of the Ghostie Boys grinning at him. He was pretty sure his name was Xavier. Unlike Jace, the rest of the *Dead Serious* crew had been surprisingly chill. Luke could see why the show had fans. As long as Jace played his part, everyone else just kept things moving.

"You done with that?" Xavier asked, nodding at the fruit bowl.

"For the moment."

Xavier chuckled as he helped himself. Luke was honestly grateful the food services on set were decent. He typically preferred cooking for himself and testing new recipes, but this worked fine for now.

"So, you and Sephie—"

"No," Luke quickly cut him off. "We're not together."

Xavier cackled. "You've made that quite clear. No, I was gonna ask if you'd work with her again."

"What? No!"

He wouldn't deny he was enjoying picking on the little snapping turtle, but it was obvious she was determined to hate his guts.

"I've been in this business for a while, Luke," Xavier quipped. "Did you catch that Salem limited series from a few years back.?"

"I tend not to watch anything witch-hunting related," Luke shrugged. "Someone like me would have been sent to the gallows back then. Not a great feeling."

Xavier nodded. "Gotcha. Doesn't matter. I was more getting at that I was an executive producer on it, so I get what works."

"Executive producer to a Ghostie Boy doesn't seem like a step up."

"Hey, watch the credits for *Dead Serious*. I've got a buttload of producing credits. I just appear on camera because it's fun to be stupid sometimes."

He could understand that. Everyone needed a bit of a brain break from time to time. If running around and keeping Jace out of trouble brought Xavier joy, then good for him.

He pointed his fork at Luke. "What I'm trying to get at is I know what people like. You and Sephie would be a huge hit."

Luke chuffed. "She can't stand me."

"Tropes, my dude," Xavier said. "You're total opposites. You're both wicked smart, and experts in your field. She's an adorable little spitfire and you're a gentle giant. It works. And, I think you like her."

"I took this gig because it pays well, not because I'm trying to break into the industry. Especially not whatever romcom situation you've concocted. Thanks though."

He turned to head back to set, overloaded paper plate in hand. Unable to help his curiosity, he wondered what they were getting Sephie to do right now.

"Keep the idea in the back of your mind!" Xavier called after him.

Luke turned back to Xavier and shook his head.. Great. He hadn't even made his TV debut and he was already being shipped.

At least it was with someone cute.

What the heck was wrong with him? He should be focusing on getting through this shoot and getting paid so he can get back to the restaurant. As he approached the library set, an intern raised a hand to stop him before he could re-enter. She gestured to his towering plate of food and scrunched her nose.

Right. No food allowed on set.

Luke began to wolf down his feast as the intern just stared, baffled.

"What? I'm not letting good food go to waste."

She rolled her eyes and pulled out her phone. "Could you hurry up? Jace sent me on a coffee run."

"The heck?" he mumbled through a mouthful of salami. "There's three boxes of coffee at the food table."

She looked down at her feet. "He doesn't like that kind."

Luke arched a brow. "I promise I won't set foot in that room. I abide by the rules."

She sighed, nodded, and turned to head for the exit.

"Hey," Luke called after her. "Don't fall for his fake charm. Jace'll take what he wants and move on to his next project. I've met tons of men like him."

She froze, clenched her fists, and kept walking.

Once she was out of sight, Luke crept silently toward the library. He paused at the door, munching on a slice of kiwi. Technically, he wasn't on the set yet. Leaning as close as he could without crossing the threshold, he could just make out Sephie, mid-speech.

"We admire the outside, sure. But we need to learn more about what's inside if we want to truly understand what Ashland Manor is hiding."

She was just as curious as he was. They may have been opposites in almost every way, but the desire to uncover the mansion's secrets? They shared that.

"Cut!"

Crap. That was his cue to go.

He scrambled back, clutching the remains of his food. A spike of dread shot up his spine as he bumped into someone behind him.

Had the intern come back?

Knowing he'd been caught, he slowly turned around, and found Xavier grinning smugly at him.

"Told you so."

Chapter 8

The dust was getting to be too much for everyone. Sephie had already used up the pack of tissues a crew member had offered her. Luke wasn't faring much better; his nose was a bright shade of pink. They needed to hurry up with filming so she could bring in a cleaning crew. But no, Jace insisted on leaving all the dust exactly where it was. Something about ambiance.

So far, the crew had attempted one of their EMF sessions with no results. Usually, they got at least one sketchy sound that could maybe be a ghost. Not today. Sephie crossed her arms and smirked, basking in Jace's frustration.

Samantha was doing her best to smooth things over.

"Jace, calm down. Let's pivot and shoot a mystery solving episode. Search through the library, dig for info, try to ID the last person who lived here."

"Those episodes don't do great, Sam. The last thing I want is another idiot blasting me on the socials."

The Redditors were going to devour this episode. Sephie's personal dislike for *Dead Serious* was nothing compared to the trolls on their forum. She'd been a long-time lurker, non-poster, and had spent many Friday nights laughing hysterically at the comments. Her all-time favorite? *Jace is what happens when a TikTok algorithm gains sentience and decides to ghost hunt.*

Samantha's patience was running very thin. The fact her head hadn't exploded yet was admirable.

"They do better than you think," she said. "It's just not the audience you want. There's more to the fanbase than spooky girlies. Just work with me here. We've got Sephie, she's the perfect guest for something more grounded in reality."

Aiden and Xavier were lounging by the EMF reader. Every so often they smacked the side of it, hoping a voice might finally come through.

Aiden grinned up at Sephie. "Jace, she's smart and adorable. I'm pretty sure viewers would love her."

"Hear hear!" Xavier chimed in.

Jace glanced her way. Sephie glared back. He scowled, knowing his usual flirt shtick wouldn't fly here.

"But we also have Luke. Luke!"

Luke lumbered over, looking just as fed up as everyone else.

"What, Jace?"

"Can't you do like, a possession or something?"

"Nah dude, that's not my jam. I said no séances."

"You talk to the dead!"

"Only if they come forward."

Jace threw his hands in the air and turned back to Samantha. "Jessica got the one medium who doesn't let ghosts use their body. X, how 'bout some *Exorcist* action, huh?"

Xavier raised a brow. "First, don't call me X. Second, I'm not looking like a fool on TV again. The fans only just stopped calling me secondhand Emily Rose. I didn't even deserve being a secondhand Regan."

Sephie bit back a laugh. Xavier tried his hardest during the episode filmed at an old church, but his "possession" had ended up looking more like a fish out of water.

Jace grumbled. "Fine. Where's that Ouija board?"

"Oh, absolutely not." Luke launched into a passionate spiel on why using a Ouija board was possibly the worst idea in human history, and Sephie took that as her cue to wander off again.

She slipped into the dining room, jaw dropping for probably the fourteenth time today. The cherry wood table and chairs were gorgeous, even under the thick layer of dust. Another crystal chandelier hung from the ceiling, with matching candle sconces set against dark green wallpaper. She could almost see the room lit by candlelight—how stunning that must have been. Eating in here would've been a feast for the eyes as well.

She'd already combed through most of the first floor. No leaks, no cracked beams, no mold—nothing particularly exciting. Apart from the gorgeous furniture, the house was unremarkable, all things considered. Just creaks, dust, and faded linens. It felt less haunted and more like someone had staged it for an open house a decade ago and forgot to come back.

Her lower back pulsed with pain from standing up all day. She eyed one of the dining chairs, wondering if it'd be worth risking Jace's wrath to brush the dust off. It didn't even have a cushion.

"Oh, just brush the dust off. You look exhausted."

The voice made her jump. She turned and found Luke joined her in the dining room. His nose was still bright pink and his hair somehow looked even more unruly. He must have been running his hands through it in frustration. Understandable.

"You sneak out, or did they let you explore?"

He shrugged. "Neither. Jace was still demanding the Ouija nonsense. I told Samantha I had to leave the room before I shoved him through a wall. And I know how much it would piss you off."

"A giant hole in a historic mansion wouldn't bode well with the city."

Luke stepped forward and blew a puff of dust directly into her face before plopping down in the very chair she'd been considering. She launched into a sneezing fit as he sat smugly.

Disgusted, Sephie yanked her shirt collar over her nose and, before he could react, kicked him sideways out of the seat. Then she flopped down in his place, fluttering her lashes smugly.

"What the hell?!"

"You'd think that broken toe would've taught you I'm stronger than I look."

He groaned and got to his feet, rubbing at his hip. She hoped she'd added a giant bruise to the collection she'd already gifted him. With a sigh, he used his sleeve to dust off a different chair further away and sat, arms crossed, glaring.

"Well, Scoob, have you solved the mystery of the mansion yet?"

She ignored the nickname; it was better than Persephone.

"No, I haven't. Then again, I haven't gotten back up to the library yet. Houses from this era usually have at least one journal hiding somewhere. Lonely housewives and all that." She brushed some more dust off the table before leaning her elbow on it. "What about you, Flexorcist? Can you really not let a dead person use you as a vessel, or is it because you don't want to be outed as a fraud on TV?"

"Not a fraud," he grumbled. "If there's anyone here, none of them have been compelled to come forward. And can you blame them? Jace is unbearable." He stretched his legs out and Sephie heard a few satisfying pops. "I think they're trying to convince him to wrap for today, but he's having none of it."

"Hey! Hex Girl! Ghostbuster! Where are you two?"

Speak of the devil.

Sephie looked at Luke and raised her brows. "Again with the Mystery Inc. nicknames."

"How are you so sure that one referred to you?"

"Fair. Still, I don't feel like being found just yet."

She slid down and ducked under the table. A moment later, the giant of a man wedged himself in next to her—far too close.

"Find your own hiding spot!" she hissed.

"Shut up!" he hissed back.

She went to kick him again, but before she could land it, Jace's footsteps entered the dining room. He wandered around muttering, seemingly unaware of the two adults hiding beneath the table.

Sephie held her breath as he circled the room. Finally, they heard his footsteps fade.

"Son of a…" he grumbled as he stomped away.

Sephie exhaled and crawled out, Luke rolling out behind her with about as much grace as a dropped couch cushion. He gave her a thumbs up.

"He really is that stupid."

She shrugged. "Or blind."

"No," said Rob, appearing in the doorway, "he's just that stupid."

They both groaned as Rob grinned.

"Come on," he said. "The sooner we finish this thing, the sooner you two get paid."

Sephie stood, brushing dust from her jeans. Behind her, Luke groaned as he pushed himself upright.

"You know," she said, eyeing the chandelier overhead, "if this place is haunted, I bet even the ghosts are bored out of their minds by now."

"Or maybe," Luke said, cracking his back, "they're just waiting for the right moment."

The chandelier creaked. Just once.

Sephie narrowed her eyes. She'd choose to ignore that and check on the stability of its mount later.

Rob's voice came from the hall. "Move it! I'm not staying here after dark."

Chapter 9

It was after dark.

Jace was wandering around the living room with dowsing rods, asking random yes or no questions to no one in particular. Rob was dozing at the soundboard, Samantha was texting Jessica, the cameraman wasn't even filming anymore, and everyone else had resorted to sitting on the floor. Nobody cared about personal hygiene at this point.

"Jace," Aiden groaned, "give it up, man. We're all tired."

"Is there a female spirit present?"

Xavier rolled his eyes. "We don't even know who we're trying to connect with, what's the point?"

"Is there a child present?"

"Come on," Isiah said dryly. "Just let Sephie and I hit the library tomorrow. If we can pin down something concrete, maybe someone will come forward for Luke."

Jace threw the rods on the ground. "NO!" he shouted. "I'm always the one who makes the first connection! I will find someone in here, even if it takes all night!"

"Uh no, you will not."

Samantha marched over to him and grabbed him by his shirt collar. "Not only would that violate every labor rule in your contracts, it's just idiotic. Jessica said to drag you out of here if you start getting delusional. I think this counts as delusional."

Literally dragging him by the neck, she headed for the door. Jace went limp, causing Samantha to trip.

"Oh, you're kidding me."

She let go of his shirt and planted her hands on her hips. Luke, who had been silent until now, marched over and effortlessly hoisted Jace over his shoulder like a sack of potatoes. Jace immediately began kicking and screeching.

"Make Macho Man put me down!"

"Nope."

"Okay, wait wait wait. I'll make a deal!"

Luke turned to the rest of the crew and raised a brow. Aiden rolled his eyes. "Let's see what he has to say, but don't put him down."

Luke adjusted so Jace could see them. His face was turning a very dramatic shade of purple.

"I'll stop for the night, I promise, but let's stay overnight."

Xavier's jaw dropped. "Heck no!"

"Yeah, I was really looking forward to crawling into my bed," Sephie added. She inched closer to Jace, eyeing him suspiciously. "Why do you want to stay anyway?"

"Maybe the house will get used to us if we stay overnight and they'll be more willing to come out of hiding?"

Luke turned to Sephie and gave a small shrug, Jace bobbing on his shoulder. "I hate to agree with him, but he's got a point."

Sephie threw her hands up. "Ghosts aren't real! And I haven't seen anything wrong with the architecture. I honestly don't think this is worth an episode anymore."

"Do you want to get paid?"

A somewhat distorted voice came from behind her. She turned to find Samantha holding her phone up, Jessica was on speakerphone.

"Sephie, I like you, I want you to get paid. If this episode doesn't happen, neither does the money. Give it one more day and I'll renegotiate your contract so you can at least get paid for your time already spent here. We supply the crew with luxury sleeping bags and pillows, you won't just be left out in the cold."

Sephie scowled. "Is that even worth it, Jessica?"

"Hey," Luke murmured, "You've been wanting to get inside this place for years now, right? You're just gonna give up because of frat boy here?"

She gnawed at her lip. He was right, and she hated it.

"Fine, but I'm not promising I'll stay the entire time."

"Wonderful," Jessica replied. "Call me tomorrow evening if you want to pull out. I'll fix everything with the producers, I promise."

Luke dropped Jace unceremoniously. He crumpled into a heap, groaning and clutching his stomach. No one paid him any attention. Samantha was furiously typing. Rob was packing up gear. Xavier, Aiden, and Isiah were already halfway up the stairs.

"Alright," Samantha called out, "they're bringing in the sleeping bags. Everyone pick a room and try to get some rest."

Jace, realizing no one was going to offer him sympathy, grumbled as he dragged himself upright. Brushing off the thick layer of dust he'd managed to roll in, he zeroed in on Sephie. The mask slipped back on, and he flashed her a million-dollar grin.

"Wanna be bunkmates?"

Sephie groaned audibly, her eyes rolling so hard she was amazed she wasn't staring at her own brain. Without a word, she spun on her heel and made for the stairs. To her horror, she heard Jace's footsteps right behind her.

"Wait, Sephie, come on, I'm sorry."

She kept walking, not even sparing him a "screw you."

"Oh, don't be a bitch."

She stopped so fast he ran straight into her. Turning around, she shoved him. Hard. An audible *oomph* escaped him as he stumbled back, barely managing to stay on his feet.

"What the hell?!"

"I'm not a bitch just because I have zero interest in a douchebag who habitually cheats on his gorgeous girlfriend." Her voice was low and venomous. She was too tired to censor herself and frankly, Jace had it coming.

His face pinched in on itself, like a very angry raisin.

Or, more accurately, a butthole.

"Rita? We're not even serious. Don't worry about that."

Sephie's brows shot up. "Oh? Is she aware of that? Because that beautiful house you share sure looks serious."

"I—it's just a smart financial move! We have an open relationship!"

"Right," she said, cocking a hip, a smirk tugging at her lips. "If that were true, she'd have men hanging off her, and you'd be a little less desperate. Didn't you get that house before *Dead Serious* took off? Wouldn't be shocked if her name's the only one on the mortgage."

He didn't respond and stood there, waves of fury rolling off him, his silence was all the confirmation she needed. Sephie stepped closer, calm and deliberate. Her height had never been a hindrance when she was mad. She jabbed a finger into his chest. He flinched.

"Stay. Away. From. Me."

She turned again and marched up the stairs.

"You're insane!" Jace shouted after her.

She didn't look back. "All the more reason not to piss me off."

Chapter 10

After claiming a bedroom with a somewhat clean floor, Sephie decided to head for the library. She had no intention of staying for the rest of filming, so she was determined to squeeze as much information out of the mansion as she could. Pulling her phone out for the first time since that morning, she found dozens of notifications from none other than Thalia. She rolled her eyes as she scrolled through them, all useless drivel about how hot the Ghostie Boys were. She sighed and pushed the call button.

"Seph! I thought you died!"

"Not the worst place to die, but no. I wasn't allowed to use my phone on set."

"How is it? Is Jace as hot in real life as he is on TV?"

"He's pretty to look at, but his behavior ruins it."

"I'm still so jealous."

"Nothing to be jealous about, Thalia," she looked up at the wallpaper, amazed it wasn't peeling. "He basically just accosted me. He's gross."

"He just has a flirty personality."

"Flirty does not equate to trying to get me to sleep with him when I obviously have no interest."

There was silence for a short moment.

"Ew."

"Yeah, ew," she managed to force out before sneezing. "God and the dust in here is just unbearable."

"Why didn't you call in your crew?"

"That's another thing, Jace won't let me. It needs to look 'ooky-spooky,' or some crap."

"Okay, you've successfully convinced me that he's horrid. Happy?"

"Very," Sephie deadpanned, even though she kind of wanted to jump for joy.

"But there's still three other Ghostie Boys. Hook a girl up?"

She rolled her eyes. "Thalia, there's more to life than men. Like, I don't know, a career?"

"I'm working on it," Thalia snapped.

Oops. Struck a nerve.

"I know. I'm sorry. You're just—"

"Just what? Go ahead."

"Being like Gran. I love her, and I love you, but vicariously living through me instead of getting your own life back on track is annoying."

Thalia let out a deep sigh.

"I know I do that," Thalia said finally. " I am sorry. There's just... not a lot going on right now. And seeing you jump back into investigating is kind of amazing. It should be celebrated."

Sephie swallowed. Thalia might be a little scattered and more than a little impulsive, but she was still her sister. Still loving. Still loyal.

"I'm sorry for the jab. I know you're working on adult things. And I'm glad you're happy for me for getting back into the paranormal. But it doesn't matter, I'm bowing out tomorrow."

She yanked the phone away from her ear just in time to avoid the shriek.

"WHAT?!"

She stared down the long, dim hallway. The library was at the far end, shadows curling thickly around the doorframe.

"Being inside Ashland Manor isn't much better than being on the outside. There's literally nothing wrong with it. I'm heading to the library to see if I can at least leave with some knowledge."

"It's your dream location!" Thalia squeaked. "And you *don't* give up. You just don't."

"First time for everything."

"What happened to my stubborn older sister? This person talking to me can't be her."

"Dr. Alias said there's no harm in walking away from something that's hurting you."

Thalia made an exaggerated scoffing noise. "I'm not a therapist, but I highly doubt he meant this."

"Potato, potahto. Let's call the whole thing off. Besides, there's a giant Greek medium here who can finish the job."

"Wait—one, what a reference. And two, why are you just now mentioning a Greek? Is he hot? Please tell me he's hot."

"Thalia. Medium."

"Sephie. Greek."

A loud crash echoed from the end of the hall. Sephie froze, eyes locked on the library door.

"Seph?" Thalia's voice somehow jumped an octave. "Seph! What was that?!"

"… I don't know. But it's the first interesting thing that's happened since I got here. So I'm gonna go find out."

"Don't you dare hang up—"

Sephie ended the call and switced her phone off. Knowing Thalia, she'd call back at least five times, which was the last thing she needed. Taking a deep breath, she slowly approached the library door, trying to keep her footsteps as silent as possible. She cursed herself for leaving her taser in her room, but it was too late to turn back now.

When she finally reached the entrance, she pressed her ear up against the door. She heard nothing but her pulse hammering throughout her head. Either there was an animal living in there, or a serial killer. She sighed, turned the doorknob, and thrust the door open with a shriek. She was met with a grunt.

"For the love of—"

Luke was stuck underneath a full bookshelf that had fallen. By some miracle, he was still alive. All that muscle was good for something. Sephie sauntered over and bent down over his head, which was sticking out from beneath the wood. He exhaled loudly.

"You can make fun of me in a second, just get me out of here."

She smirked and ducked under the shelf, using her legs to push it up just enough for him to squirm free. He collapsed on the carpet, gasping. Sephie glanced at the scattered books, searching for a journal or document of interest.

"There's nothing," Luke mumbled. "I already checked."

Dang it. Sure enough, a quick scan of the books showed only late eighteenth-century novels. Sephie crawled underneath the shelf, placed her feet on it, and pushed it upwards with her legs. Luke forced himself up and helped place it back upright. He looked down at her and smirked.

"Well, now you look like a roach."

"I'm as unsinkable as one. Now put the books away."

"Me?"

"You're the one who made the mess, clean it up."

He grumbled but started collecting books from the floor. Sephie drifted over to the other side of the room where the built-in shelves were. A sliding ladder rested nearby, broken and hanging by one post. Of course. With her luck, the journals would be on the very top shelf, which was completely unreachable.

"Hey, Flexorcist!"

He walked up behind her. "Yeah, Scoob?"

Ignoring the nicknames was just easier.

"Help me get to the top shelf."

"Do you see how tall that is? I could maybe boost you partway, but I'm not being responsible for your death. You'd definitely haunt me."

"Sure would. Now pick me up."

"No."

"Luke, come on—"

A lock clicked.

They both turned toward the door. Sephie rushed over and grabbed the handle. It wouldn't budge.

"It's locked."

Luke joined her, testing it himself. Still locked. He shoved her gently aside, backed up a few steps, and rammed the door with his shoulder. Then again. And again.

"Yes, because that's working so well," Sephie drawled.

"I'm amazed you didn't stop me sooner."

"It's a door. As long as it's not encrusted with the crown jewels, those are replaceable." She placed a hand on the wood. "But I'm going to have to find out what this is made of. That's remarkable craftsmanship."

Luke raised an eyebrow. "You can drool over wood later. First, let's figure out how we're getting out of here."

"That's what she said."

"Hysterical."

Chapter 11

Luke and Sephie gave up on escaping after about twenty minutes. The windows were locked, there wasn't an air duct system to crawl through, and Sephie had shrieked at Luke when he tried to pick the door lock with an antique letter opener he'd found. She'd unleashed a colorful string of expletives before finally tiring herself out.

Now they sat on opposite sides of the room, each trying to put as much distance between them as possible.

Luke had been willing to try smoothing things over, but the ice queen—no, more like ice sprite—seemed dead set on disliking him. He'd never met someone so small, yet so brimming with anger and spite. Maybe she ran on pettiness. Still, something must've made her this defensive. Why did he care so much about figuring it out?

"You know," he muttered, "that little tantrum didn't really help the chihuahua comparisons."

Sephie sniffed. "I told you not to mess with the lock, and you did it anyway."

"It didn't even work."

"I don't care. It's the fact that you ignored me."

Luke threw his hands up in surrender. "Fine. Whatever. We're clearly stuck in here for the night. So we can either ignore each other or try playing nice."

She literally turned up her nose and faced away from him.

What a pretentious little—

She's never been good with people.

Luke started, eyes wide, and whirled his head round to find where that voice had come from; it had appeared out of nowhere.. Sephie still had her back turned, and she hadn't moved, so it wasn't her.. Which meant only one thing: someone from the other side was trying to come through.

She's super pretty though, right? Maybe all she needs is a big, strong, teddy bear of a man to show her a good time.

Yikes. This lady spirit was bold. And somehow knew Sephie. Luke rubbed his temples, frowning. The voice was unusually clear. Normally, they didn't get this loud unless he officially invited them.

"Hey, Sephie?"

She didn't respond, didn't even bother turning back toward him.

"Sephie?"

Silence.

"SCOOB?!"

"Oh good grief, WHAT?!" She finally snapped.

Luke scratched the back of his neck. "Uh… by chance, do you have any dead relatives?"

Her nostrils flared as her eyes flashed with emotion. He immediately regretted asking.

Oh, she's all bark and no bite. Don't worry.

He disagreed. His toe still throbbed from when she'd stomped on it earlier.

"Not really the kind of thing you ask someone when you're trying to get to know them," Sephie said tightly.

"It is when you're a medium."

She scoffed. "Will you shut up if I tell you?"

"Yes."

She grumbled something under her breath, then turned to face him. "My grandma died during my freshman year of college."

Luke softened. "Did she meant a lot to you?"

Sephie nodded. "Everything. She's the one who got me into old things. Preservation. History. All of it."

My sweet girl.

So her heart wasn't entirely black, he thought

Doing the calculations in his head, he guessed that her Grandma passed around five or six years ago. Grief was a complex thing and affacted people differently. If Grandma was still hanging around the veil, something was still connecting her to Sephie, anchoring her to the mortal coil.

"It hit me hard," Sephie added, her voice quietened. She pulled her knees into her chest. "My grades slipped. I almost flunked out."

Luke wanted to know more but didn't press.

"I'm sorry for your loss," he said gently.

"…Thanks."

She pushed herself up and wandered over to the bookshelves. Luke let her go, figuring she was smart enough—and graceful enough—not to knock anything over. He took the chance to close his eyes, focusing on the connection with whom he was now fairly certain was Sephie's grandmother. Not that it took much effort, she seemed perfectly content to blab his ear off.

What are you doing? Go after the girl!

Luke shook his head. A downside of his gift: while he could hear spirits in his mind, he had to respond out loud. He didn't know why it worked that way, but it did. And considering Sephie already didn't like him, the last thing he wanted was to look like he was talking to himself.

What do you mean, no? That girl hasn't touched a man in lord knows how long. She's chomping at the bit.

Okay, so relentless and blunt. He saw where Sephie got her abrasive nature from. He waved a hand in the air as if dismissing the voice.

Oh, just grow a pair and—

"Nope!"

"Huh?" Sephie's voice floated out from behind the shelves.

Crap.

"Sorry," Luke called. "I was… talking to myself."

She emerged from behind a bookcase, giving him a puzzled look.

"Talking to yourself, huh? You sure that's not just what's happening every time you claim to speak to the dead?" She wiggled her fingers in mock-spooky fashion. "I think you need to talk to a professional."

"Already do."

"What?" She arched an eyebrow.

"Don't act surprised. I hear voices in my head. When I first connected with my cousin, my mom thought it was a psychotic break. She sent me to a therapist to make sure I wasn't schizophrenic."

Sephie raised an eyebrow. "I think you need a second opinion."

They exchanged withering looks as she made her way back to the floor, rolling onto her side and resting her head on her arm. She muttered a curse under her breath.

"Are you going to try sleeping?" Luke asked.

"Might as well," she mumbled. "Everyone else is apparently getting the deepest sleep of their lives if they haven't heard us by now. We'll get out eventually."

He couldn't argue. Carefully, he lowered himself onto the rug, only to get a faceful of dust. He sneezed violently, rolling off the rug, and onto the hardwood.

God, this house was filthy.

From across the room, Sephie giggled.

Bless you.

"Thanks."

"What?"

Damn it, Ghost Grandma!

"Nothing. Sorry."

"Freak," she muttered.

Luke sighed and closed his eyes. It was going to be a long night.

Chapter 12

Sephie expected to wake up stiffer than she already was, especially since she was lying on hardwood flooring without a pillow. She honestly hadn't even remembered falling asleep. Her last thought was rolling on the floor, glaring at Luke. But as she floated back to consciousness, she felt something warm, soft, and downright cuddly against her body. She smiled and curled in closer, wanting to enjoy the peaceful moment before she had to wake up and face the reality of yesterday. Jace and crew would probably be busting down the door any second, forcing her and Luke to play nice.

Wait, where's Luke?

Something heavy landed on her thigh.

Her eyes popped open to find Luke's face a breath away from her, so close their noses were almost touching. A thick wool blanket covered them, and feather pillows wereplaced under their heads. Sephie desperately hoped it was his *hand* on her thigh and not something else.

"Luke?" She whispered.

He didn't respond.

"Luke!" She hissed, jabbing his arm. Her finger met pure muscle.

"Ouch! LUKE!" She smacked his shoulder.

He groaned and adjusted slightly, a crackling sound releasing from his spine. And Sephie thought *she* had back issues.

"I was comfy," he muttered. "Why'd you wake me?"

"Why is your hand on my thigh?!"

His eyes flew open and he tossed the blanket off, revealing their legs intertwined. Sephie flailed away, nearly kicking him in the face in the process.

He ran a hand down the side of his face. "It's too early for this. Where'd the blanket come from?"

"We'll deal with that later," she said, digging her cell from her pocket. "I'm calling Jessica and leaving. You can join me if you want."

Her phone screen remained black as she held the power button.

"What the hell? I had, like, 70% battery!"

Luke pulled out his own phone. "Same. I hate to break it to you, but that usually means ghosts are present."

"Shut up." She headed for the door. "I'm just gonna scream until someone lets us out."

"Cool, I'll be here. Judging you."

But when she reached the door, it was already wide open.

"…Huh." She blinked at it. "Weird. Come look at this."

Luke dragged himself upright and joined her. "I didn't hear it open."

"Me neither…"

They creeped into the hallway.

Silence.

The whole house was completely still, no voices, no movement, not even the usual creaks.

Sephie squinted down the corridor. She thought she remembered which rooms everyone had claimed. Maybe they were still asleep?

Then, without warning, a single candle on a hallway table flared to life.

Luke jumped. "Oh. Hello?"

The candle immediately extinguished.

Luke frowned. "Guess it doesn't want to talk yet."

"Oh stop with that crap," Sephie scoffed. She cupped her hands around her mouth, "Xavier? Aiden? Somebody?"

Nothing.

Luke grabbed her hand. "C'mon. Maybe they're downstairs already."

She rolled her eyes and yanked her hand from his, but followed him anyway. They descended through the lower foyer and into the main living room. Still, no one was here.

Sephie checked her phone again and nearly grumbled at the black screen.

"Hey, Scoob," Luke said. "We've got company."

She looked up to find a shadow waving at them through the main window. They hurried over and pulled the curtain aside. Outside stood Jace, Xavier, Aiden, Samantha, Isiah, and Jessica, all huddled on the lawn, among camera equipment, looking very confused. Jessica waved again, pointing for Sephie to open the window. Sephie reached for the lock, to find it wasn't there. Not broken. Not damaged. Just... gone.

"Can you hear me?" Sephie called.

Jessica nodded. "Yes! I called you!"

"My phone's dead. So is Luke's."

Jessica turned and said something to Samantha, who stepped closer. "Are you the only ones still in there?"

Luke stepped next to Sephie. "Sure seems like it. What's going on?"

"What's going on," Jace shouted, "is that they kicked us out of the house last night! They're trying to take all the credit!"

Sephie rolled her eyes. "Yes, Jace. Luke and I dragged five full-grown adults and filming gear down two flights of stairs in the middle of the night without waking anyone."

"Well *someone* did!"

"Why didn't you just come back in?" Luke called.

"You don't think we tried???" Samantha snapped. "Every door's locked, every window too!"

Sephie groaned. "We had issues with the library door locking last night, the front door must have done the same thing. Hang on, meet us over there."

The group walked around the house as Sephie and Luke made their way to the front door. Luke reached for the handle, only to find just like the library door, it wouldn't budge; this one seemed to be completely frozen, the knob not budging one iota.

"Any luck?" Isiah's voice called from the other side of the door.

"Nope," Sephie replied.

"I'm calling the fire department," Jessica proclaimed.

"No!" Sephie pressed her face to the wood. "They can't tear anything down, we haven't even filed the paperwork yet!"

"Then what do you want us to do?"

"Call the preservationist I gave you the number for. He'll know how to pop a window or something!"

"This is so dumb!" Jace shouted.

Suddenly there was a burst of yelling, scuffling, and "Wait, stop!" outside.

She and Luke shared a concerned look, then ran over to the closest window. To their horror, Jace shoved Aiden and Xavier into the bushes and now stood holding a large landscaping rock.

He grinned at them. "Might wanna back up."

"Jace, don't—"

He hurled it.

Luke tackled Sephie to the side, shielding her.

She braced for the crash of breaking glass, but it never came. She opened one eye and saw that the window had *caught* the rock.

The glass looked as if it had transformed into cloth, bowing inward and cradling the stone in mid-air.

"… What?" Luke murmured.

Springing back into action, the glass pulled taught before releasing the rock like a slingshot. It flew through the air, landing smack dab in the middle of Jace's face. He landed on his back, sobbing as blood began to gush from his nose.

"Holy hell," Sephie breathed.

Luke looked around the room. "Uh, thank you?"

Sephie swore she heard a floorboard creak in response.

Chapter 13

"I spy with my little eye…"

Luke's stomach growled in response to Sephie's monotone rhyme.

"I'm starving."

"Yeah, me too. But we can't really help that, can we?"

They'd been sitting in the middle of the foyer for the past two hours, having spied everything their little eyes possibly could. They certainly could've had a normal adult conversation, but that would mean trying to get to know each other. And even though this was barely their second day of knowing each other, they both understood they were destined to be enemies.

Jace, after throwing the biggest fit over not wanting to leave the house, had been the first to bolt. Granted, he needed to seek medical attention for what was most likely a broken nose. His looks were the only thing he had going for him; maybe this would ruin his career.

Much to Sephie's dismay, Aiden and Xavier attempted to break down the front door. After kicking, shouldering, and using a makeshift battering ram, the door remained pristine, and was just as unyielding. They were both willing to stay and keep trying, but Samantha and Isiah convinced them to head back to the hotel. Jessica was the only one left and was trying to reach the preservationist Sephie mentioned. At one point, she'd attempted to shove a granola bar through the mail slot, but it was too wide to slide in.

"I'm hitting the kitchen," Luke announced, getting to his feet.

Sephie frowned. "I don't think that's the best idea."

"My stomach might start eating itself soon, I'm so hungry. There's gotta be something pickled hiding in there."

"If you end up with botulism, don't say I didn't warn you!" She called out as he disappeared down the hall.

Being stuck in a house with a sick Luke would be even worse than with a healthy one. The Flexorcist was probably the biggest baby when he didn't feel well, something about him just screamed "man-sick."

Jessica tapped on the front window and gestured for Sephie to come over. With a groan, she forced herself off the marble floor and trudged over.

"Please tell me you have good news."

Jessica cringed. "You and Luke can get to know each other?"

"If that's the good news, I don't want to hear the bad."

Jessica sighed. "The preservationist? He's in Italy for the next three months."

Sephie's mouth went dry. "I… I'm going to actually die in here."

She put her face in her hands. They had no food, no running water, and apparently no preservationist to pop a window. Ironic, really, to die inside the house she'd been dying to get inside her whole life.

Jessica rapped on the window again. "We'll get you guys out, I promise."

"I hate to be a downer, but it seems unlikely," Sephie muttered. "Maybe skip the fire department and find a construction crew."

"You were right, I have to file a buttload of paperwork with the city first," Jessica drawled. "And I can't guarantee they could get in."

"Pretty sure a wrecking ball could."

Jessica bit her lip. Sephie narrowed her eyes. She was hiding something.

"Do not tell me you have a wrecking ball on the way."

Jessica hesitated. "Okay, well… I may or may not have let Xavier take a swing at one of the walls with a sledgehammer."

"WHAT?!"

The mansion. The beautiful, irreplaceable manor. There was probably a massive hole somewhere she hadn't seen yet. Jessica raised her hands.

"Breathe. It's not what you think. It's like what happened with the window and the rock: he went to smash the bricks, and they just… caved in and snapped back. The wall absorbed every blow."

Sephie dragged her hands through her hair. This had to be a dream. Maybe she was still locked in the library, warm and cozy beside Luke…

"Sephie?"

She blinked the thought away. "Sorry, I'm exhausted. I don't know what's going on with this place, but we'll figure it out somehow."

Jessica smirked. "I know you don't believe in it, but this really sounds like a haunting."

"Stop," Sephie waved her off. "I need to worry about finding food before I spend my final days next to a starving himbo. Maybe you can drop something down the chimney?"

"Hey, Scooby-Doo?!" A voice called from way down the hallway.

Jessica gave her a confused look.

"Don't worry about it. I'll go see what he needs. Go back to the hotel, you look just as tired as I feel."

"I just want to make sure you're okay."

"I survived Lucy's stal—" She caught herself. "I've survived worse. Get some sleep."

Jessica looked concerned but nodded. "If you're sure. I'll send someone to check in regularly. Maybe we'll try the roof and see about that chimney."

"SCOOB?!"

Sephie gave a small wave before heading to the kitchen. If Luke was screaming, he hadn't choked on anything yet. Maybe he'd found something edible.

She stopped in her tracks as she pushed open the swinging door.

The kitchen, which had been as dark and grimy as the rest of the house the night before, had transformed. Every speck of dirt was gone. It looked like a professional cleaning crew had scrubbed it from top to bottom. Luke stood at the cast-iron stove, stirring something in a pot. He looked over his shoulder and grinned.

"There's plenty of fresh ingredients in the pantry! I'm making some soup."

"Wha…?" She ran towards the pantry and flung open the door. Three bags of potatoes sat in the corner, one shelf overflowed with fresh fruits and vegetables; and the other lined with rice, oats, and grains. Everything looked new. No mold. No rot.

"Luke?"

She walked back out to find him holding two bowls of steaming soup.

How was it finished already?

He handed one to her.

"I figure we'll both feel better once we're not hangry. And yes, I'm just as weirded out about…" He gestured around them. "This. But we need to eat."

Sephie wanted to investigate every inch of the kitchen. Find the supplier. Trace the source of the firewood. Figure out how everything got so clean.

But her stomach had other ideas.

Luke looked absolutely ridiculous across from her, the little kitchenette was clearly made for much smaller individuals. It felt very *Beauty and the Beast* coded, they just needed some dancing utensils to put on a show for them. Honestly, she half-expected a spoon to start singing.

She stifled a moan as she tasted the soup. Hot, rich, satisfying.

Luke smirked. "Glad you like it. It's my Mom's recipe."

Apparently, she hadn't stifled it enough. "I guess… compliments to the chef," she muttered.

He winked.

He actually winked.

"Don't do that." She took another spoonful. "Now, thoughts on this becoming a fully stocked, usable kitchen overnight?"

"You're not gonna like my answer, Scoob."

"Ghosts?"

"Sort of."

"Never mind, then. If that's really what you think, do your job, Flex."

"Can you at least come up with a better nickname? I'm not anywhere near an exorcist."

"'Stay Puft Marshmallow Man' doesn't roll off the tongue as easily."

"Hey!"

Suddenly, the table shook. Hard. Their bowls toppled, soup spilling into their laps.

Luke shot to his feet and started unbuckling his pants.

Sephie threw up one hand and tried to brush hot soup away with the other. "Help! I don't want to see that!"

"Grow up. You should probably take yours off too unless you want blisters on your—"

"Fine!" she snapped, standing and peeling off her jeans. The soup really had been hot.

She couldn't resist glancing sideways at him. His legs were like tree trunks— thick, tan, annoyingly perfect.

Why'd he have to be so pretty?

He grinned. "Nice undies."

She looked down, immediately wanting to melt into the floor. Bright pink panties with dancing skeletons stared back at her. Her only clean pair.

"You shouldn't be looking at my undies!"

"Kinda hard not to," he said cheekily.

She turned to storm out but paused when she realized what was making him laugh harder.

She'd forgotten about the writing on the back.

"BONE ME," it declared in bold, black lettering.

Chapter 14

"Come on, it's kind of funny."

Sephie whipped around on the staircase, white knuckling the railing and gritting her teeth.

"A giant oaf making fun of my underwear when we're trapped in a house together? Forgive me if I don't see the humor in that."

His shoulders slumped slightly. "Okay… yeah, I get that. I'm sorry."

She gave a curt nod and resumed climbing, Luke following close behind.

"If it makes you feel any better," he added, "I have no interest in you."

"Good," she snapped, "the feeling's mutual."

"The heck are you marching upstairs for anyway?"

"I stopped by the laundry room yesterday. Maybe whatever kook is living in the walls cleaned it, too."

He chuckled. "The fact you believe a squatter is cleaning instead of ghosts is stupid."

"A squatter is a tangible, real person. Spirits are make-believe."

They reached the second floor and Sephie headed in what she hoped was the right direction.

"What's with the personal vendetta against the dead, huh?"

"I don't have anything against the dead. I hope they're all living their best afterlife. I do have a vendetta against frauds who sell false hope to grieving people."

Luke went silent, but Sephie ignored him. She'd found the laundry room.

The door opened easily. Inside, the tile floor sparkled, she wouldn't have minded walking barefoot. The walls were covered in blue paisley wallpaper, and a large window let in a generous amount of natural light. A washing basin stood in one corner, a folding table in the center, and an old-school crank dryer rested in another.

"Well," Luke said, "your wall-dweller cleaned up this room too."

Sephie rolled her eyes. "Whatever, it'll work. Shoot, wait, there's no running water."

"Yes, there is," he walked over to the basin and pointed. Sure enough, there was a spigot rising up from the floor.

"Oh..." she stared at it. "I... I was wrong."

He smirked. "See? Not a Velma. What were you wrong about?"

"I swore the manor was built in the early 1800s, but running water wasn't as widespread until later."

He turned the water on and filled the basin halfway. "Doesn't mean you're wrong. The wealthy got running water far sooner than the general population. Just judging by the fact that this is a literal mansion, I'm guessing the owners were wealthy." He dropped his pants into the basin. "That, or someone could have upgraded later."

So she hadn't even considered other options, she hated that he made sense.

She opened a nearby cabinet and found it fully stocked with bar soap. A washboard lay on the bottom shelf.

"Apparently, liquid detergent hadn't been invented yet," she grumbled, grabbing two of the white bars. She dropped her pants into the basin with his and handed him one of the soaps. "I guess we can scrub, but they'll need to soak."

"Great," he drawled but got to work. She considered waiting her turn, but the idea of getting her pants back sooner pushed her to kneel beside him.

They scrubbed in silence for a while.

"Seriously though," Luke finally muttered, "what's your issue with ghosts? Non-believers can't be convinced, but you get downright angry."

Fine.

They were stuck here together. Might as well have something resembling a normal conversation.

"I know I said I went through it when my grandma died. Well, not only did my grades slip, I started becoming more withdrawn than usual, if you can imagine that." She focused on the soap-smeared stain. It looked good enough. She grabbed a rag and wiped her hands dry.   "I had a boyfriend at the time who got really into tarot and crap like that. He took it upon himself to set up a séance with some loon to try and reach out to Gran."

She frowned. She hadn't talked about this in forever and really didn't like dragging old memories up. Why was she telling her tragic, dead grandma tale to her newly sworn enemy?

"I'm sure you can imagine, the psychic ended up being a complete sham. She'd tried to stalk me on social media beforehand to get info, but I rarely post anything personal. She ended up guessing for a lot of it, and it just made me mad. Gran was a World War II vet, and the lady said some... interesting things about the other side."

Luke paused, soap slipping from his fingers. "Are you saying she was a Nazi sympathizer?"

Sephie gave a dry laugh. "I'm saying she had some deeply questionable ideas about the 'peaceful energies' of the era. It was disturbing. Offensive. I nearly punched her." She felt her hands balling into fists.

"Anyway, instead of helping me with the grieving process, it set me back a few steps. I dumped the boyfriend, kept to myself for a few months, brown-nosed my professors for extra credit, and life went on."

She looked up and pinched her palm hard to focus on that pain instead of the internal. No way she was crying in front of this man. That grief had been tucked away, and she wanted it to stay like that. She swallowed the tears and looked at Luke.

He looked almost... solemn?

"Scoob, you're the one who needs therapy."

"I'm already in it. I'm good."

"Yeah," he stood and crossed his arms, "sure you are."

"I'm not arguing with a himbo about therapy."

"You can't call me a himbo when I just gave you a history lesson on plumbing."

"Ugh. Whatever, Flex."

He blew a raspberry at her.

"Real mature."

"You're the one who's emotionally unavailable and lacking in people skills."

"Oh, shut up."

Suddenly, the faucet sputtered and roared, water gushing out in a frenzy. Luke grabbed the handle, trying to twist it closed.

"Help?!"

"If a big muscle man like you can't turn it off, I doubt I can," Sephie snapped.

Water was nearly spilling over the edge. She groaned, ran over, and placed her hands on top of his.

The handle turned instantly. The water stopped.

They both stared at each other in silence.

"... Um, I didn't move it," Luke said.

Sephie looked down at their hands, then pulled away fast. "This is getting weird."

"Weird enough to make you believe in ghosts?"

She ignored him. "I'm going back to my room. Hopefully, we don't have to see each other in our underwear for the rest of the day."

He stood, knees cracking. "I think I'm gonna explore more. Come with?"

"What? No."

"Come on, we can make it fun. Discover what other rooms the poltergeist has redecorated."

"I honestly just want some pants."

"Don't want your booty to keep telling me to—"

"Stop!" She cut him off. "How about we just explore different rooms? We can yell for the other one if we find anything interesting, okay?"

He shrugged. "If it makes you feel better."

"It will." She turned to head for the exit when something frilly and white caught her eye. A pair of bloomers rested on the table.

She glanced around the room, heart thudding, then snatched them and shoved her legs in.

"I'm so confused, but I got pants. So fine, we don't have to split up."

"Oh good, you're at least smart enough to not be a Fred."

Chapter 15

"I'm sorry, there must be a gas leak or something, repeat that?"

Luke rolled his eyes at a very confused looking Rob. The cameraman had somehow been the first crew member to check in on the hostages. He was sent with a goody bag full of bottled water, protein bars, and baby wipes. Sephie had no clue how he was going to attempt to get the bag inside, but thankfully, they didn't need the supplies now.

"A leak isn't possible. It was built too early for natural gas, dude. It's all fireplaces and such."

"Oh never mind the specifics, just repeat what you just said."

"We have food, water, and clean rooms," Sephie stated again.

Rob's mouth hung open. "How are you two so nonchalant?"

He hadn't been present for the house slingshotting a rock into Jace's face, so was experiencing the sentience for the first time.

"Trust me, we're weirded out too," she clarified. "We were just too hungry to care where the food came from."

"Hungry, huh?" Rob cocked an eyebrow at Luke's boxers.

"Hey! Not cool!" Luke barked. "There must have been an earthquake or something, it spilled hot soup on both of us. Our pants are currently soaking in the laundry room. We found the bloomers for her."

"An earthquake in Maryland. Yeah, sure," Rob scoffed. "Any luck with your phones yet?"

Sephie shook her head. "Nope, still dead. I feel somewhat better knowing we have basic necessities, but I'd appreciate it if someone kept checking in."

Rob gave a thumbs up. "Will do. Beds comfy?"

"We haven't tried them yet, we were locked in the library last night," Luke replied.

"Ah," Rob chirped, "Well, I hope there's a king-size somewhere. Have fun you two."

"Rob!" Sephie shrieked, but he'd already turned away and was heading to his car. Either the house was creeping him out or he had better things to do. She crossed her arms and grumbled.

Luke gave another one of his stupid smiles. "He really wants us to bang, doesn't he?"

She huffed and stomped back to the stairs. "I don't understand why. You'd crush me in two seconds anyway. I'm not hooking up with anyone that could kill me."

He snorted, but once again, trailed behind her. "I don't know, girls seem to like larger guys. Something about climbing them like a tree."

"Ew."

"Again, no interest in you, you've got nothing to worry about. Where are you wandering off to now?"

"I *swore* I saw a dropdown for an attic somewhere. Seeing that we didn't have any luck in the library, maybe any info on the previous owners is stored up there."

"And I'm assuming you need me to pull it down, cool."

"You're just as curious as I am, right?"

"Yup."

"Then, for the umpteenth time: Shut. Up."

She tried to keep her voice down, not out of politeness, but just in case… well, something heard her. Ghosts weren't real. Possessions weren't real. But something was up, and every time she and Luke had gotten snippy, the house reacted. It didn't feel like a coincidence. Her eyes darted around as they climbed to the top floor, waiting for part of the ceiling to drop on her head. Thankfully, it seemed like she'd gotten away with being snarky this time.

"You're worried about the house," Luke said.

"Am not. Well, only in the preservationist sense. But it seems perfectly fine."

"That's not what I meant, and you know it. You're just scared."

She gritted her teeth. "I'm. Not. Scared."

"Sure you're not, Scooby Dooby Doo."

She bit back a retort because while she wasn't scared, she was concerned.

The hallway on the third floor wasn't nearly as dark as it had been that morning. The sconces were lit, their flames flickering warmly against the plum wallpaper. The long rug running down the hallway looked freshly scrubbed. Sure enough, hanging from the ceiling was a chain.

Without a word, Luke grabbed Sephie by the waist, lifted her, and settled her on his shoulders before she could squeak in protest. He held her legs tight as he walked toward the entrance.

"I feel like Yoda."

"You're not as cute as Yoda."

The rug suddenly bunched up beneath his feet.

"Stop!"

He froze.

"Okay, she's cute, I admit it," he said aloud.

The rug flattened back out.

"… I'm choosing to ignore that," Sephie said in a low voice.

He squeezed her calves. "I have a feeling the house won't let you. Thanks for the heads up, by the way."

"You trip and die, I die. I was protecting myself."

He tried to shrug, but it didn't work with her perched on his shoulders. "Ceilings are higher than I thought. Think you can reach it?"

She squinted upward. "Barely. I'll probably have to stand."

"Good lord. Okay, be careful."

Gripping his head tighter than necessary, she planted her feet and slowly stood, teetering but determined. She reached and grasped the chain. It gave slightly, thankfully appearing unlocked.

"Okay," she said, "I'm going to step off you as I pull this down. Try to catch me before I break my legs."

"You're what—"

She jumped. The attic stairs creaked open above her, and Luke caught her mid-fall.

Sephie dusted herself off with a grin. "You may have two left feet, but you think fast."

"Thank you?"

"Just take the compliment. C'mon."

They climbed the stairs, every creak making Sephie wince, but nothing fell through. They didn't realize how dark the minuscule attic was until they both crawled into the small space. The air was thick with dust. Sephie felt blindly along the floor—just dirt, dust, and creaky boards. Apparently, their ghostly housekeeper hadn't bothered with this area.

Her hand brushed something warm and familiar.

"It's just my thigh, don't freak out."

"Oh, don't flatter yourself."

"I didn't mean that."

She crawled further, fingers grazing more floorboards, when a crash sounded across from her, followed by a muffled scream from Luke. She sighed.

"You okay?"

"I did Karate for fifteen years and never got injuries like these."

"Fifteen years and you're not more graceful?"

"Don't worry about that. I think I found a box. Try to climb out and I'll hand it to you."

She crawled toward the hatch and smacked straight against his butt on the way. She frowned as he most definitely giggled.

Half-stumbling down the stairs, Sephie turned just as Luke handed her the chest. It was stained black, with ornate carvings spiraling across the lid. She bit her lip, wondering what treasure they'd possibly come across.

Once they were both back on the landing, Sephie knelt and opened the chest slowly. Nestled inside was a journal, a bundle of yellowed letters tied with ribbon, a heart-shaped locket, and a blueprint.

Luke leaned over her shoulder, brows knitting.

"Well, at least we found a journal."

Sephie lifted the blueprint gently, careful not to tear it. A rendering of Ashland Manor sprawled across the page: kitchen, laundry, bedrooms, attic…what was that? Her finger stilled on a section that looked off. A room drawn in darker ink, clearly added later. Her brow furrowed.

"What's this?"

Luke hummed. "No clue."

"Curiouser and curiouser."

"Well, you know what that means, right?"

She groaned. "You're really taking this Mystery Inc. thing too far."

"You're the investigator!"

He had a point. She double-checked where the random room was. It was drawn on the side of the house, near the garden. A hidden cellar, perhaps?

Luke leaned over the blueprint. "It's probably a wine cellar or something. I think we kind of confirmed these people were rich, so it'd make sense."

"Maybe it's where they used to keep the bodies," Sephie said absently, flipping through one of the letters.

He didn't reply.

She glanced up at him. "Sorry, too dark?"

Luke didn't answer. He was sniffing the air, brow furrowed. "Do you smell that?"

She paused and took a slow breath.

"… Bread?"

"… I definitely didn't bake any bread."

Giving each other a worried glance, they hurried toward the staircase.

If the house had somehow baked bread, it could definitely burn it.

Chapter 16

"Look at you, the happy homemaker."

Luke glared in Sephie's direction. He'd found a pair of oven mitts and had pulled a golden-brown loaf from the oven. It smelled delightful.

"Well Ms. Investigator, how did this bread come to be?"

Sephie rested her head on the kitchen table. "I'm convinced I've gone crazy and got locked up in a madhouse. The psych nurses are always huge like you. Just in case they have to take down a patient."

He laughed. "Anyone could take you down, pipsqueak."

A cabinet door slammed open with a loud *bang*.

"Pipsqueak isn't a bad thing!"

A mug in the cabinet inched toward the edge.

"She's tiny and cute and adorable and I just want to scoop her up!"

The mug slid back to its spot. The cabinet door gently closed.

Luke chuffed. "I've dealt with stone tape nonsense before, but this is a whole other level."

Sephie exhaled. "It's getting harder to say ghosts aren't real."

"Yesss, come to the dark side."

"I said harder, not that I've accepted it."

"Hey, it's something."

He set the bread by the kitchen window and frowned, remembering all the locks had disappeared. "I guess we'll just have to be patient."

She shrugged. "We've got nothing else to do."

He pulled the mitts off and sat across from her, his large body once again looking ridiculous in the too-small chair.

"Just because I'm nosy," she said, "when did you have to deal with this supposed stone tape stuff?"

He grumbled. "*That* was annoying. A woman sought me out because she kept seeing her dead husband at their stables. The man was obsessed with his horses, pretty sure he loved them more than he loved her."

Sephie chuckled. "So, he was a horse girl?"

"Basically. He was there so much when he was alive his energy just stuck. His ghost would go through his prep routine, then disappear as soon as he tried to lead a horse out."

"Did you release him?"

"Oh, I released him. He wanted to make sure his wife knew he was perfectly content," he smirked. "Especially now he doesn't have to deal with her. What's left is purely his energy. It's not hurting anyone, just pissing the wife off. She got angry when I told her there was nothing she could do. I think she brought someone out to bless the stables, but I doubt it did anything."

Sephie raised an eyebrow. "You think that's what's going on with this house?"

He shook his head. "Nah, with stone tape, the energy isn't aware of the living. It's just a loop. This place is absolutely aware. It's reacting."

"Reacting however it damn well pleases," she muttered.

Luke groaned. "Speaking of, if it's gonna keep us locked in, we won't be able to get outside to find that cellar entrance."

"Crap." She hadn't thought of that.

"Maybe there's a hidden door somewhere? Who knows? Jace is gonna be pissed if we figure out everything about this place."

Sephie's eyes lit up. "Then that's exactly what we need to do."

Luke frowned. "But then we don't get paid."

She leaned in. "Flex, would you rather get all the credit for solving the mysteries of Ashland Manor, or get paid for an exploitative reality show?"

A flicker of sadness crossed his face.

"I really need the money."

There was a moment of awkward silence. They just sat, the scent of fresh bread wafting through the air. Sephie glanced out the window and saw the sun was setting. They'd spent nearly a full day locked in Ashland Manor.

"You want to talk about it?" She finally offered quietly.

"Share my own personal family trauma?" He said with a half-hearted chuckle. "Sure, why not?"

He leaned back in the chair. "My cousin who died had a dream of opening a little restaurant one day. He wanted to take a bunch of our family recipes and share them with the world. When he was gone, it became my dream." He crossed his arms, staring out the window. "Starting the business was easy, it's maintaining it that's proven to be difficult. The few customers I do have really like it, but I need a marketing person and some more staff. All of that takes money. I never wanted to exploit my gift, but Jessica tripled the initial offer."

"Yeah, she did the same for me."

He nodded. "I'm assuming the city would only hand over the manor if actual experts were involved."

"Most likely. And if that soup you made earlier is on the menu, you deserve a line out the door."

A soft clicking noise echoed from the window.

They both turned. The lock reappeared.

Luke blinked. "The house is determined to force us to be nice to each other."

Sephie reached over and flipped the lock. "Apparently."

She went to open the window, but could only crack it a few inches. Frowning, she pushed the bread closer to the crack, letting the cool breeze wash over it.

"We're not friendly enough to leave the house yet."

Luke shrugged. "But at least we know what we have to do."

***

By the time the bread cooled and they'd eaten sandwiches, the sun had long since set. Realizing the house wasn't letting them out tonight, they decided to save the cellar hunt for tomorrow. Two lit candles were placed at the bottom of the stairs as if encouraging them back to their bedrooms for a good night's rest. They climbed to the top floor in silence, the flickering candlelight casting shadows across the walls.

"This is my room," Sephie said quietly as they reached her door. "Good night, Flex."

The knob wouldn't budge. They both sighed. This was becoming more annoying than creepy. Luke scratched his head before scooping her up into a bear hug.

"What the heck?!"

He twirled her around and shushed her, giving her one final squeeze before setting her down. He simply gestured to the door when she gave him a confused look.

She tried the knob again, finding it turned easily.

He smirked. "We've gotta be nice, Scoob." He looked upward. "Those nicknames aren't used with malice by the way! It's our thing."

A breeze drifted down the hallway in response, causing Sephie to shiver. Luke simply reached over, hesitating for a moment. She gave a quick nod, and he gently stroked her bicep. She tensed at first but her body betrayed her and relaxed at his touch, almost leaning into it. She hated how much his warm hands soothed her.

She sighed. "Good night, Luke."

"Good night, Sephie."

Unsurprisingly, the bedroom was also tidy. The queen-size bed had freshly laundered bedding and fluffy pillows. The wallpaper was soft white with pale green stripes. Framed photos hung on the walls, though it was too dark to make them out. The fireplace crackled gently.

A long white nightgown hung on a closet door.

"Oh," Sephie breathed, "well, thank you very much."

She slipped out of her sweatshirt and bloomers and into the buttery-soft silk. It was without question the most expensive pajamas she'd ever worn. The moment she slid under the covers, her body relaxed. The pillows cradled her head perfectly.

As sleep began to overtake her, one last thought passed through her mind.

This still doesn't mean I believe in ghosts.

Chapter 17

Sephie shut the door with a quick click, and Luke felt himself slump a bit. Better than her slamming it in his face, sure, but it still felt like she didn't fully trust him.

Then again, they'd only just met, and under wildly strange circumstances. She had no reason to trust him. Still, if they were going to be stuck in a spirit house for an indefinite amount of time, he at least wanted her to feel comfortable.

As he made his way back to what he'd claimed as his room, he took time to study the hallway's details. He could see why architecture and design appealed to Sephie. Once the house tidied itself, the place had gone from a creepy Shining-esque corridor to something downright cozy. It was... soothing.

His room, thankfully, looked good as new. The bedding not only looked clean, it smelled clean. There was no dust in sight, just a whisper of lavender in the air. He took a deep breath and sighed in appreciation. Something white and billowy hung on the closet door. He frowned and walked over to inspect it. A nightshirt?

"You gonna give me a sleeping cap while you're at it?" he asked, voice dry.

Something soft and silky plopped onto his head.

"I didn't mean it," he said, pulling it off with a grin, "but thank you."

The cap vanished. He sighed, stripping off his flannel. He had to admit, the nightshirt was like slipping into a cool, calming hug. Letting out a long exhale, he moseyed to the bed. Thankfully, it was a king. There wasn't much worse than falling off a too-small mattress, which unfortunately was an experience he knew too well.

The fireplace flared to life with a low, steady burn.

"Oh," he said gently, "thanks, but I probably shouldn't sleep with a fire burning."

It's a sentient house. Not like it's gonna burn itself down.

He groaned. He really wanted to sleep, and not deal with Sephie's outspoken grandma.

"Look, Ms. Blake?" he said aloud, pulling back the covers.

Maternal side, so no. Just call me Flo for now.

"Well, Flo, I'm willing to work with you. Just not right now." He slid under the covers, eyelids already heavy.

"I'm pretty sure I know the answer," he mumbled, "but you're not the one causing all these house shenanigans, are you?"

Nah, this is purely coincidental. I've been wanting to talk to Sephie for a while now, but the stubborn girl's been skeptical her whole life, so there's been no real way to connect. And that dipshit of a boyfriend made it worse.

Luke closed his eyes, nodding slightly. "Well, I guess you got lucky a matchmaking house stuck us together. Can't guarantee she'll listen to me, though."

He was certain she wouldn't. He'd managed to melt a bit of her icy exterior, but she was locked in her "ghosts aren't real" stance. If locked doors, conjured food, and rooms cleaning themselves hadn't convinced her, nothing would.

Well, you need to get her to listen to you.

Ugh.

"Flo, I really need some sleep. It's been a day."

Not until you promise you'll get my girl to open up. She's hiding something, and it needs to come out.

"I'm not a therapist. And we already argued about that."

What's she calling you? Flexorcist? Come on, Flex!

Luke groaned again and threw up a mental wall. He didn't like using that particular tactic seeing how tiring it was, but sometimes, it was necessary. He'd picked it up from a more seasoned medium during a retreat a few years ago. Typically, he used it for harmful, aggressive spirits, not nosy, pushy grandmas.

Flo's voice cut off immediately.

He sighed and let himself sink into the bed, sleep tugging him under quickly.

Luke didn't usually dream. Not normally, anyway. But that night, for whatever reason, he did. He floated on something that felt like a blend of whipped cream and goose feathers. Every inch of his chronically sore, oversized body melted into the mattress. He needed to find out what this thing was made of. Whatever it was, it was magic.

A small, warm form appeared beside him. Not threatening, inviting. It felt like comfort wrapped in nostalgia. He slowly turned to his side, draping an arm over it. The warmth bloomed in his chest like glowing embers.

As he drifted, a soft sound tickled the edge of his consciousness, a faint, unmistakable giggle.

Even half-asleep, Luke knew exactly who it was.

Flo.

Chapter 18

Sephie got the best night's sleep she'd had in ages. Amazing how an abandoned, once-musty old house could pull that off. It felt like resting on a cloud, her body weightless, almost floating through dreamland. The fireplace kept everything warm and cozy, radiating just the right type of heat. She could almost feel the sun streaming over her face, gently encouraging her to wake.

As she opened her eyes, she was met with a familiar sight: Luke.

"For the love of—" she muttered, rolling onto her back. Somehow, she was more relaxed than she'd been in quite some time. Her sleepy state simply wouldn't allow her to freak out. Staring at the ceiling, she relished this last bit of quiet before the day started. The green and white wallpaper was gone, replaced with a simple beige and light brown one. The bed and linens were the same, but Luke had found a king-sized bed. Probably for the best, given how large he was. A matching fireplace simmered out, the remaining embers glowing orange.

Luke stirred, stretched in his sleep, and promptly grabbed her, pulling her flush against his chest. She squeaked as his massive frame engulfed hers, his beard brushing the top of her head and tangling with her hair. His heartbeat echoed against her ear, and something tickled her nose.

Crud. He had chest hair.

And he smelled really good.

Nope. Bad Sephie.

"Luke?" She whispered. He didn't stir. Of course.

Bypassing the gentleness, she tickled his ribcage. He let out the lowest chuckle she'd ever heard, then squeezed her tighter.

"Morning," he muttered, voice thick with sleep.

He had to have been dreaming of someone else.

She tickled him again. "Luke," she said, firmer now, "it's me, Sephie."

His eyes fluttered open. The second he realized who he'd been cuddling, his expression changed from a lazy contentedness to complete shock. He slowly let go and rolled onto his back, putting a generous amount of space between them.

"I take it you didn't wander in here and climb into bed with me?"

"Nope."

"And you don't sleepwalk?"

"Nope."

"So, the house did it."

"Yup."

He stretched again, and his spine popped loud enough to make her wince.

"You need a chiropractor."

"It's the price one pays for working out. Wanna tickle me again?"

"Oh, screw y—"

The fireplace roared to life, flames licking dangerously close to the edge of the hearth.

"I mean," Sephie gasped, "I like your muscles because they keep me warm!"

The fireplace fizzled out.

"Why does the *house* want us to bang?"

Luke laughed. "Maybe it's taking a page out of Rob's book?"

"Huh."

Sephie chewed on her lip. Maybe that was the case…

"What's going on in that noggin of yours, Scoob?"

She looked at him. "What if this is all part of the TV show?"

He rolled onto his side, arching a brow. "What do you mean?"

"Think about it," she mused, "The production company wanted to hop on the reality dating train and figured the best way to do that was to piggyback off one of their most popular shows. They found two complete opposites, locked them in a house under the guise of ghost hunting, and decided to try and bring them together through special effects or something."

Luke flopped back into the pillows. "Honestly? You should be a producer."

"So you think there's a possibility?"

"Nope."

"But you just said it was a good idea!"

"Yep. I think it's a brilliant idea. An idea the *Dead Serious* producers would never come up with."

"Fair point." She joined him in snuggling back into the pillows. "What time do you think it is?"

"No clue, and oddly, I don't care. I'm comfy."

"Ditto."

They lay there for a while, staring at the ceiling. Sunlight peeked through a gap in the curtains, making the leftover dust sparkle in the beam. A bird chirped outside. Somehow, the air smelled faintly like flowers.

This was nice.

"You know," Luke said, amused, "we're basically having pillow talk."

She smacked him lightly on the shoulder, just making him chuckle again.

"Hey, if this is a reality show, I can work with it," he said. "Historic mansion to explore, free food, incredible sleep accommodations, I'm basically getting paid to have a staycation."

"Still worth it even though you're stuck with me?" She quipped.

He faced her again. "Sure is, Scoob."

"Whatever, Flex."

"You think we could sue if anything goes catastrophically wrong?"

She shrugged. "We signed the media release forms already, so they would probably lean into that. I read every inch of that contract though, and it was specifically for *Dead Serious*. Unless there's some loophole, I don't know how they could cover their butts."

"You're like, stupid intelligent. What'd you get your college degree in?"

She smirked. "The easiest one could possibly get; business."

"Not too fond of school, were we?"

"Not in the slightest. I only went because my parents demanded I do something with my life. So here I am, with a college degree and student loans, doing the same job I've had since high school."

She didn't resent people who loved school. But for her, it had been a costly mistake. Even if she walked away from paranormal research for good, she'd just get a barista job and keep researching weird old places as a hobby.

Her stomach growling, announced it was time for them to start their day.

"You need a Scooby Snack?"

"That and coffee. Guess I'm gonna have to figure out a French press."

"I know how to use one, no biggie."

Right, restaurant.

"This is feeling too much like a one-night stand and the guy ends up being nice."

"… Thank you?"

She tossed the covers off and swung her legs over the side of the bed. But instead of touching the floor, her feet slipped into satin. Looking down, she spotted a pair of Victorian house slippers already on her feet.

She held up a foot. "House took it as a compliment."

Luke leaned over the edge of his side. "I got a pair too. And they're actually big enough." He gave her a sideways smirk. "So whether it's ghosts or production, someone's been getting personal with our feet."

She rolled her eyes and looked up at the ceiling. "Whoever you are, can I at least get a tank top or something? I'm not exploring this place dressed like a Victorian lady."

Luke gasped in mock horror. "How dare you want to expose your clavicles!"

"It already stuck me in bed with a man I'm not married to, I don't think they're concerned with me being a hussy."

Chapter 19

"Great, now I'm gonna have to waste money on a French press."

Sephie was already on her second cup of coffee. Luke managed to explain how to use the press while he went to work on breakfast. He smirked as he stirred the egg hash he'd put together.

"It wouldn't be a waste, you clearly like the coffee." He tossed her the oven mitts from the night before. "Do me a favor and get the biscuits out of the oven, please."

"You're standing in front of it."

He widened his stance.

"I'm not pulling biscuits out of a hot oven between your legs. You want some roasted nuts with that?"

He chuckled and stepped aside, giving her room. She pulled out the very flaky-looking biscuits, the warm, buttery smell wafting into her nose as she carried them to the table. The window still only opened a few inches, but neither of them complained. They were just glad the lock hadn't disappeared yet.

"Order up."

Luke joined her at the table with two plates loaded with hash: peppers, onions, and some kind of green herb mixed with the eggs and potatoes. Sephie hadn't realized diner-style breakfast could look so bright and pretty.

She took a delicious forkful and giggled at him across the table.

"Maybe if we keep being nice enough, the house will give you a bigger chair."

He tore into a biscuit. "I like this one. Feels quaint."

"You look like King Kong."

"Do not forget I could crush you with my fist."

She rolled her eyes. "I'm assuming we'll be able to get the rest of the soup out of our pants, but we still have to wait for them to dry. Let's hope more clothes appear."

"This is pretty damn domestic. I think we deserve more bloomers, at least."

The image of Luke in a pair of lacy bloomers appeared in her head.

Why did he look cute?

"Hey!"

They both looked up to find Aiden at the window.

"What the heck?"

Luke shrugged. "I see Rob didn't update you. We've got food, water, and apparently clothing."

Aiden stared, then smirked. "Only thing I heard from Rob was that you two seemed to be getting along better. I didn't expect to find a Victoria and Albert on vacation."

"A who?"

Sephie huffed. "Queen Victoria and Prince Albert? One of the greatest love stories ever told?"   She looked at Aiden. "I appreciate the reference, by the way. Luke over here is too much of a meathead to understand."

"Hey!"

The French press's top popped open and launched coffee grounds in Sephie's direction. They missed by a few inches, splattering against the window.

Sephie grumbled. "I'm sorry for calling you a meathead, you're very smart."

Luke stared at the grounds. "Apology accepted."

The grounds began to drip down the glass, leaving trails of brown sludge behind. The house, apparently, was going to make them clean it up.

Aiden's mouth hung open. "Um, what was *that???*"

"Sentient house," Sephie and Luke answered in unison.

"Sentient—this has got to be a joke. What have you two been up to?"

Luke raised a brow. "You mean to say the *Dead Serious* crew didn't rig this place with special effects and hidden cameras reacting every time we're mean to each other?"

Aiden blinked. "NO!"

Sephie rested her chin in her hand. "I dunno, they might not have told any of the Ghostie Boys. No offense, Aiden, but I wouldn't trust you guys to keep a secret like that."

Aiden shook his head. "I'm insanely confused. You two are obviously fine, so I'm going back to the hotel. Enjoy the rest of your breakfast."

He wandered off toward his car and Sephie just shrugged.

"I guess if they have hidden cameras around here without our knowledge, we could get out of that contract."

"True," Luke replied. "Although maybe we should just give them a show? You'd make enough money to not investigate as much, and I could put more into the restaurant."

"And there'd be residuals. Probably sponsorships," she added.

"You don't seem like someone who'd want to be in the spotlight, though." He cleared their plates and took them to the sink. "How long were we supposed to film again?"

"A week," she sighed. "I guess if they let us out of here on day seven, we'll know what's really going on."

"Yeah, I guess." He glanced at the coffee grounds now pooling on the window ledge, streaks of brown goo behind them. "Let me grab a rag. Then we can check on the pants situation."

***

"Uhhh…"

Sephie stared at the neat piles of folded clothes that appeared on the folding table.

"What?" Luke walked up beside her. "Oh."

They stepped closer to inspect the latest offering from the house. Luke held up what could only be described as a pair of boxers, but made of linen. Sephie lifted a pair of briefs that looked like someone had trimmed the legs off bloomers. Matching stays came with them.

"I think," she said, amused, "the house is trying to give us modern-day clothing. It just… doesn't know how."

Luke chuckled. "Hey, I'm grateful for a new pair of underwear. At least it's not those wool drawers men used to wear."

She frowned. "Who on earth thought that was a good idea?"

"I don't know. I'm amazed dudes were able to do the nasty." He gave her a look. "You want me to go change in my room or something?"

She turned away. "Just don't look."

"Okay."

Nervously, she stripped out of the nightgown. Behind her, she heard Luke doing the same. Her hands shook a little as she pulled on the stays, the makeshift underwear, the house's version of leggings, and a tee with… a gramophone on the front?

It had tried to make a band t-shirt.

She just had to figure out where she dropped her boots.

"Hey, Flex—" She turned to find a shirtless Luke hunched over the table, searching for a shirt. Her eyes widened. "I'm so sorry."

"What?" He looked down at himself. "Not like I'm butt-naked or anything. And you've seen me in boxers and a nightshirt. Chill."

The nightshirt had concealed the massive muscles hidden under his flannel. He didn't have chiseled abs, but he was big. His arms and shoulders looked like boulders, his chest was broad and solid, and sure enough, a trail of curly hair ran down his stomach, all the way to—

"Scoob?"

She blinked a few times.

He smirked. "Ah. Go ahead and lust for a second."

Her face went hot. "I'm *not* lusting."

"Suuure."

She bolted forward, haphazardly scooped up her pile of clothes, and scurried to the exit.

"I'm gonna put these away in my room. Meet me in the foyer in ten, we'll go over the journal."

She heard his laugh just before she slammed the door.

Chapter 20

After Luke found a shirt and Sephie splashed some cold water on her face, the two met again in the foyer. Sephie held the leather journal in her hands, staring at the clasp on the front.

"I always feel like I'm invading someone's privacy when I do this," she grumbled.

"Try actually talking with the dead person when you're holding their personal belongings," he muttered back.

She went to undo the clasp, only to find it stuck. She let out a long sigh.

"Don't freak out," Luke whispered, before wrapping his arms around her waist from behind. He leaned over and gently placed his chin on the top of her head. "Try it again."

She easily undid the strip of leather.

"I guess I'm good at cute," he said softly.

She attempted to ignore him as she opened the journal and read aloud.

This journal belongs to Mrs. Cora Jane Ashland, born November 23rd, 1811.

"Well I'll be," Luke sighed, "we found the owner."

"Possibly," Sephie corrected. "She might be part of the family lineage."

Luke shook his head. "Not with that birth date, it wouldn't line up."

Dammit.

"Yeah, you're right."

"You know you don't have to be right about everything all the time, right?"

She glared at him. He let go of her waist and held his hands up defensively. They both turned their attention back to the journal, grateful for the distraction from the awkwardness. Sephie continued to read.

Monday, January 2nd, 1832.
I am, at last, Mrs. Augustus Ashland.
I hardly know how to express the happiness that overflows from my heart,

though I daresay this journal shall try to contain it. I find myself lingering over the name as I write it. Mrs. Ashland. Although, Cora Ashland doesn't roll off the tongue as easily. Never mind that.

"Corashland… Cora Ush…she's got a point," Luke said.

Sephie couldn't help but giggle at him. "Cora Ashland. You just have to make sure that slight pause gets in there."

"Cora Ashland. It's pretty once you get it."

The wedding was nothing short of an enchantment. Gus spared no expense, and I daresay I have never seen such joy upon his face as I did when the vows were spoken. The celebration began long before the ceremony itself. A somewhat unorthodox arrangement, I admit. But Gus insisted joy need not follow order. And so, we dined and laughed and danced until my cheeks ached from smiling and my slippers could bear no more. Uncle Ellis and his ensemble played long into the evening, and though Mother fretted about the impropriety of such liberties, even she was caught joining in.

At the stroke of midnight, as we were pronounced husband and wife, a volley of fireworks burst across the sky.

"A New Year's wedding? That's kind of brilliant, and I'm stealing it," Luke hummed.

"It's corny," Sephie said dryly.

A breeze stirred through the foyer, flipping the pages of the journal and threatening to slam it shut. Sephie turned and wrapped Luke in a sudden bear hug, her head barely clearing his ribs. The breeze stilled.

"Sorry. If you think it's a cute idea, then it's your wedding, and that's what matters."

"Apology accepted. Now keep reading. I want to see what else the lady of the house has to say."

Sephie flipped the pages back.

We arrived at the estate shortly after, and I confess I have not yet the words for what met me at the door. The house is vast beyond all reason. Gus has spoken of its construction these past years, but no amount of imagining prepared me for the reality. He assured me during our entire courtship it would be worth the wait. As much as I hate to admit it, he was correct.

"Hey, she's like you!"

Sephie ignored him.

When I was but sixteen, I fancied myself ready to be a wife. But now I see at sixteen, I understood nothing of love, nor of the world, nor of myself. Gus and I were children then, with no business getting married. But we waited. We grew. And now, at twenty, I am no longer that impatient girl. I am a woman, his wife, and more grateful than words allow for the time we took to become so. We are married. Truly, wholly married. And we do not simply reside in a house, we have a mansion.

"Wow, she got married at twenty versus sixteen. Remarkable." Sephie rolled her eyes.

"Oh stop, it really is. Sounds like her hubby wanted to make sure they'd be comfortable going into marriage. And a longer courtship gave them time to figure out if they actually liked each other. Mature decision, I think. She probably could've snagged someone else while she was waiting, but she didn't. They obviously loved each other."

He had a point. Again.

Gus is asleep already. He is unaccustomed to such revelry and retired shortly after our arrival. He promised me a fairytale, and I believe he has given it. I'll use the time to explore this giant building, there are rooms I'm not sure we'll ever use.

"Dear lord, can you imagine actually being a homeowner at twenty?" Luke crossed his arms. "I'm lucky my rent hasn't gone up that much."

"Gus' family must've been loaded. Moving right into a custom-built, three-story mansion after the wedding of the century…" Sephie could only dream of money like that.

"Well, we've got some names. The original owners were Augustus and Cora Ashland. They started construction around 1828, moved in at the beginning of 1832. I'd kill to have access to a public library right now. I could probably find something more, unless the city managed to hide everything."

"Who knows?" Luke shrugged. "Hey, didn't you say there were portraits in your room? Maybe Cora and Gus are in some of them."

Sephie nodded excitedly, and they headed for the stairs.

This was fun.

Why is this fun?

Chapter 21

"How did you not notice this before?"

Luke and Sephie were staring up at Cora and Gus' wedding portrait. Cora was stunning, with feline features, piercing eyes, and a tall, willowy frame. She wore a Victorian wedding dress, complete with layers upon layers of silk and tulle. Gus looked studiously handsome. He was slightly shorter than Cora, with an athletic build framed by his suit. A pair of round spectacles accentuated his kind eyes.

"I was tired and didn't have much light, okay? I wasn't paying attention to portrait details," Sephie said. That wasn't entirely true. She had wondered about it. But taking a deep dive into the art wasn't exactly her top priority after waking up in Luke's bed.

Luke turned his attention to another photo of Gus standing in front of a row of buildings, hands in his pockets and a huge grin on his face.

"You think his family was in real estate?"

Sephie leaned in. "Possibly? It would make sense. It was definitely one of the biggest ways people made money back then. And they did build the house."

Her gaze drifted back to the wedding photo. The couple couldn't have been more different, yet they looked completely in love. It was kind of heartwarming. Only five portraits were hanging here; there had to be more somewhere.

"Did you see any more portaits in the library?"

Luke shook his head. "Not hanging up, but maybe there's a photo album or something on a shelf-" he cut himself off. "Wait, what if the house fixed the ladder?"

Sephie grinned. "Only one way to find out."

They headed down the hall toward the library, Sephie flipping through the journal as they walked. She read aloud.

Friday, January 27th, 1832

We have resided in the house for nearly a month now, and I must say, it is most splendid. Gus saw to every detail with such care. There is a proper library, a well-appointed kitchen with all the modern conveniences, and even a designated space for laundering. Mother continues to insist we hire a maid to handle chores, particularly the washing, but I find comfort in doing it. I need something to do while Gus is away at business, and it pleases me to feel as though I am offering something of value to our new household.

Still, I almost feel as though something's missing in this mansion. I just cannot put a finger on it.

Luke reached out and stopped her before she collided face-first with the library door.

"Maybe no more reading while walking," he said, twisting the doorknob easily. "Apparently, we're still being nice enough to keep doors unlocked."

"Let's hope nice enough for a renovated library."

Sephie's jaw dropped as they stepped inside. The already impressive room had undergone a full-on Beauty and the Beast transformation. The massive window's curtains had been restored—lush red velvet, now elegantly roped back with gold cords to let sunlight flood in. The hardwood floors gleamed, and both remaining walls now boasted built-in shelves, packed to capacity. Two sliding ladders stood in opposite corners.

"Whoa," Sephie breathed, "I think this is the biggest transformation yet."

"Insane," Luke agreed. "I thought it was weird to have free-standing bookshelves in here. I wonder who plastered the wall up before."

"Someone who clearly didn't respect books. Ooo, a reading seat!"

She bolted over to the cushioned bench built into the window. The wood matched the floor; the velvet upholstery matched the curtains. It was the perfect little corner to lose yourself in.

Luke smirked. "Shiny object syndrome much?"

She shot him a look. "It's cool and you know it."

He nodded, already moving toward one of the ladders. "I'm gonna try climbing up to the top shelves and see if anything interesting's up there. Enjoy your throne."

She stretched out on the cushion, perfectly content. Birds chirped outside, drawing her to look out the massive window. The garden below looked vibrant compared to before. She squinted, trying to spot a cellar entrance, but didn't find anything.

"Hey Luke, I'm not seeing—"

CRASH.

"God—" She leapt to her feet and rushed toward the shelves. Luke was dangling from the top, having kicked the ladder out from under him. A few books fell, including a large leather-bound one. Sephie planted her hands on her hips.

"Can't leave you alone for two seconds?"

"I'm *totally* fine."

"I'm sure you are." She started dragging the ladder back toward him. "You are the Flexorcist, after all. But I don't think there's a smart way for you to scale down."

"And you thought you'd be able to climb this thing like a spider monkey."

She held the ladder as he carefully stepped back onto it.

"Why'd you end up like that anyway?"

"There's a hidden compartment up here. I reached for it and slipped."

"You should have waited for me, I wouldn't have fallen."

She bent down and picked up the large book. It was indeed a photo album. She glanced at the other books: *Emma, Little Women, Frankenstein, The Picture of Dorian Gray,* and *Dracula.* Cora and Gus seemed to appreciate the classics.

"I wonder why these were hidden away with the album?"

Luke, now safely on the ground, picked up *Emma.* The brown leather was worn at the edges, and the pages yellowed. He carefully cracked it open, and his eyes nearly bugged out of his head.

"Scoob, this is a first edition."

"WHAT?!" Sephie stopped herself from snatching it out of his hands. "Should we have gloves on or something?!"

"All things considered, it's in good shape. I think as long as we're careful." He gently closed it and placed it on a nearby table.

Sephie blinked.

Had that always been there?

She brushed it off as they knelt to examine the rest. *Frankenstein* didn't seem particularly special, but the others were all first editions, *Little Women* and *Dorian Gray* were even signed. They moved each book to the table in silence as if transferring holy relics, both of them exhaling deeply once the final book was placed.

"Well," Luke muttered, "aside from *Frankenstein*, that explains the hidden compartment."

"*Frankenstein* is an odd favorite."

"*Frankenstein* is brilliant, ya pleeb."

The ladder creaked.

"Pleeb is a compliment."

The ladder rolled.

"Did I say pleeb? I meant… Sweet Pea."

The ladder stilled. Luke exhaled sharply.

"Let's take a peek at that photo album."

"Sure thing, Snookums."

He grabbed her hand like it was the most natural thing in the world and half-dragged her to the reading nook.

She stared at their clasped hands, making a face. He chuckled.

"Don't do that. I wouldn't call Sweet Pea the best save, so stick with the facade."

She gave him the cheesiest grin she could manage and twisted out of his grip to flop onto the cushion. He grumbled but sat beside her as she opened the photo album.

A smiling Cora greeted them on the first page, perched on the rolling ladder, placing a book on a not-yet-full shelf.

"I guess Cora was the reader, then?" Sephie mused.

"Sure looks like it. There's a whole shelf dedicated to Jane Austen."

"Men can like Jane Austen."

"That they can, I'm one of them. But you really think Gus was collecting romance novels back then?"

Not a chance.

The next page showed the couple at the beach, wearing modest 1800s swimwear. Gus held a parasol and was mid-lick on an ice cream cone Cora held out to him. Utterly adorable.

"Ah-hah," Sephie said triumphantly as she flipped the page to find Cora in what looked very much like a wine cellar. "Unless they visited a winery or something, this has gotta be around here somewhere."

Luke hopped up. "Ready for more exploring, Scoob?"

"Let's find ourselves a cellar."

She clutched the album tightly. Luke reached for the door—only to find it locked. He jiggled the knob, but it wouldn't budge.

"… Not again." He took one of Sephie's hands and looked around. "Hey, this is my lady and she's… really cute and stuff."

The door stayed firmly shut.

Sephie set the album down and leapt up, wrapping her arms around Luke's neck. He instinctively grabbed her lower back so she wouldn't fall, her feet dangling. He inched over and tried the knob again.

Nothing.

He carefully set her down, and they gave each other a concerned look.

They were stuck. Again.

Chapter 22

"Persephone Blake is the most stunning woman I've ever laid eyes upon."

Sephie smacked Luke on the shoulder.

"Cuz that'll help," he whined, rubbing his arm.

"I hit pure muscle, shut up. And you know I hate my full name."

They'd tried everything they could think of to appease the house. Many hugs and compliments later, their efforts were proven fruitless.

"If I had a literal Greek Goddess's name, I'd milk it for all it's worth," Luke mumbled.

"Persephone was a little twit."

Luke gave her a look.

"Yeah yeah, I know, it's not real, but do you know how overdone that story is nowadays? Everybody romanticizes the crap out of it." She crossed her arms. "Hades kidnapped her, she was dumb enough to eat the food, and got stuck being a part-time wife to the guy who captured her."

"It's just a myth," Luke said, scratching his head. "And she's the Goddess of Spring. That's cool, right?"

Sephie didn't answer.

"I don't know why it bothers you," he continued, "but I'll be more careful, promise."

A book toppled off a shelf in the middle of the bookcase, landing with a soft *thump* at their feet. Luke picked it up, stared at the cover, then looked upward.

"Okay, look, that's not funny!"

Sephie grabbed the book to see what Luke meant.

The Art of Conversation by Roger Boswell.

Sephie gave a dramatic eye roll. "I mean, if the house literally just wants us to talk, haven't we already been doing that?"

Another book fell. This one landed title-up: *The Importance of Being Earnest*.

"Har har!" Sephie shouted at the ceiling. "You think you're hysterical, don't you?"

"Scoob," Luke said, "if it wants us to talk more, maybe we should?"

Sephie grumbled. They'd already shared dead relative trauma, what else could they possibly talk about, the weather?

"Look," Luke said, "I get you want to keep to yourself, but we're gonna need food at some point. I'm not keen on eating you, seeing as you have no fat."

"I'll take that as a compliment," she snapped, stalking back to the window seat. "But fine, might as well. Even though I could probably get a few meals out of you."

He wrinkled his nose but followed her. They settled onto the cushion in silence before Luke sighed.

"I guess I can start?"

"Start where?"

"I dunno. When I was a kid?"

Sephie leaned against the window, waving at him dismissively. A sharp woosh cut through the air, and Luke caught something mid-flight, right next to her ear. Wide-eyed, she turned to find him holding a small blue book. She snatched it from his hands.

The Ladies' Book of Etiquette, and Manual of Politeness.

"Cute. Fine, sorry." She turned toward him, giving her full attention. "Are you from Maryland originally?"

"I am, Baltimore. You?"

"Baltimore?" She arched a brow. "I would've pegged you for Chestertown. Tree City and all that. I'm from Annapolis."

"The woodsman getup is a personal choice. That, and it's easier to find husky sizes." He shifted slightly. "But yeah, Baltimore. Parents are still together, only child, lost the closest thing to a brother I ever had…"

"Your cousin, right? What was his name, if you don't mind me asking?"

Luke blinked, surprised she cared, then smiled. "Angelo. He got the more Grecian-sounding name out of the two of us."

"I'm guessing that's your dad's side, given your last name. Where's your mom from?"

"Boston," he chuckled. "She's of Irish descent, but the absolute definition of a Boston woman. Imagine that accent interacting with my Yiayia growing up. They both claim there's a language barrier."

"I find it hilarious that I'm the one with the Greek Goddess name, and there's not a lick of Greek in my family."

"What's your background?"

"White," she said, accentuating the 'h.' "Very white."

He erupted into a laugh. "So your parents were trying to be 'different' with your name."

"Pretty much. I got to be the guinea pig. My sister, Thalia, got off a lot easier."

She hoped her family wasn't worried. Surely someone on the crew had reached out to them.

"Your name's better," Luke said.

"What?"

"Queen of the literal Underworld versus a muse? Come on, no contest."

"Hm." She still hated the full name, but relating to the Queen of the Underworld made her feel a little better. "Do you serve any Greek food at the restaurant?"

"Ha, not yet. I've been leaning more into the cozy cottagecore-type stuff. Soup, good breakfast, lots of potato dishes." He smirked. "What's hilarious is, Angelo was a vegetarian."

"Isn't that, like, the cardinal sin of being Greek?"

"Pretty much. Yiayia was the living embodiment of *My Big Fat Greek Wedding.* 'What do you mean he don't eat no meat?!' Drove her nuts."

Sephie laughed. "Gran was similar, except she wanted me to eat. She was positive my growth was somehow stunted. Both my parents and Thalia are tall. Then there's me."

"You being tall would give you too much power." He peeked out the window. "And I take back my take back. You *are* tiny and cute."

She couldn't help but grin. "Thank you. Your... largeness is pretty endearing." She ran a hand through her hair. "Have you always been so tall?"

"Nope. I was like you-. Shortest one in every class. Then I shot up in tenth grade. It's wild, suddenly being in a giant body out of nowhere."

That explained the random clumsiness.

"That garden really is gorgeous," he mused. "I wish I'd gotten a better look at it before we got stuck in here."

He looked out the window like a golden retriever desperate to be let outside.

No, more like a Saint Bernard.

Either way, it was cute.

"You think that's enough to open the library door?" She asked.

They walked over together. Luke reached for the doorknob.

Still locked.

She sighed. His stomach growled.

Sephie put her hands on her hips. "You can eat paper, right?"

He scowled. "Technically, yeah. But I'm not eating anything from a collection like this. It's gotta be priceless."

"True." She stared at the door and frowned. "What more do you want from us?"

A familiar thump sounded behind them. They rolled their eyes and turned.

The Scarlet Letter.

"Is it calling me a harlot or saying you have a secret love child?" Sephie quipped.

Luke was suspiciously quiet.

"Do *not* tell me you actually have a secret love child."

"No!" he nearly shrieked. "No kids. Not yet, at least."

"Oh, so you want babies?" Sephie grimaced, imagining some poor woman having to deliver a half-giant infant.

"Someday, yeah. Wait, never mind that." He exhaled. "I think it wants me to tell you something I've been hiding."

"Good grief, out with it then." She was getting annoyed again, and could really use some more coffee, she was beginning to feel her 4pm withdrawl headache creeping into her skull.

Luke stared at his feet. "You're not gonna like this."

"I'm sure I'll dislike dying in here more than whatever secret you're keeping."

He looked up, a stoic expression on his face.

"Your grandma's been trying to come forward since last night."

Chapter 23

Sephie just stared at Luke, feeling numb. She'd just started to like him. He was goofy but endearing, had his himbo moments, sure, but he was undoubtedly smart. And he obviously cared deeply for his family.

Why'd he have to go and pull this?

She sank to the floor, crisscrossing her legs like a little kid. She put her hands in her lap and began picking at her cuticles. Luke carefully took a seat next to her.

"Don't do that," he said gently. "You'll bleed."

"What do you care?"

"Sephie, don't act like that—"

"Shut. Up."

Uncomfortable silence settled in the room again. Sephie did everything she could to keep the tears from falling. How dare he listen to her talk about Gran and then try to use it against her? She couldn't remember giving him anything specific, nothing he could use to tug at her heart.

"You're just like the rest of them," she whispered.

"I promise—"

"Shut up."

Luke scowled. "You know, it's great you stick to your guns, but maybe work on listening to other people before you come to your own conclusions?"

She huffed, and it came out as a strangled sob.

"Sephie, look," he inched closer. "What the heck do I have to lose? You don't like me, you're not paying me, I literally get nothing out of this." He flinched. "Well, except getting your Grandma out of my ear."

She sniffled.

"Please don't cry."

"I'm not."

"Oh, you're like that."

She finally looked at him and glared. "Like what?"

"Putting on a whole tough guy act to keep from opening up."

"Shut up, Freud."

"Now there's a wackjob."

A giggle escaped her before she could stop it. Luke gave a small smile.

"I'm not Ed Warren, I'm not that Nazi your gross ex found and I'm not Teresa Giudice."

"The heck does a Real Housewife have to do with ghost talking?"

"Ghost talking is a new one. You know, the Long Island Medium?"

"Flex, that's Theresa Caputo," she snorted through her tears.

"Oh. Well, shows how much reality TV I actually watch. But anyway," he waved a hand, "I'm not a fake. And if you have any doubts at all, you have permission to punch me."

"Because that'll do a lot of damage."

"You gave me friction burn and broke my toe, I'm sure you'd find a way to do *some* damage."

Again, he had a point.

Sephie took a long breath. Even if he was a fraud, what else could hurt her at this point? She'd gone through enough therapy to keep it together.

"Fine."

"What?"

She managed to keep any more tears at bay. Looking at Luke, she grumbled, "Fine. Let Gran come forward."

He exhaled and nodded. Then, his head jerked suddenly. "Jeez, she was just waiting for permission."

Sephie frowned. "Luke, what's Gran's name?" She knew she hadn't given him that.

"Florence Paul Addison Adkins. What a mouthful. And before you ask, your middle name is her maiden name."

"Okay." That was too good to be a lucky guess. He could have researched her family tree, though.

"I'm gonna use your full full name, so fair warning. But Persephone Addison Blake? Really?"

Sephie rolled her eyes. "Trust me, I know. Mom said they were naming me after Gran. Imagine the shock when she got to the hospital and saw *that*."

"I guess interesting names are something you have in common."

"It's why she went by Flo." Whoops. She just gave him something. But would could he possibly do with a nickname?

Luke closed his eyes and nodded.

"Mhm." He was really putting on a good act. Although Gran did like to talk. If she couldn't speak directly to her granddaughter, she'd definitely take advantage of a middleman.

Ghosts aren't real.

"Um."

Sephie glared. Luke flinched.

"Flo was... a little too curious about your love life?"

Sephie grumbled. "Gran, I'm glad you're so open to women exploring their sexuality, but that is not me." She leaned back on her elbows, stretching her legs out. "I didn't feel like having a ho phase."

Luke laughed. "She says it wasn't a ho phase, she just liked having fun with boys."

Good ole Gran.

"What all did she say to incite that?"

"I'll let you know ahead of time this is the most ridiculous connection I've ever made."

"Sounds right. Go on."

He took another deep breath. "She said, 'Sephie, get your head out of your butt and be nicer to this young man. He looks like he'd be a....'" His cheeks flushed red. "...fun ride."

Sephie turned a brilliant shade of pink, eyes wide..

There was sex-positive, and then there was Flo.

"I..." Sephie desperately tried to change the subject. "Can Gran just get us out of here?"

"She's not connected to the house, so no. She came forward here because you're here and apparently need her."

Sephie finally laid flat on her back. The floor was hard and not remotely comforting, but she didn't care. She just wanted to feel... nothing.

"She was gone when I really needed her," she whispered. "And yeah, I know, she was ninety-eight and needed to go. But nobody else seemed to understand."

"This is me, not Flo. You want to talk about it?" Luke reached over as if to stroke her arm, but ended up just setting his palm beside hers.

Sephie sighed.

Here goes nothing.

"My last investigation job was four months ago. A girl, Lucy, inherited her grandma's Victorian house a few years before, and was convinced it was haunted." She closed her eyes. "I'm always able to chalk up the paranormal occurrences to houses being, well, old. Lighting, reflections, and structural issues can explain away most of it."

Luke's glance looked slightly suspicious, but he just nodded. "Gotcha. Yeah, I've had some clients who I just couldn't connect with anyone. I'm sure something else was causing their issues."

Sephie opened her eyes and stared at him. He looked genuinely sincere.

"Long story short," she continued, "the ghost of hers ended up being an ex-girlfriend. I finally caught her one night when I was there and chased her. She got the upper hand, grabbed my shoulder, and put a knife to my throat..." She swallowed. "It was the grabbing that got to me more than the knife. I... I guess it's not the first time someone grabbed me like that. That gross ex? Brandon... he... he used to do it. Not in a violent way. Just this firm hold on my shoulder, like he needed to keep me in place."

Luke gave her hand the most feather-light of touches. "I deserve the broken toe."

"No, you didn't. Lucy ended up moving out of state. And it... hurt. That house was her biggest connection to her grandma, and she just left it. I was so mad that one person could ruin that by not taking no for an answer. Mix almost getting sliced open with already resurfacing grief over dead grandmas... I kind of isolated myself."

There. She admitted it.
Luke ground his teeth for a moment.

"The way I see it, you don't open up because it never seems to end well, physically or emotionally."

She nodded. She knew this. Dr. Alias knew this. She had just chosen to ignore it, it was always easier.

"I was going to give up doing paranormal investigations. Write a book, make a buttload of money, retire in some mountain-top cabin. I just wanted to leave it all behind."

"Flo says you shouldn't give up something you love—and get paid for—just because of one experience." He stood and offered his hand. Sephie took it, and he helped her up.

"Lord. She's also saying you and I should become 'business partners,' so you have a better sense of security on investigations."

Sephie wrinkled her nose. "She didn't say 'business partners,' did she?"

"Oh, she very much did not."

"Gran," Sephie looked upward, exasperated. "I haven't had a partner since... yeah. I'm good."

Luke blinked. "Wait, you've been single for how long?"

A faint click echoed from the door, cutting him off. They both turned to face it, just in time to see it swing open on its own.

Chapter 24

Sephie nearly bolted out of the room. Luke couldn't blame her. Even though the library transformed into one of the grandest things pulled straight from a fairy tale, going over personal trauma still made it feel suffocating.

But he had to talk to her, just a little more. No more secrets. They were only causing problems.

"Sephie?" he called out.

Damn, she was fast. No wonder she had been able to take down Lucy's stalker. He winced as the image of her being thrown to the ground, a knife glinting above her, flashed in his mind. It was the kind of image that left a sickly feeling in your stomach, whether it was your memory or not.

Shaking the thought away, he jogged down the hall, hoping to catch up.

"Hey, Sephie?"

She turned, her curls bouncing like they had minds of their own. The corners of her mouth quirked upward just a bit. Not a smile, more like a smirk. But still, it was better than her usual razor-sharp glare she'd mainly shot his way. He'd take it.

"Sorry," she said. "I just needed to get out of there. Never thought I'd say that about a library."

Luke chuckled. "I feel you."

"What's up?"

He awkwardly clasped his hands behind his back. There wasn't an easy way to explain another strange overlap in their already bizarre situation.

"I know Lucy."

She blinked. "Oh?"

"Yeah."

There was a beat.

"Uh… anything else?"

"Aren't you curious?"

"I mean, unless she was an ex-girlfriend of yours or something."

He shook his head. "No. She was my first client, I guess?"

"Guess?" Sephie crossed her arms, and a touch of her glare made a comeback.

"Yes, guess," he grumbled. "One of my family members sold me out, and I had people show up at my doorstep the next morning. Lucy was one of them, but she was different to the rest."

Sephie nodded, her eyes softening a little.

"It was soon after her Grandma died. She was trying to connect with her because she felt undeserving of the house for whatever reason. I think she just needed closure."

"So, do grandmas come through pretty often?"

"Not any more than anyone else," he said with a dry smile. "And hers didn't come through. One of her second cousins did. Apparently, Lucy's the only one in the family who isn't a money-hungry piece of crap, so she inherited the house."

Sephie frowned. "That makes me hate what happened to her even more."

Luke shrugged. "Not like she sold the house. She went through a lot and needed a change of scenery. Can't blame her."

"I guess." Her arms dropped to her sides, and she frowned. "Seems like a lot of odd coincidences going on."

That there were. Departed grandmas, old houses, shared connections... Luke was beginning to wonder if it meant something.

Sephie wasn't like the other loved ones who came to him hoping to speak to the dead. She didn't want answers handed to her, she wanted the truth. He liked that about her. More than he probably should.

Luke glanced down the hallway. It was quiet again. Eerily so.

"Hey," he said, quieter now. "You okay?"

She gave a sound between a scoff and a laugh. "No. But I'm not totally losing it if that's what you're asking."

He stepped closer. "I meant it when I said you don't have to be alone in this."

Her gaze flicked up to his. "I believe you."

They stood like that for a moment. Somewhere far off, the house creaked. Not ominous, just... a reminder it was always listening.

"I don't think it's random," Sephie said suddenly. "Any of this."

"No?"

She shook her head. "You, me, this house, Lucy. It just all seems to be connecting in some way. Like one of those boards with red strings attaching a bunch of photos."

"Well," Luke said, "that would imply there's some Charlie Day attempting to connect everything."

He didn't want to say fate. As much as he believed it, Sephie was just starting to enjoy his presence, and he didn't want to screw that up.

The hallway light flickered once. They both looked up.

Luke furrowed his brow. "Did you—?"

A sharp bang echoed through the silence.

They froze.

Another bang, harder this time, and more rhythmic.

They ran to the window at the end of the hall that overlooked the front door. Rain misted the glass, but through the distortion, they saw a shape pressed against the window downstairs, frantically smacking at the frame. Another shape was standing closely behind, apparently not as concerned.

Luke squinted. "Who's that?"

"Good god," Sephie sighed. "That's my sister."

Another sharp bang crashed against the glass, this time, it was followed by a loud, shrill voice.

"SEPHIE?! Come to the door!"

Something crashed downstairs. Of course it did. The house made it crystal clear that it didn't plan on letting anyone, or anything, inside unless it wanted them there.

But with the way Thalia was pounding and shouting, Luke wasn't sure the house could hold her back.

Sephie rolled her eyes. "I suppose I should let her know I'm okay." She cocked her head towards the stairwell. "You coming?"

He nodded, almost smiling.

Meeting the family is going to be… interesting.

Then he caught himself, and mentally slammed the brakes.

Easy, Romeo. He and Sephie were barely friends. Trauma buddies, if anything. No need to start imagining Thanksgiving dinner.

Chapter 25

"Oh thank god!"

Luke and Sephie stepped into the foyer to find Thalia pressed up against the front window. Jessica was behind her, arms crossed, blinking up at the sky. Sephie rolled her eyes. Thalia's voice had already pissed someone off. She walked over to the window and cocked a hip.

"Hey, Sis. I was wondering if they contacted you."

"Too late, in my opinion." Thalia shot a glare at Jessica. "One would think the families of kidnapping victims might get a phone call."

Jessica stepped up beside her. "They haven't been kidnapped. They're just stuck. And they have food and water. We were focused on getting them out."

Thalia wrinkled her nose. "*What* are you wearing?"

Sephie looked down at her gramophone shirt. "What, not a fan of Edison?"

"Who?"

"Thalia, you are not that dumb. Think."

She bit her lip and then something lit up in her eyes. "Oh, he discovered electricity."

"There you go."

Luke stepped next to Sephie. "*This* is your sister?"

"Sure is."

Thalia got a good look at Luke and immediately went goo goo eyed. "Oh hiii. Sephie, who's this?"

"Oh brother," Sephie groaned. "Thalia, this is Luke, the medium I told you about."

"Oh! The Greek!" Thalia literally fluttered her eyelashes. "So I was right."

She was referring to Luke just *having* to be hot. "Oh shush."

Thalia wiggled her fingers under her chin. "Hi Luke."

Luke, either oblivious or uninterested, gave her a flat "Hi" back. Sephie smirked. The last thing her sister needed was another man to derail her already scattered priorities.

Thalia pouted. "Um. So, have you figured out how to get out of there yet?"

Sephie frowned. "Isn't that supposed to be their job?" She nodded toward Jessica.

"Trust me, we've been trying." Jessica held her phone up to the glass. Sephie squinted and saw a mass influx of emails, text messages, and missed calls in the notifications. Jessica sighed and shoved it back in her pocket.

"People are either too busy with other projects, or they want nothing to do with Ashland Manor."

"What?" Sephie blinked. "You'd think every preservationist and historian would be dying to get their hands on this place."

Jessica shrugged. "I don't know, a lot are worried because there is no information about this place. They're afraid they'll mess something up."

"Oh," Sephie perked up. "We did figure out who the original owners were! A young couple, Augustus and Cora Ashland, they moved in at the start of 1832."

Jessica's eyes lit up. "Now that's amazing news. I might be able to get some info based on that. Maybe they had a kid or something who changed their name?"

Sephie nodded. "We'll keep digging. There seems to be plenty of hidden treasure in here."

Luke sighed. "So, we're still stuck. Hey, where's my family?"

"They know you're safe," Jessica said. "They can't make it for a few days—work."

Sephie patted his arm. "They still love you, Flex. Thalia here is just unemployed."

"Hey!" Thalia squeaked. "I'm between jobs!"

"Yeah," Sephie snorted, "between getting fired and not wanting a new one."

Thalia's face flushed. "What's got you so pissy?"

"I've been through a lot in two days, Thalia. Cut me some slack."

Luke glanced between them, concern flickering in his eyes. Thalia looked guilty.

Sephie sighed. She hadn't meant it. "I'm sorry. That was mean."

Thalia softened and gave a sheepish grin. "It's okay. And you're right. I'll send out more applications when I get home."

Luke chuckled. "You weren't kidding when you said you were nothing like her."

"And I wouldn't have it any other way."

Jessica tapped on the window again. "Hey, so you two are still fine?" They both shrugged and nodded, having accepted their current situation temporarily.

"Cool. I have to go check on Jace at the hospital, then I'll start digging into the Ashland family tree."

Thalia perked up. "Jace, like *Dead Serious* Jace? Oh please, please, please, let me come meet him!"

"What?! No!" Jessica looked at Sephie for backup.

"I don't know, maybe they'd hit it off."

Luke lightly bumped her side. "Have you not been complaining about how gross Jace is? You're really gonna send your sister off to be his newest plaything?"

"Hey!" Thalia squeaked, "I have no interest in him, I want to give him a piece of my mind for picking on Sephie!"

Sephie sighed. "Thalia, go home. I'll introduce you to one of the other three Ghostie Boys as soon as I'm out of here."

Thalia grinned. "Promise?"

"Yeah, yeah."

***

"Your sister is a piece of work."

"She's something."

They were back in the kitchen, Luke cooking again. Somehow, this domestic routine was comforting. Sephie never imagined herself in any sort of relationship similar to this. Brandon tried to convince her to move in for months before she'd dumped him. She'd preferred quiet meals alone. It was more efficient. No... ick... small talk.

But eating with Luke? That felt natural. Just like spending time with him did. And it helped he could cook.

He pulled something off the stovetop and placed it into matching bowls.

"Calling her out on her unemployment was kind of mean."

"She *is* unemployed. I apologized."

Luke tsked as he set a grilled chicken salad in front of her.

"I'm assuming there's no ranch?"

Luke mock-gasped. "You peasant."

Sephie rolled her eyes. "Oh, yeah, like you actually use a red wine vinaigrette."

He chuckled. "Nah, you're right. I love me some ranch. But we're gonna have to make do with olive oil."

She shrugged. It was better than nothing. The salad looked fresh, and the grilled chicken was perfectly seared. She took a bite and smiled. Somehow, even his salads tasted good.

"So did the muse go to college too?" Luke asked between bites.

Sephie nodded. "Yeah."

"If I remember correctly," he dramatically stroked his chin, "Thalia was the muse of comedy?"

"That she was."

"As hilarious as your sister appears to be, I doubt she wanted to be on SNL."

Sephie smirked. "She studied marketing. She's really good at it."

He raised a brow. "Oh?"

"Yeah." She took another bite, chewing slowly. "Unfortunately, she's also really good at getting guys to buy her drinks. Not a full-blown alcoholic or anything, but she did get fired from her dream job after sleeping through a big meeting." She bit her lip. The memory of her usually bubbly sister curled up in bed for days, crying after the fashion magazine let her go, still made her chest ache. "She moved back in with our parents and pulled herself together. But honestly? She's scared to try again. And... yeah, she's kind of lazy."

Luke hummed. "If we ever end up getting paid, I'll hire her."

Sephie dropped her fork. "What?"

He smiled. "She needs a job, I need someone good at marketing. Seems obvious to me." He picked up her fork and handed it back to her. "And I'll be fair, don't worry. She screws up, I'll let her go."

He offered that as if it were no big deal.

Luke cleared the plates, still somehow managing to make himself at home in the undersized kitchen.

"You don't have to do that," she said.

"Do what?"

"Hire Thalia."

He set down a plate of chocolate chip cookies.

Her eyes widened. "When did you make those?"

"I didn't," he said, sitting again. "The house did."

Of course it did.

"And honestly," he said through a mouthful of cookie, "I want to hire your sister. I know you decided we were mortal enemies, but I'm starting to think we're at least meant to be friends. I mean, I'd like to still hang out once we get out of here."

Friends.

Once she gotten past her pettiness, Luke really was easy to be around. He annoyed the hell out of her, but in a fun way. They were in similar "fields," if you could call them that, and they already knew each other's baggage. It did feel like a friendship.

She smiled. "I guess we are friends."

"Still calling you Scooby-Doo."

She took a bite of a cookie. Delicious.

"I wouldn't expect anything different from The Flexorcist."

One of the cabinets gently creaked open. They both looked up to find a single bottle of wine sitting inside.

Sephie's mouth dropped open slightly. Luke scratched his head.

"That definitely wasn't there before."

"Nope."

"You like wine?"

"Not usually," she said, eyeing the bottle. "But it's gotta be good if it's in here, right?"

His eyes twinkled. "I know we should be looking for the mysterious entrance into the cellar, but I'm up for some day drinking if you are."

She giggled. "Hey, it's rude not to accept a gift from a sentient house."

Chapter 26

Sephie's past experiences with wine hadn't been the best. Her mom had let her have a sip of her apricot wine when she was sixteen because she was curious. That sip ended up being spat right back into the cup, with her mother muttering about, "Well, now I can't drink the rest of that."

Thalia went through a boxed wine phase in college. Sephie tried to share a glass with her a few times, but she could only liken the stuff to sour grapes. Thalia teased her about her "refined tastebuds."

Luke offered to try the house wine first. He'd dug through a kitchen drawer, found an 1800s corkscrew, and was currently fiddling with the bottle. It looked different from most wines Sephie had seen. While it was red, it had a dark amber tint to it. No label, but Luke guessed it was some kind of port.

They'd finally entered the dining room for the first time since hiding under the table on their only day of filming. Out of all the rooms so far, this one looked the most Gothic and mysterious. The scones' light glittered off the chandelier, casting dancing flecks over the dark green wallpaper. The long cherrywood table and chairs had been polished until they gleamed, any trace of dust erased. Matching green cushions had been added to the chairs. Sephie felt like she'd walked into a chapter of *Dracula* and was just waiting for the Count to make a grand entrance.

"Please don't break anything," she muttered, watching Luke nearly let the corkscrew slip.

"I won't. I've opened many a wine bottle in my day. Greek, remember?"

"I thought France was wine central?"

He gave her a mortified look. "Scoob, Greek Gods? Mount Olympus? Dionysus???"

The cork popped. Luke grinned and sniffed the opening, closing his eyes and nearly moaning.

Sephie grimaced. "Flex, chill."

He chuckled. "Sorry, this is good stuff." He poured a little into a glass and swirled it.

"Please don't go all wine critic on me."

He waggled his eyebrows. "Oh you know I'm going to."

"Just don't do that weird mouth thing."

"People do that because it enhances the taste," he said, swirling the glass dramatically. "I think it's pretentious. Just drink the damn wine."

He took another sniff from the glass this time. "It smells like... I don't know, like somebody melted a candy bar and shoved it in an old leather book. With like, a little orange peel thrown in."

Sephie furrowed her brow. "Why would anyone want to drink leather?"

Luke shrugged. "It's the only thing you can compare the notes to. You usually don't taste it."

She imagined chewing a piece of leather on a skewer. It'd be like the worst bubblegum ever.

Luke took a small sip, swished it in his mouth for a second, then swallowed. He closed his eyes again, smiling.

Sephie blinked at him. Surely, it couldn't be *that* good. "Well?"

"It's like roasted nuts and dried apricots. There's just enough of a kick to it that you don't feel like you're drinking straight syrup. I feel like I should be sitting in an armchair, plotting world domination while drinking this." He offered her the glass.

"Not even gonna pour me my own?"

"If you seriously care about backwash, I can. I just didn't want to waste another glass if you end up hating it."

She nodded and sniffed. It smelled like… wine. Sour grapes with maybe a touch of citrus and poor decisions. Bracing herself, she took a sip.

Instant regret.

It took everything she had to force it down instead of spewing it back up.

Luke gaped at her, horrified. "You seriously don't like it?"

She shook her head furiously, tears pricking the corners of her eyes from the tartness lingering at the back of her throat.

"I don't think I've ever met anybody who just didn't like wine," he said, bewildered.

She coughed and wiped her eyes. "You have now. I want a mudslide."

He gave one of his low giggles. "Those weren't invented until the '70s, so I doubt the house will hook you up there." He poured himself another glass, swirling it again. "Want to dig into Cora's journal? See if she wrote about the cellar?"

"Good plan," Sephie croaked. "I left it in the kitchen. I'll go grab it."

Luke took a seat at the dining table, swirling his glass and raising an eyebrow theatrically. "I need a fluffy white cat to stroke or something. Mua ha haaa."

"Wow," she mused as she walked out, "you couldn't be intimidating if you tried."

She thankfully heard him chuckle behind her. How many hidden talents did this man have? He talked to dead people (allegedly), cooked, and made wine sound like the most interesting thing in the world, just as long as she didn't have to drink it.

Cora's journal was still sitting on the kitchen table, next to a new glass of brown liquid. Sephie eyed it warily as she moved closer. She picked up the glass, sniffed it, and laughed.

"Luke?" she called as she walked back to the dining room. "The house tried to make me a mudslide."

He gave her a look. "Tried and succeeded?"

"It's basically chocolate milk, vodka, and whipped cream." She took a gulp. "But I can actually drink it, so A for effort."

"You know there are college students out there getting sloshed on just that."

"Oh, absolutely," she said, sliding into the chair across from him.

This table fit his large stature much better. They should probably eat in here from now on. Although she did love watching Luke cook.

Flipping ahead a few pages, Sephie scanned until she caught sight of the word cellar.

Wednesday, June 6th, 1832
I find myself dreadfully idle.
Somehow, I have managed to design and furnish every chamber of this three-story house to my satisfaction. My library shelves are in proper order, and I have tested every recipe in Aunt Alma's wedding cookbook, some with great success, others with mild catastrophe.

Gus, in his infinite wisdom, insists I ought to find a suitable hobby. I have suggested, more than once, that I might secure some modest employment, but he responds only with laughter.

Truly, if he would only agree to the construction of a wine cellar, I might at least apply my palate to something of real use. Heaven knows I've the tongue for it—and more sense than most of the so-called sommeliers I've met.

"Dang, Cora was smart as hell." Luke mused, pouring himself more wine.

Sephie took another sip of her faux mudslide. "I'm guessing the only jobs available to her at the time weren't her thing. Can't blame her, I wouldn't want to be a teacher either."

"Or work in a mill." Luke shuddered. "I read an account of a girl's hair getting caught in a machine and it ripped her scalp off."

Sephie ran a hand through her hair, just imagining how much pain that poor girl must have gone through. She was definitely going to need a shower soon. So far, they'd only used the bathrooms to use the toilets, and the pull chains had been an experience on their own. What she assumed was the main bathroom did have a shower, but Sephie wasn't entirely sure how much she could trust it.

"Hey," Luke waved his hand in front of her. "Skip ahead to whenever Gus gave in and built the cellar."

"Oh, sorry."

Friday, August 17th, 1832

I have prevailed! Gus has granted his consent for the construction of my very own cellar.

Admittedly, I hoped it might come to fruition rather earlier in the season, as I shall now have no hope of being prepared for the grapes' timely arrival. Still, I remain grateful for the opportunity, even if slightly delayed. I have promised Gus that I shall oversee the entirety of the work myself, seeing he couldn't distinguish a Merlot from a muscadine were they labeled in block letters.

I'll place the entrance near the side garden, discreet yet accessible. I'm rather annoyed I have to purchase grapes from outside vendors for the time being, but with proper dedication, I remain confident that one day I may produce my own. If I apply myself with the full force of my faculties, I dare say I might establish a proper winery.

As for a name, I've already devised one: Cora's Folly. Is that not deliciously absurd? I find it utterly delightful.

Sephie took another gulp of her drink. There was more in it than she thought, but she wasn't complaining. That slight, floaty feeling was beginning to buzz pleasantly in her head.

"I wonder if the cellar actually ever came to be," she mused, swirling her glass, "or if it was just a dream."

Luke was already on his third pour of wine.

"I didn't think of that," he mumbled. "Like, they added it to the blueprint but never built it? What about the photo of her in the wine cellar?"

He hiccupped, and Sephie giggled.

"No guarantee that was actually her cellar," she said. "Maybe they were on a rich-people trip to France."

"Or Greece!" Luke declared, holding up a finger, nearly knocking over his glass.

"Whoa buddy, how much of that have you drank?"

"I'm good," he said, holding up the bottle, which was somehow still nearly full. "See?"

Sephie glanced at her own glass and frowned. It, too, looked as if she'd never touched it. That didn't make sense.

"Flex," she said slowly, "I think the house wanted us to have some fun."

His cheeks were flushed. "Hm?"

"It's refilling the alcohol."

Luke stared at the still-full bottle of port, then gulped.

"Aw, man."

Sephie burst out laughing. "You're such a lightweight."

"Am not!" he slurred. "This must be magic ghostie wine." With that, he laid his head down on the table. "Whoa, I wanna go to sleep."

"C'mon, big guy," Sephie said, grabbing at his muscular arm. "Let's get you upstairs for a nap."

She managed to haul him to his feet for a split second before he sank to the floor almost in slow motion. Curling his huge body into a fetal position, he sighed happily.

"This is comfier than I thought," he whispered happily.

"Luke!" Sephie cried.

His only response was a loud, contented snore.

Sephie couldn't help but laugh under her breath and crossed her arms. Around her, the house creaked and settled, as if pleased with itself. She had the strange feeling they'd passed some kind of friendship getting drunk together test. And the house was celebrating right along with them.

Chapter 27

After double-checking Luke was definitely out for the count, Sephie decided to do some more adventuring on her own. She'd done a speed run of the house on filming day, but most of the rooms were too cluttered to properly explore. Now things were (hopefully) cleaned up, it felt like the perfect time to poke around, and maybe even attempt a shower.

She hummed to herself as she climbed the stairwell to the second floor. Aside from the sentient house scolding her every time she was mean to Luke, being in the mansion had become kind of nice. While she'd taken a "break" from investigating to deal with a fun little thing called PTSD, she hadn't really taken the time to just... exist. Granted, this was technically a job, but the house was making sure it didn't feel like one.

Sephie started exploring the second-floor rooms in order, pleasantly surprised when the first door on her left was unlocked. A study greeted her. This room was more in line with the dining room's aesthetic: dark mauve wallpaper covered the walls, a mahogany desk and matching drawing table sat on one side, and a baby grand piano occupied the opposite corner. A medium-sized window let the afternoon sun stream in through cracks in the heavy black velvet curtains.

"I wonder if this was Gus's room," Sephie muttered to herself.

An honest-to-goodness cuckoo clock suddenly came to life. The little bird thrust out of its perch, loudly announcing that it was 2 PM. Startled, she rested a hand on the desk and looked up toward the ceiling.

"Okay, Gus's office, study, whatever. Got it. Thanks."

She brushed her fingers along the polished wood, wondering how many papers had passed over it when Gus was still alive. She and Luke were fairly certain his family had owned a lot of real estate, but Gus had also dreamed of becoming an architect. That would explain the drawing table—and his massive involvement with building the mansion.

The piano didn't make much sense. It had been considered more of a feminine instrument in the 1800s; men only played it if they were pursuing music professionally.

Cora definitely didn't seem like the piano playing type, but neither did Gus. Maybe it was decorative? But that didn't make much sense because everything in this house felt placed with intention.

Aside from the beautifully designed room, Sephie didn't see anything useful. She stepped back into the hallway and pulled out Cora's journal, hoping it might offer a hint about which rooms held the best secrets. She opened it and flipped back through the months she'd skipped.

Tuesday, February 14th, 1832

To my surprise, Gus stayed home from work today in honor of St. Valentine's Day. I don't believe he's taken a weekday off since I've known him, it felt almost scandalous.

He tried to make me breakfast in bed, bless him. I woke to the unmistakable scent of burning eggs and rushed to the kitchen to find him covered in flour, holding a pan full of what could only be described as charred remains. Needless to say, I ended up cooking the meal myself.

Sephie couldn't help but laugh. Gus sounded like the most well-meaning dolt but in an endearing way.

We spent the morning finalizing our plans for the garden. Gus seemed confused when I told him I had no intention of growing fruits or vegetables. I had to explain that gardening is more than utility, it can be beauty, too. Perhaps one day I'll grow food, but for now, I want to focus on flowers. We've planned something lovely together. Whether I can convince him to help with the actual planting come March is another matter entirely.

Sephie made a mental note to check the March entries, doubtful Gus ever helped. Designing a building was one thing; designing flower beds was another.

We went to The Gilded Fork for supper. They still serve my favorite duck, and Gus remembered. He'd even made reservations before the wedding, knowing how difficult it would be to get in. Dessert was a lemon cream that nearly melted off the spoon.

It would have been the perfect evening... except he brought up starting a family.

I know he wants to carry on the Ashland name, and I want that too. Eventually. But we've only been married a little over a month. I've explained to him I want us to grow into this life together before we change it further. It may not be the common way of things, but I believe it's the right one. He said he understands. I think he means it. But I know it hurt him to hear.

Sephie frowned. So they had wanted children. Did that ever happen? If so, what became of the rest of the Ashland family? Why hadn't anyone claimed the manor?

Then again, Cora might've only written she wanted children because that was what was expected of her. Sephie had no doubt Cora would have been an amazing mother—but the way she thought, the way she lived, seemed different from most women of her time.

A sudden tinkle of piano keys pulled her from the thought.

She froze.

Hesitantly, she crept back toward Gus' study. The melody drifting through the hallway sounded like a variation of Moonlight Sonata. If she didn't know better, she'd think Luke had woken up, found the piano, and decided to showcase yet another hidden talent. But he seemed pretty knocked out.

"… Cora?"

She didn't believe in ghosts.

The sonata continued, swelling slightly as she approached the door.

"… Gus?"

The music stopped. Sephie flung open the door to find nothing. She took a deep breath and stepped cautiously back into the study. Everything looked exactly the same. Arching a brow, she crossed to the piano. It sat there, elegant and silent, untouched. She planted her hands on her hips and looked up at the ceiling again.

"Help me out here. What did I miss?"

No response.

The house had called her back in for a reason. The piano looked ordinary enough. No art or photos on the walls. Nothing on the drawing table. Had she checked the desk drawers?

A single high C rang out from the piano.

That was it.

She slipped into the chair behind the desk, taking a moment to marvel at how comfy it was. Cora knew what she was doing when it came to interior design. She pulled open the three drawers on the right side, frowning as each one turned up empty.

"Hm," Sephie murmured, running her fingers along the underside of the desk's top. This was exactly the kind of house that would have secret compartments. Sure enough, her fingertip caught on a hidden latch. A grin spread across her face as a concealed drawer popped open. Inside was a single object: a key.

Sephie groaned. "Of course it's a key. I'm sure you're having a grand old time sending me on a wild goose chase, huh?"

A soft tinkle of piano keys answered her, almost like a giggle.

Chapter 28

Luke awoke still buzzed. He rolled to his side, and the dining room began to swirl around like a state fair ride. Sheesh, that was some strong stuff. Silently, he gave kudos to Cora, wherever the heck she was. He tried shifting again, but the moment he moved, his stomach began to swim right along with the room.

Okay, so he was still a bit more than buzzed.

He vaguely remembered Sephie saying something about the house refilling the bottle.

Thanks, bro. Appreciate it.

Even so, alcohol didn't usually knock him out like that. He was sure Sephie had gotten a kick out of it, but it was definitely embarrassing. She'd probably come up with a new nickname for him. Tipsy McGee, or something equally humiliating. Knowing her, it'd be hysterically witty. Like her.

Speaking of Sephie, where was she? He glanced around through the hazy glow of the spirits (yes, he did giggle to himself about that), careful not to move his head too much. There wasn't anything in his stomach to come back up, but he didn't want to take any chances. He could imagine the ways the house would punish him if he spewed stomach acid and port somewhere.

With his body feeling heavy as lead, pushing himself upright proved to be useless. Wherever Sephie was, he knew she could take care of herself. Luke resigned himself to lying on the floor for a bit, snuggling his cheek against the thankfully dust-free rug. He swore he could still feel the amber wine coursing through his veins. That, combined with the spinning room, coaxed his eyes closed again.

He knew he looked like an idiot. He could feel a goofy grin stretching across his face. If the house had done this, which it definitely had, it was probably trying to get him and Sephie to bond in some weird way. Granted, it wasn't the strategy he would've gone with, but whatever. The house probably assumed Sephie would fuss over him, so of course, she hadn't. She was most likely using the quiet time to explore other rooms in the house, not having to worry about him causing a ruckus.

Luke kind of wished Sephie stayed to look after him a bit. The thought of her playing nurse made his heart flip-flop. Not that it would ever happen. He highly doubted Sephie ever took care of her romantic partners when they were sick or something. Sephie was all about personal responsibility. Taking care of your own damn self.

Crap… was he beginning to like-like her?

"Gus?"

A voice, smooth as honey, pulled Luke back to a state of semi-consciousness. *Gus?* He opened one eye, just a sliver, half-expecting another stone tape moment. He almost hoped it was. Maybe it could help them figure out if there was a wine cellar somewhere nearby.

"Gus," the voice giggled, "did you sample my new batch?"

Slowly opening his eyes completely, Luke was met with an Amazonian of a woman. Her tall, willowy frame stood above him, hips cocked, an amused smirk on her lips.

Cora.

She rolled her eyes, and the smirk turned into a large smile. "My love, while I'm glad you enjoy my recipes, I'd prefer if you'd ask first before you get carried away."

His head was still throbbing, so he wasn't completely comprehending the situation. This was new; he'd seen stone tape experiences, dealt with a sentient house, and made connections with the dead, but not in a physical form like this.

He tried pushing himself upright again, but it felt like marbles were rolling around inside his skull. Cora reached out and grabbed his shoulder, stabling him before he flopped back on the rug. Her hand was warm and her grip was sturdy; she was solid. Real. He rubbed his temple. The cool press of a wedding ring met his skin. Sobering up a bit, he held his hand out in front of him; it was far smaller than his usual bear paws. His eyes trailed up the crisp white sleeve of the button-up shirt he was now sporting.

"Sweetheart?" Cora asked gently.

Yeah, this was definitely new.

Luke somehow managed to get to his feet, though his legs felt like jelly. Cora didn't let go, keeping him steady.

"Sorry, dear," a voice that wasn't his said from his mouth. "Just couldn't resist."

Cora giggled and began leading him from the dining room. She was taller than him now, which confirmed it: he wasn't in his own body. He looked up at the beautiful nymph who was now his wife and felt all of Gus's love for her. His stomach filled with butterflies, threatening to tip into nausea.

These two had been soulmates.

Cora half-dragged him up the stairs. He didn't know what was happening, but he felt safe.

"My dear, what are we doing?"

"I think you need a quick bath," Cora said. "Then I'm going to tuck you into bed. Hopefully, if we get you comfy, you won't have a nasty hangover tomorrow."

That wasn't how it worked, but he didn't care at the moment. He just knew a gorgeous woman, who Gus was very much enamored with, was going to give him a bath. The butterflies in his stomach were threatening to move a little lower. Hopefully, the alcohol still in his system would dull any reaction. He might be in Gus's body, but it'd still feel creepy.

"Gus?" Cora asked as they slowly climbed the stairs. "I certainly hope you don't feel like I'm taking advantage of you at the moment, but are we still alright building the cellar?"

Perfect.

"Take advantage of me all you want, my love," he found himself chuckling. He could just picture Sephie gagging. "We are okay to go ahead with the cellar. I obviously adore your wine. Almost as much as I adore you."

She beamed, and Luke could feel the pure warmth bloom in Gus's chest.

"I just don't know where to put the second entrance," Cora muttered.

Second entrance? This was the information he needed. He couldn't wait to get back to Sephie and tell her everything. If he got back. And if she believed him. Luke was fairly sure this was a telepathic dream of some kind, but he'd need to do more research on it.

"Perhaps," he offered, "we put an entrance somewhere in the pantry?"

Cora hummed. "You don't want to put a secret entrance behind a trick bookshelf?"

Luke laughed. "As fun as that would be, I think the tunneling required would mess up the foundation of the manor."

Cora stuck out her bottom lip, and he could feel Gus just wanting to lean into her and kiss her. He wasn't going to act on it, it felt wrong. To distract himself from Cora's gorgeous mouth, he began to take in his surroundings. His vision was clearing. The "real world" version of the manor had nearly caught up to how it looked in its heyday. Depending on how long this dream lasted, maybe he could find the ballroom.

"I suppose," Cora interrupted his thoughts, "that a pantry entrance makes the most sense, doesn't it?"

He nodded. "Not as much fun, but yes. I'll contact Duncan tomorrow, we can start mapping it out."

Who the heck was Duncan? Luke made a fuzzy mental note to see if he and Sephie could find any more information on him.

"We can attach the library to the next room over," he added. "If you're dead set on a secret entrance."

"Really?" Cora nearly squealed. It was amusing hearing her sultry voice jump an octave.

He squeezed her hand. "Of course."

Cora stopped in front of a door that must have led to one of the master bathrooms. She gave Luke a quick hug before opening the door. "I love you."

Gus's love surged up, and Luke didn't fight it. He pressed a soft kiss to her cheek, watching her melt.

"I love you too. Always."

She reached for the doorknob, and he froze at the now familiar jangle.

"Oh, not again," Cora groaned. "Sweetheart, we really need to oil these doors. It's kind of embarrassing, getting locked out of rooms in your own home."

So, this had always been a thing. That almost made more sense. If locked doors had consistently been a problem, the house was definitely using it to its advantage. Sneaky little thing, wasn't it?

"Gus, can you give it a go? It always seems to work when you do it."

Luke smirked. "I guess I have the special touch, huh?"

"Oh, you do." Cora waggled her eyebrows, and Luke felt sparks in Gus's groin... *Focus.*

He stepped forward, expecting resistance from the knob. But it turned effortlessly. The door practically flew open.

Luke stumbled forward and crashed hard into the bathroom.

"Oh hell!"

Sephie?

Chapter 29

Sephie hoped she'd find a "weird" room on the second floor, but aside from the study, it was all spare bedrooms and two bathrooms. According to the blueprint, there was supposed to be a ballroom on the ground floor, but she somehow hadn't found it yet. Knowing the house, it was probably too embarrassed to be seen in any state but its full glory and had locked the doors.

She hadn't noticed anything that could be unlocked with the key she'd found. There'd been the random chest at the foot of a bed, but none had visible locks. Granted, she hadn't opened every single one to see if there were more hidden compartments, but she hadn't had the patience. The sun was beginning to set, and she felt slightly gross, so she decided on having a bath. While the one shower in the house did appear to be in working order, it almost looked like some sort of torture device. It was huge, had an odd platform at the bottom, and seemed to have originally utilized recycled water. Hard pass.

One of the guest rooms on the second floor had a bathroom attached with a giant tub. She'd tested it earlier, and like the basin in the laundry room, the water seemed to be up to date with modern plumbing. She couldn't imagine boiling water to fill a tub manually. No wonder personal hygiene sucked in medieval times.

As if it had read her mind, the house had already filled the tub with hot, lavender-scented water by the time Sephie entered the bathroom. She couldn't help but smile and glance around.

"Hey, thanks. I really appreciate it."

A slight ripple of the water seemed to acknowledge her.

Sephie cautiously stripped off her clothes and sank into the tub. The house had obviously seen her undress before, but something about taking a bath seemed more intimate. Stifling a moan, she relaxed as the water surrounded her tight muscles. She hadn't sat down in a while, and her back especially was paying for it.

It was pretty impossible to say she didn't believe in ghosts now. The only reason she hadn't said it out loud was because of pure stubbornness.

Well, and she didn't want Luke to be right. Again.

That little moment with Gran had been pretty damn convincing. She was positive she hadn't let any information slip beforehand, and with their phones useless, there was no way he could've dug up anything on her. If Gran were here right now, which she kind of was, she'd tell Sephie to swallow her "god damn pride" and let someone else in. Then, when Sephie insisted she was fine on her own, she'd try to create another Bumble account for her.

Gran had not only had her fun before settling down with Gramps but also for as long as she was physically able to after he died. Sephie had met one too many of her one-night stands during visits. Once Gran couldn't mess around herself, she'd tried to live vicariously through her granddaughter who was not interested in any intimacy whatsoever. Why she'd picked the emotionally unavailable one over the flirty, fun one, Sephie would never understand.

It wasn't that Sephie didn't crave certain aspects of a relationship. Before Brandon, the more intimate parts, the kind that let her focus on pleasure, were always nice. The fact that even making out with Brandon had felt like a chore should've been a giant red flag. That, and the fact she never introduced him to Gran. After the fake séance stunt he'd tried to pull, Sephie had sworn off men completely. There was nothing one could do that she couldn't do for herself.

She slid beneath the water, pushing all actual thoughts from her head to let herself be. The warmth was so comforting. She massaged her scalp and rose back up, grateful as whatever the lavender-scented stuff was lathered in her hair. A little neck pillow appeared on the tub's edge, and she happily leaned against it.

It felt as though nothing could ruin this moment of zen.

CRASH.

Of course.

Cracking one eye open, Sephie expected to see a sconce had fallen off the wall. She was literally taking a bath the house had drawn for her, what could she possibly have done to piss it off?

She was horrified to see Luke standing at the bathroom entrance, hands thankfully covering his eyes.

"Oh hell!"

"Sephie! I'm sorry! I didn't see anything, I promise!"

He sounded just as mortified as she felt, so he clearly hadn't barged in on his own. She flung her arms over her chest and sank further down in the water as if it would cover anything.

"Crap, hang on."

Eyes squeezed shut, Luke waved his hands blindly in front of him, feeling around for the door. Sephie looked around the room, praying for a towel to appear. No such luck. She grumbled.

"I apparently don't have anything to dry off with," she called out. "Just move forward a little, the door's right there."

Luke carefully shuffled ahead and touched the door, sighing in relief. He gripped the knob and Sephie heard the all too familiar jangle. He groaned.

"It's locked. It's fricking locked."

"I gathered. Hold on, I'll find my clothes."

Putting dry clothes over her sopping wet body wasn't appealing, but it was better than being naked in front of Luke. She peered over the end of the tub and let out an exasperated groan.

"What's wrong?" he asked.

"The house took my damn clothes."

He immediately turned his back to her and dropped to the floor. She looked over and saw how tense he looked. He ticked her off, but he wasn't a creep.

"I swear I'm not looking, I just couldn't keep my eyes closed any longer."

"It's okay. I mean, it's not okay, but... I..."

"I know what you mean."

"Okay, good."

She quickly dunked her hair under, rinsing the last of the suds out. So much for a long, relaxing bath. This stupid house was going too far this time.

"Hey!" she called out. "We played along with all your other matchmaking attempts, but this is bordering on harassment!"

"I'm really uncomfortable," Luke added.

"See? So if you don't mind, at least give me a robe."

Something pink and fluffy dropped out of the air and landed next to the tub. Sephie looked over to find one of the shortest bathrobes she'd ever seen. It'd barely cover her butt, but at least it was something.

"Luke, it gave me something. I'm climbing out of the tub, don't move."

"Wasn't planning on it."

The air was freezing on her wet skin. It was highly unpleasant and, quite honestly, felt unfair. She just wanted to relax, and the house apparently took it as an invitation for some hanky-panky. She picked up what looked like a child-sized robe and wrapped it around herself. Sure enough, the hem sat right at the top of her thighs, barely covering anything. At least it was something.

"Okay," she grumbled, "I'm covered."

"That doesn't sound convincing, Scoob."

"Have I shown *any* indication that I want you to see me naked?"

Slowly, cautiously, he turned to face her. Then, he erupted into laughter.

"Is that robe for a dwarf?"

Sephie shrugged, then immediately yanked at the hem, feeling air in places she definitely shouldn't. She shuffled over to try the door, finding it still locked. Keeping her arms glued to her sides, she gazed around the room and said, "You didn't even give me some sultry robe, you really think anything's gonna happen?"

Nothing.

Luke ran a hand down his face. "Maybe we should do something?"

"This is getting awfully voyeuristic."

The drain made a horrific gurgling noise as the last of the bathwater disappeared, like the house was letting out its own exasperated groan. She jiggled the doorknob again. Still locked.

"Oh, for—"

Finally losing the last of her patience, Sephie leapt into Luke's arms. Well, more like crashed into him, wrapped her arms around his neck, and dangled there. He was in too much shock to even grab her.

"You want something?!" she shrieked. "Here!"

She slammed her lips against his cheek, practically punching him with her mouth instead of kissing him. Luke froze, stiff as a board, letting her hang off his neck with her mouth smushed on his face. She held it for approximately six seconds before releasing him and dropping to the floor.

The door swung open.

"You perv!" she shouted as she stormed out of the bathroom.

Luke stayed glued in place, the only movement was his hand wiping her spit from his cheek.

Chapter 30

Dammit.

Dammit dammit dammit!

Luke couldn't force his feet to move. He wanted to chase after Sephie and apologize, even though he had nothing to apologize for. Instead, he stood frozen, hand still resting on his cheek where she'd just slapped a smooch on him. To make matters worse, Cora offering to bathe him, kissing her cheek, and now Sephie kissing his cheek, he was completely sober. And something was stirring in his lower stomach.

How humiliating.

She literally punched you with a kiss, you moron! Quit it.

Luke knew Sephie was going to need space for a while. A long while. He shook his head and looked around the stunning bathroom again. It was encased in white marble, the scent of lavender still lingering in the air. The lighting was dim and comforting, and a little neck pillow rested neatly on the edge of the tub.

"You know," he muttered, "I can tell you put a lot of thought into trying to give her a relaxing bath. Why'd you have to go and ruin it?"

Though the tub had been drained, it gave a gurgle—like it was sassing. He frowned but held his tongue. No way he was risking getting locked in again. He closed his eyes, counting backward from ten until his blood pressure dropped back to normal. People seriously underestimated how effective that trick was. After one last glance around the bathroom, he gave a small wave and stepped back into the hallway.

He'd need to talk to Sephie soon. The ghost dream, vision, possession, whatever the heck it was. Hopefully, after everything else the house had thrown at them, she'd believe him. Luke was fairly positive even her stubbornness was useless against what had just played out.

The image of her tugging at the hem of the minuscule pink robe flashed back into his mind, and his cheeks flushed. Once again, Sephie's adorable qualities were consuming his thoughts.

He definitely liked her. He wasn't going to deny it anymore. She was tiny and cute and could probably cut his throat with a spoon, and he adored that. Maybe it was time to start acting on the house's attempts at getting them together? Maybe if he genuinely acted on his feelings, it would help them get out faster. Then he could ask her out on a proper date.

She'd either punch him or say yes. There wasn't really much to lose.

The candles lining the hallway flickered as Luke made his way toward the kitchen. Amusingly, it had become the most frequently visited room in the house. He was either cooking, discussing their still-trapped status with guests, or, now, hunting for the entrance to Cora's wine cellar. He'd made a mental note to "not drink any more haunted wine," when he saw a figure at the window. He grumbled.

"Hi, Jace."

The pretty boy's face definitely looked worse for wear. Both eyes blackened, nose bandaged and splinted. And yet, he still managed to glare through the glass.

"Don't 'hi Jace,' me. Where's the goblin?"

Luke crossed his arms and stood to his full height. Jace visibly shrunk into himself.

"If you're talking about Ms. Blake, which is the only way you should be referring to her, she's resting. We've had a hell of a day."

Jace went to frown and immediately winced, hand flying up to touch his nose.

"Ouch! This is all that little brat's fault! How am I supposed to film looking like this?"

"I guess you'll have to rely on that dazzling personality of yours," Luke smirked. "And how exactly is this Sephie's fault?"

"Why do *you* get to use her actual name? She give it up or something? Wouldn't surprise me."

Luke nearly growled. "Don't talk about her like that. And even if we did do anything, we're both adults. What's it matter to you?"

Jace pouted like a five-year-old whose toy had been taken away from him.

Ah.

"You think she's hot."

"Do not! I have no interest in the Lydia Deetz wannabe. Especially after what she did to my face!"

Luke rolled his eyes. "She didn't do anything, the house did."

"What?!"

"The house threw all of you out and just returned the rock you tried to throw at it. It's been taking care of us, and it's obviously trying to tell only me and her something. You're the ghost hunter, Jace, shouldn't you know all about sentient houses?"

Something shifted in the kitchen behind him. A quiet creak, as if the house agreed.

"Now, I get that you love blaming everyone else for your problems, but I'm not having it. Go take a nap. You'll feel better."

Jace swiped a hand down his face and winced again.

"God dammit! Whatever, keep hiding the goblin from me. I'll pay her back eventually."

He turned and began stomping off to wherever his driver was waiting. No way he'd driven himself there with eyes looking like that. Luke darted over to the window, pressing his face close to the glass.

"You'd never have a chance with her! She's far too good for you!"

Jace slumped a little as he continued stalking off.

Good.

***

After crouching down far more than what his large body was typically capable of, Luke finally found a hidden door behind the grain shelf. A cartoonishly silver lock decorated the front.

"How the heck did I miss that before?" he muttered.

Expecting resistance, he tugged, and the lock immediately dropped into his palm. He blinked, chuckled, and tucked it safely into his pants pocket before crawling through the newly opened entrance. No way was he leaving the padlock behind. Not after the other times the house had locked him in.

Thankfully, the entrance led into a broader corridor that let him stand up fully. Ahead was a staircase, and nearby hung an oil lamp. He scrunched up his nose; hopefully, there were more lights down there. Being alone in the dark within the very pit of a ghost house did not sound like a good time.

Feeling like a final girl in a slasher movie, he held the lamp out like a shield, lighting each step as he descended. Down, down, down, until both feet hit solid ground. Another oil lamp hung nearby. As Luke stepped toward it, it flared to life. He grinned and looked upward, silently thanking the house. More lamps ignited one by one as he moved deeper into the room, revealing shelf after shelf of wine bottles.

His grin widened.

He'd found it.

Carefully, he picked up a bottle that matched the one the house had gifted. This one had a beautifully designed label with Cora's Folly stamped in loopy script. There was no way Cora had made this much wine and not sold it. There had to be records somewhere; ledgers, invoices, something.

He wished his phone actually worked so he could take photos. Dragging Sephie down here at some point wasn't exactly ideal. And he wasn't about to haul any bottles upstairs without proper permission… though he had no idea how he'd get it. Cora and Gus hadn't stuck around as ghosts, so it wasn't like he could just ask. The house itself had made it clear it was acting of its own accord, fueled by the massive energy their love had left behind. Flo had been the only person to come through, and she'd basically shut up since finally connecting with Sephie.

He should've been used to this place by now, but watching each gas lamp extinguish one by one as he walked back up the stairs still gave him goosebumps. It reminded him of the Brown Mountain Lights back in Appalachia. That was another thing he needed to debate Sephie about. Surely she had some super logical explanation about why they just couldn't be paranormal. He smiled to himself, just imagining the rage pouring through her tiny body as she told him how wrong he was.

As he went to push open the cellar door, he found it stuck. Frantically, he searched through his clothes, only to find the padlock still resting comfortably in his pants pocket. Groaning, he banged on the door.

"What's the point of locks anyway if you're just gonna pull this?"

He knew the damn house would be laughing if it could.

Chapter 31

Sephie slammed the door hard as she stormed into her bedroom. The fireplace roared to life in response, crackling with a bit too much enthusiasm. She felt a fire of her own ignite behind her eyes, her nails digging crescent moons into her palms.

"Shut. Up."

The words came out low and sharp, startling even her. The flames immediately extinguished, leaving nothing but a faint whimpering hiss. Sephie swore she heard a whine echo through the air like the room had been scolded. After nodding firmly, she marched to the closet and began rummaging through the bundle of clothes they'd been gifted earlier. All she wanted was something, anything, that properly covered her lower half.

"I'll admit, The Flexorcist is pretty damn adorable, but you're pushing it!"

No reply.

"Look," she sighed, softening slightly. "We've stopped being jerks to each other. We're friendly now. I'm assuming you're used to being full of love after Cora and Gus, but maybe just focus on the 'cordial' part of our relationship for now, okay?"

The floorboards creaked submissively.

"Thank you."

A giant, fluffy towel dropped onto the bed, followed by an oversized black shirt that was clearly meant for Luke. Sephie quirked a brow but eagerly wiped away the last droplets of water from her arms and legs. She began to scrunch at her hair, attempting to get all the excess water out. Damn curls always took forever to dry anyway, so no use in wrapping them up in the towel. Slipping the shirt on, she found it went down to her calves, much more like something she'd actually wear to bed. Maybe the house was finally starting to understand her. She squinted and peered upwards.

"Do I get underwear?"

Something red, lacy, and frilly smacked her right in the face. Frowning, she managed to hold back a protest. Any underwear was better than nothing, and it wasn't like anyone else would be seeing them. She slipped the scrap of fabric on, still feeling breeze where she definitely shouldn't have been.

"Okay, you misogynistic pile of wood," she muttered, hands on her hips. "You're being pretty unfair with all this."

Again, no answer. It learned to play dumb.

With an eye roll, Sephie stomped across the room and stood in front of the portraits adorning the wall. Her gaze landed on Gus and Cora's wedding photo, the epitome of romance and devotion.

"Stupid happy couple," she mumbled. "So perfect that it's the only type of love this house acknowledges."

She could practically hear Dr. Alias's voice in her head: *Just because you're unhappy doesn't mean you get to force that emotion on other people.*

God, she hated how right he always was. Although technically she was dealing with a house and not a person.

He was her fourth therapist. The first three had all dropped her after two sessions. She'd become a pro at answering questions with a flat "I'm fine" and shutting down any real attempts to help. But Dr. Alias was different. He didn't flinch when she bit back, instead he challenged her. After a month of verbal sparring, she'd finally cracked and confronted her emotions somewhat. It had been enough to appear as a semi-normal human.

Letting out one more sigh, she turned away from the smugly content wedding photo and walked over to the bed. She probably should eat something, but seeing Luke again was currently the last thing she wanted. Curling up in the delightfully cloud-like bed and pretending the whole bathroom incident never happened sounded far more appealing.

Her stomach betrayed her by growling.

"You'll survive without the lumberjack's cooking for one night," Sephie muttered. But as she flopped down on the bed, something felt off. The mattress wasn't letting her sink in like it had before, the pillows felt stiffer, and the blankets felt smothering instead of comforting.

"Oh, motherfu—"

The house was still managing to punish her limits.

Muttering curses under her breath, Sephie shoved the covers off and slipped her feet into the slippers that materialized on the floor.

Fine, she'd go to the kitchen, take a quick nibble of whatever delicacy Luke had whipped up, and then head right back to bed. There wasn't any use fighting with the house at this point; it'd just continue to be ornery until it got what it wanted.

***

The foyer was quiet as she made her way toward the kitchen. The flickering candles cast lazy shadows against the walls, almost mocking her. She half expected to see Luke at the counter, cooking something ridiculous and delicious.

The kitchen was empty.

Frowning, Sephie looked around. No Luke. No food. No sign he'd even been there. Those were plenty of red flags for Sephie to understand something was wrong.

"Luke?"

She began opening cabinets, peeking under the table, even checking the oven. Ridiculous? Maybe. But in this house, who knew where he could've been hidden away?

"Luke?" she called again.

A scratching sound followed by a frantic pounding came from the pantry. She rushed over and the sounds grew louder. A bag of oats had been pushed to the side, revealing a once hidden door with a giant silver padlock. Sephie cautiously inched closer, fearful the house was messing with her again.

"Luke?"

"Sephie! Thank god, yes!"

She crossed her arms. "How do I know it's really you in there and not the house playing another trick?"

"Oh, come on! I don't know, ask me something the house wouldn't know?"

"It hears everything."

"Then how about you just trust me?!"

She bit her bottom lip and gripped the padlock. How was she supposed to open it?

Then it hit her.

"Hang on, I think I have the key. I probably left it in the bathroom."

"Key???" Luke squawked. "But the padlock's in my pocket!"

Sephie groaned. "Then you're the one that got tricked. Give me a second."

As she turned to leave, something glittered next to a jar of peaches. The silver key.

"Thanks," she muttered as she snatched it up. Maybe transporting the key to the pantry so she didn't have to trek back upstairs was a peace offering, of sorts.

The lock clicked open easily, and Luke barreled out, grabbing her shoulders and pushing her away from the hidden doorway.

Every alarm bell in her body screamed. Fight-or-flight mode kicked in, but this time, her body chose to override it completely and simply freeze. Her muscles tensed, her brain started to fog, and the impending blackout began to pull her under.

"Crap," Luke cursed, releasing her immediately. "I'm so sorry. Breathe. Count backwards from ten."

His voice sounded like it was underwater.

Ten, nine, eight...

"You're safe, I promise."

Seven, six, five...

"I needed to get you away from that entrance, that was just asking for another locked in situation."

Four, three, two...

Then, she felt arms around her. Strong and grounding, but not restrictive. It felt instead like being anchored by warmth.

One.

Her vision began to clear. Luke was still holding her, concern etched on his face.

"Sorry," he said again, beginning to back away. "I panicked. I know you're no-touchy—"

Before he could finish, she pulled him back in and buried her face against his chest. He stopped speaking and stroked her hair gently instead.

"You're okay," he whispered.

And for the first time in a long time, she kind of believed it.

Chapter 32

Sephie nibbled on an apple dipped in peanut butter while Luke furiously whipped egg whites. She said she was going to bed, but he insisted on making dessert. Why he'd picked something that required a meringue was beyond her.

"You really don't have to do that," she muttered again.

"I told you, sugar helps everything," he replied, pausing to flex his fingers. "I do wonder how little old ladies used to make this without electric mixers."

"I thought that'd be easy for you with those biceps of yours."

He held up the whisk and inspected the white fluff clinging to it. It flopped slightly. Satisfied, he spooned the mixture into a glass baking dish with care.

"Is that stiff enough?"

"That's what she said," he giggled, sliding the dish into the oven. "It doesn't have to be too stiff."

"Will it fall if I scream at it?"

"Not a soufflé, so no," he said, joining her at the kitchen table.

She offered him another apple slice. When he declined, she dunked it in more peanut butter. Luke said that whatever he was baking needed ninety minutes. She suggested checking out the mysterious cellar again, but he immediately vetoed the idea.

"Are you scared of the dark?" she asked, amused.

"What? No," he replied far too quickly.

"So, you are."

"Am not."

"Come on, we've shared trauma. You can share your fears."

He sighed and buried his face in his hands. "Fine. Yeah, the dark and I don't get along."

"See? That wasn't so hard." She passed him another slice, which he shoved into his mouth.

"I'd have thought dealing with ghosts would make the dark less terrifying."

Luke shrugged. "It's not ghosts I'm worried about. It's the physical things I can't see."

"Anyone trying to kidnap you is going to think you're Jason Voorhees."

He chuckled. "Maybe. Still spooky not knowing what's around you."

A sweet vanilla scent was already drifting from the oven. Sephie was convinced the house amplified good smells. Maybe Luke could replicate that at his restaurant. Didn't Burger King do something like that with fries?

"So, what are you scared of?" he asked.

Sephie blinked. The thought of fries had momentarily transported her away from their conversation.

"Death."

"Well, who isn't?"

"I know, basic answer. But honestly, that's it."

"Spiders?"

"Nope. They're important to the ecosystem."

"Water?"

"Not a beach fan, but that's mostly because I burn."

"Fire?"

"Pretty sure my parents thought I was an arsonist at one point."

Luke's next question was cut off by loud voices outside, more like shouting. They glanced out the window to find Jessica and Jace approaching.

"Aw man, he came back," Luke groaned.

"Back?"

"Ha! There she is!" Jace pointed straight at Sephie.

Jessica sighed. "You said you'd stay in the car."

"I lied."

"I should've known."

"Hey, you! Hobgoblin!"

Sephie squinted. *Hobgoblin*?

Technically a household spirit, so kind of fitting. But she doubted Jace knew that. She glanced at Luke, who looked like he might explode.

"Pretty boy stopped by earlier when you were getting settled. I thought I scared him off."

Sephie looked at Jessica, who was doing a poor job of dragging Jace back to the car. He definitely wasn't looking pretty. His nose was bandaged, and his eyes were ringed in purple bruises. He slapped Jessica's hand away and stomped up to the window.

"Thanks to you, I'm unemployed!" he shouted, jabbing a finger at the glass. Sephie swore it dented inward. They didn't need the house going haywire again. She stood and moved closer to the window, arms crossed.

"You're not unemployed," Jessica said flatly.

"I will be! No one wants to look at this face!"

"You needed a nose job anyway," Sephie deadpanned.

Luke burst out laughing as Jace clenched his fists.

"You brat. I'll ruin your career."

"I'd love to see you try, Marcia, Marcia, Marcia," Sephie spat.

"Besides," Luke chimed in, "everyone else seems to think the two of us could easily take your job."

Jace slapped the window now, with it visibly puckering this time. Terrified, he immediately pulled his hand away. Jessica seized the moment, grabbed his wrist, and yanked, sending him stumbling backward.

"OUCH! You broke my wrist!"

"I did not. Go wait in the car."

"I will not—"

"Jace," Jessica snapped, arms crossed, brow raised. "Go back to the car, or you can kiss that next marketing campaign goodbye."

Jace sulked off. "Doesn't matter with me looking like this!"

Jessica turned back, exhaling. "It's for boots. Whatever."

Luke joined Sephie. "Anyway, what's up, Jessica?"

"Took some digging, but I think I found someone connected to the Ashlands. No kids, but maybe a friend or employee. Name's Pischner."

Luke glanced at Sephie.

"I haven't seen that name yet," she said. "Though there are still parts of Cora's journal left to read."

"At least it's something," Luke said.

Jessica's phone buzzed. She frowned at the screen, typed out a quick message, and stuffed her phone away.

Sephie narrowed her eyes. "Jessica?"

"Hmm?"

"What's wrong?"

"Oh, nothing. Just work stuff."

"Work stuff to get us out of here?"

Jessica deflated. "That was another medium I had hopes for. She basically said it's a lost cause, so let it go."

"You mind me asking which medium?" Luke asked.

"Marna Hallowstein?"

Sephie gritted her teeth. That woman was most definitely a fake. She was one of the many so-called "mediums" she kept her eye on. Multiple of the woman's former clients ended up seeking her out after wasting money. She'd ended up solving their "ghost problems" with her typical ways; research and common sense.

"Uh, hey," Luke hissed, "maybe check with Sephie or me before you reach out to any mediums? Marna's an imposter in every way. Even her name's made up."

Sephie looked up at him. "You know her?"

"Unfortunately, yeah," he replied. "Allie Hone. She was at a small educational get-together a few years ago. Lied even back then."

The fact Luke acknowledged Hallowstein was a con artist made Sephie's trust in him grow more.

Jessica shrugged. "I was just trying to help. You know anyone legit who we could call in?"

Luke raised a brow. "Not anyone with experience in sentient real estate," he said. "Would you believe this isn't a common thing?"

Jessica nodded toward them. "I don't know what's common anymore. You two still okay? I have to go lock Jace up somewhere."

Sephie giggled. "Like an asylum? Yeah, we're fine."

Jessica gave a small nod and smile before heading back to her car.

"Now *she* thinks we're banging," Sephie said.

"Totally," Luke replied.

A soft ding echoed behind them. They turned to find what might have been an egg timer perched on the counter. The numbers didn't even make sense, and it was very crooked. Bless the house, it was trying.

Luke opened the oven and stared.

"I might not know much about baking, but I don't think you're supposed to open the door," Sephie called out.

"No, you're not," he admitted, pulling out the dessert. "But it's done."

"You said ninety minutes."

"I did. But this is definitely house magic."

They both looked up.

"Thanks," they said together.

They laughed. Sephie watched the way Luke's eyes lit up when he smiled. He really was like a giant teddy bear.

"So what is this sugar miracle?"

"Pavlova."

"Like the ballerina?"

He grinned. "Didn't peg you for a ballet nerd, Scoob. But yeah. It's supposedly named after her tutus. I don't know. It's delicious."

He tapped the top gently. "Still a bit warm. Want to help me make whipped cream when it cools?"

"That's what she… said? No. Never mind."

They both laughed again. The scent of vanilla and sugar filled the air as if the house itself was settling into something sweet. Sephie couldn't help but feel like maybe this haunted place was starting to feel like home.

And that honestly terrified her.

Chapter 33

They'd decided to risk it and enjoy the Pavlova in the library. While they'd both somewhat forgiven the house, the library was one of the more enjoyable places they'd been locked in. Just in case, they brought along extra apples and peanut butter, two blankets, and a candle. They'd made a cozy little nest in the middle of the room, munching on the sweet, marshmallowy dessert.

"This is really friggin' good," Sephie said, muffled between bites.

"Thanks," Luke smiled. "It's basically just sugar, vanilla, and eggs, but it's always the simplest things that taste the best."

Sephie was pretty sure she could eat the entire dish, it was that good. She'd have to make sure Luke hired Thalia; maybe she could keep scoring free food after they were free from this house. Although if they actually stayed friends (which she really wanted), she'd probably end up his official taste tester. That sounded like a great plan.

Dr. Alias would be so proud. Look at ole Sephie Blake—constant loner, introvert, rude as hell—making an honest-to-goodness friend. The sentient house had been annoying, but she and Luke wouldn't have even crossed paths if not for it. She looked over at him and found him flipping through Cora's journal.

"Any mention of a Pischner?"

"Not yet, just more about the wine cellar and how excited she was."

"Were there more bottles down there, by the way?"

He nodded. "Yup. Fancy labels and everything."

She nibbled her bottom lip. "She had to have sold at least some of them. How the heck did they keep everything so secret?"

"Oh wait," Luke said, handing her the journal. "This might be something."

Monday, September 3rd, 1832
Duncan arrived early this morning to begin surveying the grounds for my cellar. He presented a remarkably detailed drawing, far superior to the modest little square I penciled onto our household plans. According to his design, the primary entrance shall be positioned near the garden, precisely where I'd hoped. But more thrilling still: I shall have my secret passage through the pantry.

We accomplished little else today, but he permitted me the honor of breaking ground. I took one of my gardening spades and unearthed a single patch of soil. It may seem a small act, but to me it felt most significant. With that simple gesture, Cora's Folly has become something more than a fanciful notion drifting in my mind.

"Okay," Sephie said, closing the journal and taking another monster bite of Pavlova. "Good for her, but what's this 'something' you speak of?"

Luke set his plate down. "Warning: I'm about to say some more ghost, medium, woo-woo stuff."

Sephie rolled her eyes but gestured for him to continue.

"Yeah, so, I don't know if it was the house or the alcohol or what, but I had an experience? That's what caused the bathroom incident."

Instead of putting her plate down, Sephie helped herself to another serving. Luke arched a brow but kept going.

"I woke up in Gus's body, somehow. And Cora was there."

"So you dreamt up the Ashlands?"

"Kind of?" He scratched his head. "It felt way more real than any dream I've ever had. Like I time-traveled and was dropped into Gus for a minute."

Now she set her plate down. "And this has never happened before?"

"Nope."

"Interesting."

A beat passed.

"I was in a moment where Gus was apparently drunk off Cora's wine. She was taking him upstairs for a bath, and the door stuck. It unlocked as soon as I touched the knob, and then… well, I fell into what was supposed to be a very relaxing moment for you."

Sephie nodded. She'd already figured the house had something to do with Luke ending up in a heap on the bathroom floor, but this was wild, even for it.

"And this connects to a supposed Pischner how?"

"Maybe through Duncan. Gus mentioned him in the dream when Cora brought up the wine cellar. Now, Cora mentions him here. Maybe he's Duncan Pischner?"

Sephie shrugged. "Definitely a possibility. I guess we can hand the name off to whichever poor schmuck has to check on us next."

"Where's that photo album?"

She'd nearly forgotten. They moved to the small table by the bookshelf. The leather photo album was waiting, although this this time, on top of it sat a small green cloth book. Sephie shot Luke a look.

"Do you know what that is?"

"Nope," he said, wrinkling his nose. "Please be careful."

"What makes you think I'm opening it?"

"I just got trapped in a dark wine cellar by myself. I think it's your turn to deal with the spooky stuff."

Sephie sighed but gently picked up the book. It had no title, no embossing, and nothing to distinguish it. Slowly, she opened the cover. Luke leaned over her shoulder, then winced.

Mysticism and Spiritualism: Insights of Duncan Flatley

Luke groaned. "I do not like that."

Sephie frowned. "What? Doesn't that mean Duncan was a medium?"

"Big nope. Close it, please? I'm getting some bad energy off it."

He'd gone pale, gripping at his stomach as he backed away. She glanced once more at the scratchy handwriting inside, then shut it. Now probably wasn't the time to risk a Necronomicon situation.

Luke coughed. "Mysticism is pure crap. It's probably why you're so anti-medium. But they're two very different things."

"There's just too many names for all the hootenanny."

He chuckled. "I connect with the dead. Mysticism's more about becoming one with God or some kind of absolute. I personally think it was invented by someone either in spiritual psychosis or on a buttload of shrooms."

She laughed. "So, do you think Duncan had ulterior motives with the wine cellar or something?"

"Possibly. It might explain why Cora never sold any of the wine. That could lean into dark magic territory." He scowled at the book. "Hopefully, it was just a hobby. I can't see Cora or Gus not noticing something that shady. Either he hid it well, or never mentioned it."

Still didn't solve the Pischner mystery.

"Do you usually react like that to bad juju?"

His color was returning. "It doesn't happen often, thankfully. Last time was when a homophobic dad showed up yelling at his lesbian daughter."

"Ew. Why'd she ask to speak to him in the first place?"

"She was a good person and hadn't spoken to him in six years. Figured he might want to apologize. He did not."

"Wow. Backwards thinking even in death."

"Yup. That kind of energy sticks. I'm pretty sure I barfed after that session."

"We don't need that. I'll toss this in the fire."

"No!" Luke squeaked. "That's asking for more trouble. We might need it later."

Sephie frowned. She didn't feel anything bad coming from it, but she didn't want

Luke to be affected. Especially if it meant not seeing Pavlova again on the way back up.

"Oh!" She perked up. "Gus had a desk with a hidden compartment. That's where the cellar key was. We could stash it there?"

Luke nodded. "That'll work. But let's check the photo album first."

Sephie shoved the green book behind the other books on one shelf for now, then opened the photo album. Luke returned to his place peering over her shoulder, and she felt oddly safe with the closeness. They flipped through pages of Cora designing or holding bunches of grapes, Gus sketching architectural plans, the two of them looking stupidly happy together.

"How were they so couple-y?"

Luke gave a small smile. "They absolutely adored each other. That dream just proved it, I felt like I was in love with Cora. That's how strong it was."

"You get a boner or something?"

"Shut up."

Sephie laughed, but envy tugged at her. She was jealous. She knew it. But she wouldn't admit it. She'd never known that kind of romantic happiness and had accepted she never would.

Luke pointed at a photo of Gus standing among the skeleton of some grand project. Wooden beams framed the half-built structure. In the background stood another man, head tilted back like he was inspecting the work.

"Who's that?"

Sephie squinted. "I mean, I'm guessing Duncan was either Gus's employee or business partner. So, high possibility it's him."

"I'd kill for reverse image search right now."

"Ditto."

Sephie closed the album and pursed her lips. Why on earth was this so hard? She handed the book to Luke and went to retrieve Duncan's. She got the okay from him before pulling it out again.

"Anything?"

He shook his head. "No, I think it's just when it's open."

"So we won't be doing that." She tucked it under her arm. "Okay, Gus's office—"

An enormous yawn cut her off, and Luke gave one of his own. He rubbed the corner of his eye.

"We've dealt with a heck of a lot today. Maybe we should call it a night."

Ghost wine, a drunken possession, a mortifying bathroom moment, nearly getting locked in a cellar, you name it, Luke pulling her out of a panic attack, and a whole lot more nonsense. Yeah, that was a heck of a lot.

She tossed the green book to the very back of the shelf, not particularly caring if it got damaged.

"Night, officially called."

They turned their backs on the book, just in time to miss the way the shelf seemed to shift behind them.

Chapter 34

"You think we should even bother trying to sleep in separate rooms?"

Luke couldn't help but blush. She had a point. The last two nights had ended with them curled around each other. There's no use trying to fight it anymore.

In the whole two nights of knowing Sephie, their whole enemies, to friends, to lovers pipeline was moving dangerously fast.

Wait, lovers?

He needed sleep.

"Flex, hello?"

He shook his head and looked at her. Sephie had an infuriatingly cute, smug grin plastered across her face.

"I don't bite," she said, raising her brows.

"No, I know," he mumbled, rubbing the back of his neck. "I mean, I'm fine with sharing rooms, but I don't want to make you uncomfortable."

"You've seen me in my underwear, a bathrobe, and snuggled me like a Build-A-Bear. I think we're past the uncomfortable stage."

Luke chewed the inside of his mouth. He was more worried about getting *too* comfortable. He wasn't sure if waiting for the house to move one of them in their sleep, or just doing it themselves was the better idea.

"Luke, dear God, I'll sleep on the floor if you're gonna act like that."

"I'm a gentleman, I'll sleep on the floor if it comes to that. I was obviously fine when I passed out on the rug. But the house is gonna stick us together anyway."

Sephie shrugged. "Okay then, your room, or mine?"

This was beginning to sound like a one-night stand again.

"My bed's bigger?"

"Sold."

She turned on her heel and marched toward his room. Luke told his stomach to chill the hell out and followed. As they walked, each sconce along the hallway extinguished itself, one by one, casting them deeper into shadows. The action mirrored the gas lamps in the cellar earlier. He wished the house would wait for them to get inside his room before turning the lights out. Sticking as close as possible to Sephie, he realized it was purposefully doing it.

Suddenly, the carpet bunched up in front of Sephie and before he could say anything, she tripped. Without thinking, Luke dove forward and threw himself on the floor to break her fall. She landed on his chest with a soft thump. They paused for an awkward moment before she rolled off him.

"Why on earth did you do that?"

"I think some part of my caveman brain thought that was better than grabbing you."

"I appreciate the thought, though I question the execution."

"I'm tired, okay?"

She giggled and pushed herself upright before offering him a hand. She couldn't do much with his weight, but he took it anyway. Her hand was so small in his, it only made him want to keep holding it. Keep holding her.

"Flex," she said dryly. "You can let go."

Crap.

Even caught, he didn't let go right away. Sephie raised a brow but didn't seem too mad as she gently pulled away. When they looked up, Luke's bedroom door creaked open on its own.

"Lord," Sephie groaned. "If there's a rose petal trail, I'm gonna throw a fit."

The room, thankfully, looked just as it had in the morning, except the bed made. Sephie took a flying leap and landing face first in the covers.

"I never understood making the bed," she said, muffled. "You're just gonna wreck it later."

"I make mine every day."

She popped up on her hands like a startled cobra. "Wait, *you* made this?"

"Yup."

"I thought it was the house. Why? We're literally the only people here. No one's judging."

"It's a routine thing. Helps me feel productive, I guess."

She flopped back down. "Hey, whatever makes your little housewife heart happy. I'm just glad the bed's comfy again."

"Again?"

"Mine felt weird earlier, right after the whole bathroom saga."

Luke furrowed his brow. "Was that when you saved me from the cellar?"

She rolled over to look at him. "Exactly then."

"The house wanted you to come save me."

A surprisingly sweet thought.

"Flex. It locked you in there."

Oh, right.

He sighed. So, it wasn't looking out for them, it was continuing its twisted matchmaking. Hopefully, it'd be a bit kinder after he admitted to being scared of the dark. Out of all the pranks it'd played, the cellar was the closest to being cruel.

Luke started stripping off the corduroy pants and button-up shirt.. Sephie made a noise between a squeak and a gasp. When he looked over, she had both hands over her eyes.

"Maybe warn a person?"

He rolled his eyes. "Were you not just saying I'd seen you in far less already and it didn't matter? They're boxers, basically swim trunks."

"Just... just put the nightshirt on, okay?"

Luke normally just slept in his boxers, but the nightshirt was comfy. People in the 1800s definitely understood sleeping comfort. He pulled the pajamas from the night table drawer, slipped it over his head, and then carefully sat on the mattress.

"Okay, I'm dressed."

No response.

"Sephie?"

Still nothing. He leaned closer. Her hands were still covering her face, but her body was slack.

A soft snore escaped her lips.

Luke smiled. She'd passed out mid-conversation. Classic.

As quietly as he could, he circled the bed, gently moved her hands away, and pulled the covers up around her. The tense wrinkle between her eyebrows disappeared. God, she was adorable.

He tiptoed around, slid under the blankets, and settled on his side. The candle flickered out, the fireplace dimmed to a gentle glow, and the room fell into warm silence.

Luke closed his eyes.

"Goodnight, Sephie," he whispered.

He wasn't not doing great with the whole "being friends" thing.

With her soft snore as background music, he finally let himself drift.

Chapter 35

Sephie woke snuggled up against what she knew was Luke. He'd been nothing but a gentleman the night before, but she had a strong suspicion the house worked its magic once they'd fallen asleep. She inhaled deeply, wrapped in warmth. There were worse things than waking up in the arms of a big, burly beefcake.

She'd been so desperate to continue hating Luke, but the giant puppy dog of a man made it increasingly difficult. He was genuinely kind, stupidly adorable, and beyond endearing. Endearing enough to make her put up enough with his gifts. Who would've thought a medium who looked like he cosplayed as a lumberjack would be the one to make her believe in ghosts?

Slowly opening her eyes, she expected to find Luke's sweet face and mess of hair across from her. She couldn't help but squeak as a very different face came into view. The new face's eyes fluttered open, replacing Luke's brown eyes with stark blue ones. They blinked a few times, trying to get the sleep out of them.

"Honey, what's wrong?"

"Gus?" An alto, husky voice came from her mouth.

A hand, definitely not Luke's, stroked her cheek. Much smaller, but just as warm. She couldn't help but lean into the touch as his thumb passed over her bottom lip.

"Did you have a bad dream?"

She reached to rub her eyes but paused. Her hands were long and elegant, not her usual stubby fingers. Slim fingertips ran through hair that was no longer thick and curly, but fine and chestnut brown. This had to be a dream. But why was it so real?

"Cora?"

Cora?!

"I…" the sultry voice came again, unfamiliar yet hers. "I guess I did have a bad dream."

Gus tucked her hair behind her ear and booped her nose with a grin. The affection made her heart melt. Cora's heart, anyway. This man meant everything to her.

"Do you want some water? Warm milk?"

She shook her head.

Gus smirked. "A hot toddy?"

"Oh, yes please," the words escaped before she could stop them. Sephie hated whiskey. Cora, apparently, loved it. Nothing sounded better than the warm drink right about now.

Gus pulled the covers off, reached for his glasses, and climbed out of the bed. Sephie couldn't help but just gaze at him. Warmth pooled in her stomach as Cora's adoration took control. He offered her a hand.

"Coming?"

"Of course."

Her hand felt familiar in his. Cora's was like the rest of her body—long, thin, and almost waiflike. The contrast with Gus's calloused hand was striking: silk and sandpaper, but somehow, it worked.

Sephie always loved couples who seemed completely opposite, yet found balance in their differences. Maybe that was part of why her past relationships failed. There was no real contrast.

No. Brandon was just an asshat.

The kitchen looked exactly as she and Luke left it. Maybe a bit tidier. Sephie remembered Gus's lack of cooking skills in Cora's journal and winced. Hopefully, his bartending skills were better.

Gus led her over to the familiar kitchen table and pulled a chair out for her. What a gentleman. Cora's heart fluttered. Sephie stared out the window at the cloudy night sky. A few stars peeked through here and there, with the moon making the occasional appearance.

The sound of pouring liquid pulled her attention back to Gus. He worked with quiet grace, squeezing lemon, adding cinnamon and honey, and letting a fragrant blend of whiskey and citrus swirl together.

"It's been a while since you've woken up in the middle of the night," he said. "What's on your mind?"

She let out a deep sigh. "I'm not sure."

Gus stirred the liquid, and a warm citrus-whiskey aroma floated throughout the kitchen. Normally, Sephie would have gagged, but the scent was comforting to Cora.

"Stressed?" he gently teased. "Starting a business and all that?"

Cora's lips curled into a small smile. "I suppose. My wine is the best there is. I just can't help but feel…"

Sephie wasn't controlling the words and had no clue what Cora was trying to say.

Gus placed a warm mug in front of her and took the seat across the table. The drink looked amazing. Golden, steaming, and garnished with a cinnamon stick. It smelled like comfort.

"Drink. It'll soothe you."

She sipped. Expecting a burn, she was pleasantly surprised by the smoothness. It was warm, a little zingy, and entirely soothing. Her whole body relaxed.

Gus smiled. "That's my girl."

He reached across the table. Her hand met his instinctively, and he began tracing soft circles against her skin. Butterflies fluttered.

"It's normal to be afraid something won't work," he said. "Remember how frantic I was when I started out in real estate?"

A half-formed memory surfaced. Cora was his anchor back when that all started.

"Cora's Folly is going to be a big hit, sweetheart. I just know it."

She took another sip, smiling. The toddy tasted like a warm hug.

"Is the drink helping?"

"You know it is."

Gus gave a smug smile before pressing a kiss to her fingertips.

"Not that I couldn't stay up and talk to my beautiful wife all night, but Duncan and I have an early morning meeting." He slowly got to his feet and walked around the table. "Are you alright if I head back to bed?"

She nodded. "This should put me to sleep pretty soon, I'll be joining you shortly."

He wrapped his arms around her from behind. She took a deep inhale and leaned into his chest.

Wait, was that… lavender?

"Did you steal my soap?"

A vibration passed through them as he gave a low chuckle.

"I ran out. And I figured I love your scent so much, might as well have it around me when you aren't."

He kissed the top of her head, gave her shoulder a quick squeeze, then left the kitchen. Sephie felt Cora turn into a pile of goo.

Great, now she was just more jealous. This couple was the absolute definition of perfection. If the house was expecting to experience the same type of love again, she and Luke didn't have a chance of escaping anytime soon.

She finished off the hot toddy and set the mug in front of her. She mentally took note of his mention of Duncan. But the warmth from the drink was already making her eyelids droop. She tried to stand but couldn't. Her legs felt like sandbags.

So tired.

"I guess this chair is fairly comfy."

And soon, she was out cold. Cora's presence or not, the drink had done its job.

Chapter 36

"Scoob?"

Sephie muttered and stretched her arms, feeling a twinge in her lower back. Okay, apparently not dragging herself back up to an actual bed had been a bad idea. The kitchen chair, which had seemed super comfy in her hot toddy haze, was now reminding her it was simply wood and a singular cushion.

She slowly opened her eyes to find Luke staring at her, looking perturbed.

"You okay?" he asked, concern filling his voice.

She pushed her hair out of her face, thankful to find her baby hands back.

"Aside from a very sore spine, yeah, I'm okay."

"Crud, I was worried."

"Why?"

He took a seat across from her, flushed and panting like he'd just run a marathon.

"Oh gee, I don't know, I woke up and you weren't there?"

Sephie blinked. "I could've just gotten up early."

"Scoob, I ran through the entire house looking for you. I thought the place got pissed and booted you, too."

Oh.

He *had* run a marathon.

"I'm fine," she said, softening.

"I see that."

"Sorry," she added. "I'm not the nicest when I first wake up."

"Just when you first wake up?" he teased.

Sephie couldn't help but grin. "Cute. No, I'm really fine. I think I had… what did you call it? A possessive dream?"

"That's a good name. Something visceral? Full transport?" She nodded.

"Strange. I figured it was just a medium thing. Maybe you *are* a witch."

She winced, rubbing her temple and choosing to ignore the witch comment. "Ugh. I need coffee."

Luke stood and moved to the French press. "I'm on it. Who were you in your dream?"

"Cora. She couldn't sleep, so Gus made her a hot toddy, and they were their usual cute couple selves."

"Anything useful?"

"Gus said he had a meeting with Duncan in the morning. They definitely worked together. But mostly? I think the house was taunting me."

"Taunting you?"

Sephie sighed. "Showing me how perfect Cora and Gus were. Like you said, I could feel how much she loved him."

"What's that got to do with you?"

"In case you haven't noticed," she crossed her arms, "love doesn't exactly treat me great."

"Ah. So you're jealous."

She bit her lip, refusing to dignify him with a response. Luke nodded. The house, in its infinite sass, whistled the kettle to life a little too fast.

Luke poured the water over the grounds, let it steep, then handed her a mug.

"Only crazy people drink their coffee black."

He'd remembered.

"If you haven't realized I'm at least a bit loony after being stuck with me for three days, you're crazier than I am."

She sipped and let the warmth unfurl in her chest.

"Jealousy doesn't spout from nowhere, Sephie. It's okay to want love."

She didn't reply. He didn't push. The quiet between them was reflective, but not heavy.

"I know you hate people," he added.

"I do not."

"Scoob."

"I hate stupid people."

Luke let out a low chuckle. "Fine. Stupid people. But your hatred of them doesn't exactly line up with your craving for romance."

"I don't—"

A loud knock at the front door cut her off, startling them both.

"Can we just ignore them?" Luke asked.

Sephie stood, clutching her mug. "No, they'll think we're dead."

"Ugh," he groaned, following her to the front window.

"Hello?" Thalia's voice rang out, followed by more impatient knocking.

"Hey," a male voice added. "Told you—front window."

"Oh! Right!"

Thalia and Isiah came into view. Sephie blinked. Isiah was apparently the sacrificial lamb who got to deal with her shrill little sister today.

"Morning," Luke muttered.

Thalia frowned. "What happened to you two?"

"Bad night," Sephie said flatly.

"Should we be worried?" Isiah asked. "We haven't figured out how to get you out yet."

"There is no way out," Sephie said. "The only chance we have is appeasing the house. And Luke and I aren't its favorite pairing."

Thalia and Isiah exchanged a look.

"Seph, are you sure you're okay?"

"I'm intact."

"Mentally, I mean."

"I'm fine."

She stormed toward the foyer, irritated and prickly. Behind her, Luke offered them some kind of vague reassurance before hurrying to catch up.

"Scoob, pity party later. We should at least try to find the ballroom today."

She turned sharply, managing a deep breath before she snapped again. "I know. Just let me finish my coffee and—"

A crash outside cut her off, followed by Thalia's high-pitched scream.

Eyes wide, they raced back to the window.

"Hey!" Sephie shouted up at the ceiling. "You hurt my sister, I *will* burn this place to the ground!"

They peered out to find Thalia sprawled in Isiah's arms, her leg stuck partway into the porch hole Sephie herself had made the first day there.

"Oh good lord," Sephie muttered.

Neither of them moved. Instead, Thalia blinked up at Isiah like he'd just rescued her from a monster. Her fingers clutched his hoodie. His arm was around her waist. It looked weirdly romantic.

"Are you kidding me?" Luke groaned.

Isiah gently helped Thalia extract her leg but didn't let go of her right away. She wobbled slightly, and he caught her by the waist with ease. She blinked up at him again, cheeks flushed, and then burst into giggles.

A smile tugged at his lips, and he chuckled along with her.

"Oh god, they look like a Hallmark movie in the making," Sephie muttered.

"House couldn't pair us up, so it's trying the side characters," Luke said dryly. "At least it's not Jace."

A nearby candle flared to life with a smug little flicker.

"Hey, genius!" Sephie snapped at the ceiling. "They're able to leave, we're the ones stuck inside!"

The candle sputtered in response.

Luke knocked sharply on the window. The new couple jumped and immediately waved, cheeks pink, before skipping off.

Luke crossed the room and blew out the candle with gusto. The house apparently took the hint and stayed extinguished.

"We are so busting out of here."

"Agreed. But I need to finish my coffee first."

He retreated to the kitchen like a man on a mission. "I'll make breakfast then!"

"Oh, Flex? Can you make eggs?"

"Absolutely!"

What a morning indeed.

Chapter 37

Luke slammed a bundle of papers onto the kitchen table, making Sephie's plate of eggs wobble.

"What the heck?!"

"We're idiots."

Sephie frowned. "I'll admit my brain hasn't been at full power the last day or so, but come on."

He shook his head furiously. "No, Sephie. We've been so focused on the journal —"

"Yeah?"

"Hello?! There are letters, and the locket!"

He pulled the locket from his pocket and dangled it in front of her.

Oh crap.

"We're indeed idiots."

The house creaked in response.

"Oh shut up, you've put us through enough," Sephie snapped. Thankfully, there was no follow-up response.

Luke opened one of the letters and handed it to her. "Read this."

Sephie furrowed her brow. The cursive matched Cora's journal.

Friday, January 11th, 1833

My Dearest Ada,

I was heartbroken to receive your note and learn of your unfortunate circumstance. I understand your wish for discretion, but I must confess I see no course forward that does not require me to inform Gus of the situation. You have my solemn word he shall not breathe a word of it to Duncan, though surely you comprehend he must know the truth, eventually.

Still, I give you my assurance that we shall guard your confidence for as long as it is within our power to do so. I mean to help you, but I cannot do so alone.

Yours in friendship,
Cora

They sat in silence for a moment.

Mystery upon mystery. Was the house keeping them around for its own voyeuristic pleasure, or was it begging for a cold case to be solved?

"She was pregnant," Sephie finally whispered.

"Sure seems like it," Luke replied. "But who was she?"

"I'd guess Duncan's lover. But we barely know anything about him. How are we supposed to learn about Ada?"

"You done with that?" Luke pointed to her plate.

"I am now. That kind of killed my appetite."

Luke scooped up her plate and finished off the eggs.

"Sorry, I think better with more food in me."

"You can have my leftovers anytime," she mused.

He shot her an adorable smile. She blushed.

Focus Sephie.

She paged through the letters and pulled out one from a few months later.

Monday, April 8th, 1833

Dear Mrs. Ashland,

I cannot properly express my gratitude for your kindness in sending Nurse Christensen this morning. Concealing my condition these past two months has tried both my strength and my nerves, and I am certain the strain has done me no good. The nurse was swift, yet thorough, and departed before Duncan returned from his business.

We are arranging all future visits with great caution, ever mindful of his hours. The nurse instructed me to take more rest and refrain from over-exertion—but I find that near impossible, with the high standards Duncan demands of the household. Should I falter in my duties, he is bound to notice. I confess, Mrs. Ashland... I scarcely know what to do. I never imagined my life would take such a turn. And yet... here we are.

With sincere thanks,
Ada

Luke was tidying up again, more than usual. Trying to stay on the house's good side.

"Flex, Duncan was the father."

His eyes widened. "Talk about drama."

"To make matters worse, it seems like Ada was his maid or something."

Luke grimaced. "Unfortunately, it was a common occurence back then. Hell, it's still common today. Gross rich guy convinces the servant to give it up and wants nothing to do with her afterward. Jace anyone?"

"Speaking of Jace, *Dead Serious* would've milked this for tons of episodes."

"True," Luke said. "But you'd have felt like crap."

She would've.

He stood behind her and pulled another letter from the stack.

Thursday, July 25th, 1833

My Dearest Girl,

As soon as you finish reading this letter, gather what you can carry and wait in the rear garden. I've sent this note by way of my neighbor Mr. Alexander's son. He's been instructed to say nothing, and both he and his father are in my confidence. We may or may not hold leverage over them, but that's not your concern.

Duncan knows.

He called upon us to assist with the wine cellar and began hurling accusations. He claimed I was harboring secrets and conspiring with you. Which... well, yes, I suppose we are.

He lost his temper and came alarmingly close to raising his hand. I managed to trap him in the cellar and waited until Gus returned. He let Duncan out and took him for a drive to calm his fury. That should grant you ample time.

We have more than enough space here at the manor, and you will want for nothing. We will look after you. That is my solemn promise.

Always,
Cora

"I believe I called Cora a badass before?"

"Something like that," Sephie replied. "Gus helped, too. Soulmates and a good team. Ugh. Perfect."

He scratched his beard, which was bordering on scruffy now. "She'd be, what, six months along by then?"

Sephie nodded. "Sounds right. But if she wasn't showing much, Duncan wouldn't have noticed."

"Still, you'd think someone would've noticed another woman and baby living here."

"If we've learned anything, it's that Cora and Gus were very good at keeping secrets."

"Ooo, what if they were spies?"

She shot him a look. He smirked.

"What? Anything's possible."

"Possible, not probable."

"Scoob, there's no information on either of them and she, what was it," he pointed at the letter, "'may or may not hold leverage' over their neighbors?"

"Okay, I'll admit, that is fishy. But we can't focus on that right now."

She reached for the locket on the table, sunlight making the silver glint..

Wait.

"Is that…" Luke leaned in.

A tiny engraved A sat at the very bottom of the heart.

"A for Ada?" Sephie asked.

Luke gently took the locket and fiddled with the clasp. It didn't budge.

Sephie sighed and looked up. "Come on. We're trying to help."

"Hang on." Luke stepped behind her, mimicking Gus's motion from Sephie's dream. He slowly slipped the chain over her head, fingers brushing her collarbones with the lightest touch. She shivered.

She thumbed the clasp, and it now opened easily.

Inside: a sepia photo of a young woman, curvy, wild curls tucked into a bun, sitting with folded hands. She smiled softly, though there was a trace of sadness in her eyes.

Luke peered over her shoulder. "I'm guessing that's Ada."

The opposite side held a photo of a baby in a bassinet, sleeping peacefully.

"You think this was Ada's locket?" Luke asked.

"I don't think a woman would carry a photo of herself in a locket, even with her baby's photo. Seems more like something the father would keep."

"But Duncan didn't want anything to do with them."

"This'll sound weird, but maybe it was Cora's?"

Luke nodded. "Honestly, that makes the most sense. But again, if a woman and baby were living here, there should be more evidence."

A loud creak echoed beneath them.

They both looked down.

Luke frowned. "It wants us back in the cellar."

"There must be something important in there."

"I refuse."

Another louder creak.

Sephie sighed. "I don't think you have a choice."

Chapter 38

"I told you, I'm not going back down there."

Luke knew he was acting like a petulant child, but he didn't care. The last thing he wanted to do was travel back down into Cora's wine cellar.

Sephie crossed her arms. "Quit being a baby."

"I'm not being a baby. I have legitimate concerns!"

She sighed. "Flex, come on."

"Nuh uh. No way, no how."

"I need a big stwong man to keep my widdle self safe," she teased.

"You do not, and don't ever do that voice again."

She giggled and Luke felt something jump in his stomach.

He liked spending time with Sephie and didn't overly enjoy the thought of splitting up. But the cellar was dark. Especially when the house thought it was hysterical to turn off all the lights.

"Besides, don't you think it'd be better if one of us stays up here?" he offered. "I don't feel like dealing with getting locked down there."

She rolled her eyes and opened the hidden door. "I guess you have a point. Okay, stay here."

Luke heaved a sigh of relief. She grabbed the lantern hanging in the entrance, then disappeared into the darkness.

He cupped his hands around his mouth. "Please, be careful!"

"You'll come save me if I need help!" She called back.

Oh he absolutely would not. The little menace could easily handle herself. Especially in the outfit the house supplied her with today. They'd gone to get dressed before setting off and the manor had tried to recreate *The Mummy.*

Well, almost.

The house was still trapped somewhere between late Victorian and early Edwardian aesthetics. Luke ended up in khakis, a crisp blue button-up, suspenders, and brown suede boots. Sephie got black pants, a billowy lilac blouse, and black leather boots.

"I would have flipped if it tried to give me some hot archaeologist outfit," she'd muttered.   The house tried to shift one of the photos on the wall, but Sephie cast a glare so deadly it thought better of it.

For the record, Luke wouldn't have minded if she got stuck in a hot archaeologist outfit.

He dragged a bag of rice over to wedge the door open, then headed for the foyer, snatching the blueprint and letters on his way. Today, he was determined to find the ballroom. How he nor Sephie hadn't set foot in it yet, he didn't understand.

"Why've you been hiding it?" He muttered to the house.

A breeze passed through the main chandelier, causing a slight tinkling sound. Luke made sure to step out from under it as he went over the blueprint again. He wasn't about to get phantom of the opera'ed.

According to the blueprint, the ballroom should be down the hall opposite the kitchen. But he didn't remember even seeing a door there before.

He also didn't remember any candelabras.

Now the hall was lined with them, each flame bright and oddly steady. Too many candles, in his opinion. If Sephie didn't end up burning the place to the ground, it'd do it on its own.

Hey," he called, "are you trying to seduce me or warn me? 'Cause I'm opening that door regardless."

The sound of piano music began drifting through the hall.

"… Okay."

He slowed his pace, but didn't stop.

"Lovely playing. Whoever you are."

The music grew more grandiose. Luke grinned. Compliments were clearly effective. He reached the ballroom door and opened it easily. Just in case, he dragged a candelabra to wedge it open. If the house wanted him trapped, it'd have to work for it. Granted, it'd probably still find a way somehow, but he wouldn't make it easy.

His mouth fell open as he stepped into the ballroom. The hardwood floor gleamed, freshly polished. Cream-painted walls alternated with soft pink paisley panels. A grand piano stood in the corner, accompanied by a violin and a harp. Three crystal chandeliers hung overhead, sparkling with light from two massive windows on the far wall—windows Luke definitely hadn't seen from the outside.

His footsteps echoed as he walked to the instruments. Nobody else was in there. No one visible anyway. There were plenty of ghosts who enjoyed playing whatever their chosen instrument was while they were alive. He figured that's what happened here. Sephie mentioned another piano somewhere—maybe Cora or Gus had been musical.

He slid onto the bench and looked around. The room was stunning. The Ashlands must've thrown incredible parties here. Maybe that's why the house had kept it hidden; too many memories lingering in the air. An abundance of energy that could bring too much attention to the house.

Right now, it was quiet. Too quiet for his liking

He turned to face the piano and played a scale. As old as he knew it had to be, it sounded freshly tuned. He warmed up with more scales, then slipped into a sonata he couldn't name, a goofy remix of Chopsticks and *Heart and Soul,* and finally, *Clair de lune.*

Sure, it was cliché. But he couldn't help but love the composition. Debussy seemed to understand how music worked; human emotion expressed perfectly in a way words couldn't. No wonder ghosts were drawn to it.

The sound of a skirt swishing on the hardwood pulled Luke away from his musing. He continued playing even as the ghostly apparition of a couple appeared at the center of the dance floor. After dealing with a few stone tape situations, Luke was fairly used to stuff like this happening. Although, afterbeing transported into Gus's body thing, he was wary of whether the dancing couple could actually see him as well.

Suddenly, it felt as though another pair of hands pushed Luke's away from the keys, replacing *Clair de lune* with a grand waltz. Another invisible force lifted him by the underarms and dragged him to the dance floor. Luke tried to wriggle his body free, but he didn't have control over it. His heart thundered in his chest as he was dumped in the middle of the room. Around him, more dancing couples materialized. Trying to stand felt impossible, as if his legs were lead. He could barely turn his head. His vision became blurry.

"Sephie..." He tried to scream but it came out as a whisper.

He swore he saw a blurry, possibly green, shape of a man float above his head and into the chandelier. Emerald-colored flecks filled the room, giving him the illusion the room was spinning. Or maybe it actually was spinning? He couldn't tell. A bout of nausea passed through his body, and he felt faint. Something cold wrapped around his wrists and ankles, rooting him in place.

The music quickened, more frantic now, disorienting, like the ballroom itself was unraveling.

He could feel the pressure in his head building, a thick buzzing beneath his skin. His mouth opened in a silent scream.

The chandeliers flashed green. The air crackled.

He crumpled to the floor, eyes rolling back as the world fell away in a chaotic haze of music and light and darkness.

Then, stillness.

Chapter 39

"UGH! Why?!"

Sephie had just ran into the third cobweb since getting to the heart of the cellar. Luke hadn't mentioned any spiders, but then again, he was probably more focused on the darkness. She waved a hand in front of her face, hoping to dust away any more of the sticky threads.

"You know," she directed to the house, "you've done such a great job at cleaning the rest of the house—why'd you slack here?"

The gas lamps flickered in protest.

"What, are you ticked we split up?"

Another flicker, this time, it left her in complete blackness for a few seconds.

"Yup, that's it," she sniffed. "And I'm not scared of the dark. Try harder."

She knew she probably shouldn't be egging it on, but at this point, she really didn't care. As her frustration grew, more of her domineering personality came out, and the house apparently didn't know how to deal with it.

There was no response this time, so Sephie jutted her chin out and continued her exploration of the cellar. So far, she'd only found bottles upon bottles of wine, all marked with the Cora's Folly label. She couldn't comprehend how Cora had clearly created enough for an initial launch, yet there was no history of the brand anywhere.

What had gone wrong?

"What are you hiding, Cora?" she muttered, holding her lantern out in front of her. The cellar itself had been hidden, so perhaps there were more secret areas down here.

"AH!" she spat, as yet another cobweb appeared. She frantically ran her fingers through her hair, trying to remove the substance from her curls. Resting one hand on the closest wall, she carefully pulled the remaining web from her eyelashes.

"Well then, thanks for that."

The wall shifted underneath her hand.

Sephie jumped and moved the lantern closer, revealing a small door. She smirked.

"Okay, genuinely thanks for that."

She pushed, and the door slid easily to the side, revealing a secret room. Sephie was pretty sure it was a storage space, but times like these made her appreciate her size. She placed the lantern just inside the entrance, crouched down, and crawled in. A single shadow bounced off a wooden crate in the center of the room. Sephie duck-waddled closer, holding the lantern out in front of her, trying to see if there was anything marked on the crate.

It was blank. Sephie huffed and blew a stray curl out of her face. The lid was nailed shut. She could probably kick it open with her boot, but didn't want to risk damaging whatever was inside. It had to be important, right? Why else hide it?

There was no way Sephie was dragging the crate out on her own. And it was highly unlikely she'd get Luke down there again to help. There had to be a hammer somewhere in the house, given Gus's profession and all.

She carefully waddled back to the entrance, only to get hit with another cobweb to the face.

She wiped a hand down her face, not even attempting to get all the remnants. If a spider wanted to move into her hair, fine. She had enough curls that she wouldn't even notice it.

"I can't open the crate without tools or Luke's help. Chill."

All the lanterns immediately blew out, except for the one she held. Sephie rolled her eyes and headed for the exit. Acknowledging the paranormal seemed to only make things harder.

She managed to find her way to the stairs without tripping.

"I swear, if you shut that door, I'll just kick it down."

The light from the still-open door came into view and Sephie smirked. While compliments had worked, threats were a lot easier. Hanging the lantern back up, she blinked a few times as her eyes readjusted to the light. Then she noticed the bag of rice holding the entrance open.

She smiled. Luke.

Granted, the house probably still could've closed it, anyway. But it was the thought that counted.

"Luke?" Sephie called out to no response.

She wandered into the kitchen. It was empty. Cora's journal and the locket still sat on the table. Luke mentioned wanting to find the ballroom, so that was most likely where he'd gone. She moved into the foyer and toward the ominous hallway.

What had been the occasional breeze was now gusts of wind, causing the chandelier to swing wildly. Sephie scurried quickly out of the way. The last thing she needed was to be crushed by crystal.

"Luke?!" she called again.

Nothing.

This was very wrong.

She sprinted toward the ballroom doors, her boots echoing sharply off the walls. The hall was dark and gloomy, almost like it had been when they first entered Ashland Manor. Candelabras were strewn across the floor, and Sephie leapt over them like a track star.

"Where did all this Haunted Mansion crap come from?"

She refused to slow down—the doors were close now. Locked or not, she'd break through.

They opened for her.

She skidded to a stop, mouth falling open. A putrid green mist floated through the room, leaving a thick layer of grime on every surface. Sephie pulled her shirt up over her face and squinted.

"Crap! Flex?!"

Three chandeliers swayed above, as the mist swirled around her. She scanned the room for any sign of Luke. Her eyes burned, her lungs ached. Now she heard the music. Not the gentle, tinkling tune from Gus's office. The harsh, frantic notes of *In the Hall of the Mountain King* exploded around her. Whether the house was trying to drive her out or not, she wasn't leaving without him.

"Come on," she muttered. "Come on, come on, come on…"

The toe of her boot hit something solid. She heard the faintest moan. She dropped to her knees and felt the familiar biceps.

"Luke! Luke, wake up!"

He didn't move. The mist was getting thicker, the grime clinging to her skin.

Crap. She was going to have to drag him out. Somehow.

She bent down, looped her arms beneath his, and pulled. He barely budged. She didn't know if the tears in her eyes were from the mist or her own panic, but she ignored them. She darted to his legs, grabbed his ankles, and yanked. Better—but still too slow.

"God, Luke, please hold on."

A loud creak echoed from the floor. Suddenly, the room tilted, like a ramp. She picked up momentum as the doors grew closer.

"So close…"

Something caught her boot. She fell with a screech. Refusing to panic, she army-crawled to Luke, laid over him, and held tight.

"This had better work," she hissed through gritted teeth.

With one final push of effort, she rolled him over her and collapsed on top. They tumbled out into the hallway. The ballroom doors slammed shut behind them.

Sephie yanked her shirt down and gasped in the clean air. Luke lay still.

"No no no no no," she crawled over him, pressing two fingers to his neck. A pulse. Barely. But she couldn't see him breathing.

"Crap, okay."

She placed her hands on his chest and began compressions. Thank god she'd gotten CPR certified. Unfortunately, this wasn't the first time she'd had to use it.

Humming *Stayin' Alive* (yes, ironic), she pumped out thirty compressions. She was full-on straddling him now, but modesty didn't matter. Carefully, she pinched his nose shut and leaned in.

"I'm so sorry," she whispered before pressing her mouth to his.

She gave him two strong breaths. He had to be okay. He had to be.

She pulled back, ready to start again, when he coughed.

More tears fell as green phlegm sputtered from his mouth. Gross. But he was breathing. He inhaled deeply and finally opened his eyes. She blinked at him, tears dripping onto his chest. Without thinking, she collapsed against him. His arms wrapped weakly around her back.

"Holy hell," he rasped, "thank you."

She sobbed.

Chapter 40

"I can help you to the bathroom, seriously."

Luke was giving himself the equivalent of a sponge bath in the kitchen sink, an endless stream of green muck going down the drain.

He shook his head. "If I didn't feel so gross, I'd honestly just pass out on the floor right now. The last thing I want to do is climb stairs."

She shrugged. "Understandable. I'm gonna need to wash my hair at least. It collects everything."

"You're like a feather duster."

"Har har."

The water finally ran clear. Luke sighed heavily, grabbed a tea towel, and dried his head. Wiping the last few specks of green from his eyes, he looked up at Sephie. She was desperately trying to put her tough-guy persona back on, but was failing. Her eyes were red from crying, her lips were cracking from breathing through her mouth, and her curls were indeed full of dust, cobwebs, and green grime.

He handed her the towel. "I know I said it already, but thank you. I mean it."

She gratefully took the towel and ran it through her hair. Lord knows what began sprinkling out like confetti.

"I honestly just can't imagine what I would have done if..."

She trailed off. Luke didn't push. He didn't want to think about that "what if" either.

Sephie threw the tea towel into the sink—it clearly wasn't doing anything for her dream catcher of a hairdo. She put her hands on her hips and blew a curl out of her eyes. "Do you remember what happened before you passed out?"

He wobbled over to the kitchen table and flopped into a chair. "Just... green." He knew he'd wanted to check out the ballroom, and it had been breathtaking initially. After that, everything went hazy. He just knew it had become almost impossible to breathe, and he couldn't fight it.

Sephie bit her lip. "Normally, I'd blame mold or something, but that crap seemed... wrong."

"Wrong like paranormal wrong?"

To his surprise, she nodded.

She apparently noticed what she agreed with, and her eyes grew wider. "I more so mean, it's unexplainable at the moment."

"It's just a little slime, Scoob."

"Shut up, Flex."

The kitchen window cracked open slightly, then slammed closed, causing the two of them to jump. Sephie's eyes cut toward the glass, daggers practically shooting out. Luke swore he saw it tremble as it cracked open again, slightly wider than before. He chuckled.

"I'm sick of playing nice," she muttered. "It literally just shifted an entire floor to roll us out of a deadly gas, and it tries to reprimand us for name-calling? Nuh uh."

She sure was beautiful when she was mad.

He shook his head, trying to focus back on the task at hand. "Find anything new in the cellar?"

"Oh!" Sephie exclaimed. "That whole almost dying thing made me forget. There's a little crawl space down there with an unmarked crate. It's nailed shut."

"I am not going down there to help drag it up here," Luke protested.

"I figured as much. After that mess, I wouldn't expect you to. I need to find a hammer."

She marched out of the kitchen with gusto, cobwebs still snowing from her head. He figured she was going to raid Gus's office. Luke crossed his arms and leaned back in his chair. He honestly needed a nap, but he didn't want to risk being scooped up again by lord knows what. It was kind of unbelievable that what was supposed to be an "easy" job chasing around frat bros with cameras turned into a near-death experience.

And here I was thinking you'd be the one to protect her.

"Dammit, Flo, not now."

Well, it's kind of important.

Luke groaned. Sure it was. He'd throw a wall up, but he knew he'd immediately pass out again from using what little energy he had left.

"How important is important?"

I know what caused that emerald-colored fight you just had.

He sat up immediately. "How?"

The entity, or whatever the hell that was, was in my neck of the woods. Had to force its way through the veil to get to you.

"I thought you needed permission to do that."

You typically do.

Whatever attacked was extremely powerful if it hadn't connected by way of a vessel. "I'm guessing you didn't get a good look at whatever it was?"

Unfortunately, no.

"Well, we know it's dead. Whatever it is."

Or a demon.

Luke shuddered. He was pretty sure demons weren't actually a thing. If there was ever negative energy around, it was either because the soul was hurt or they were a horrible peson when they were living.it .

Sharp footsteps alerted him to Sephie's return. Amazingly, Flo went quiet. Sephie marched back through the kitchen, hammer in one hand, crowbar in the other. Luke's mouth dropped open a little.

"Where'd you find a crowbar?"

She twirled it in her hand and grinned. "I explained to the house on my way up that it had better give me something useful, or it'd deeply regret it. Both tools were on Gus's desk when I walked in. Now, I have a box waiting to be opened." With that, she strode off to the cellar.

Luke had to hand it to her, she was ruthless. He waited a moment to see if Flo had anything to add. When she didn't, he pushed himself to his feet and headed to the pantry. They'd only had breakfast maybe an hour ago, if that, but he needed to distract himself. Crafting new recipes was the perfect distraction. And he wasn't keen on any more adventuring today.

"Preheat the oven, would you?" He heard the scraping of coal dropping into the cast iron and grinned. A sentient house basically equaled a smart kitchen. He wandered into the pantry, and a fresh bowl of cherries immediately caught his attention. Scratching his chin (he desperately needed to groom hisbeard), he pondered what he could do with the fruit.

"You look like the Nutty Professor."

Sephie reemerged from the cellar, hammer in one hand, a bottle of wine in the other, and the crowbar shoved into the waistband of her pants. He carefully took the bottle from her.

"If I'm the Nutty Professor, you're Einstein."

She ran her now-free hand through her hair, scooping up the new additions of cobwebs.

"I swear, they appear out of nowhere. Granted, I didn't have the lantern—"

"I'm sorry, didn't have the lantern?" He just noticed the light source still hanging right outside the stairs. He gaped at Sephie. "How did you manage?"

She smirked and shrugged. "It kept the rest of the lanterns on. And I'm used to crawling through small, dark places anyway."

Maybe she really was a hobgoblin. Nah, too cute. Definitely an imp.

She gestured at the wine bottle. "Take a look at that label, I'm gonna hit the laundry room."

"Laundry room?"

"I told you, I'm not attempting the crazy contraption that's apparently a shower. I'm gonna wash my hair in the laundry basin."

He arched a brow, impressed.

She wandered out, somehow more relaxed than before. Luke assumed it was because she was finally slipping back into her element: exploring, researching, and being generally snarky. He liked it.

Glancing at the wine bottle, he found a different label slapped on the front. Arden Dell Ales was written in a different cursive script. Luke knew that name somehow, he just couldn't quite put his finger on it. While Cora's Folly seemed to focus more on amber port, the liquid in this bottle was a deep ruby red. Why had this been down there?

His attention turned back to the cherries. He looked back and forth between the bottle and the bowl before a large smile spread across his face. Checking various shelves, he managed to collect the rest of the ingredients his little brain concocted, which included chocolate.

"Scoob might not like wine, but I bet she'll like it in a dessert."

He swore he heard a floorboard groan. He didn't care.

Chapter 41

Sephie's neck ached from holding her head under the faucet. Thankfully, the house pitied her and made sure the water wasn't freezing cold. She'd forgotten shampoo, so she resorted to the same bar soap she and Luke used on their pants. Her curls were going to look horrendous without her usual products anyway, so no, she didn't care about looking presentable.

It took at least three times as long as it had for Luke to get the water to run clear. The sheer amount of cobwebs, slime, and dust that came out of her hair was remarkable. She was shocked she didn't see any spiders going down the drain. She shut the water off, grabbed the closest T-shirt, and plopped her hair in it to try minimizing the inevitable frizz.

Her sojourn into the cellar had been exhilarating. Even though the lanterns provided some light, she'd essentially been in the dark when she crawled into the storage space. And yet, she'd managed to pry the nails out of the crate, lift the lid, and haul a wine bottle and some tools all the way upstairs. This was what she was good at —and she was realizing she couldn't give it up anytime soon. Even if it meant changing her tactics.

Like maybe adding a medium business partner.

An audible bang echoed from the library as Sephie wandered out of the laundry room. She wrinkled her nose.

"I already had to save a life today. I'm not investigating creepy noises on my own."

Another bang made her jump, but she kept walking toward the stairwell. Sephie from a few days ago would have dashed straight to the library to investigate. After nearly losing Luke, she knew better.

"Tomorrow maybe. When I have Luke with me."

A nearby candle flickered—not in malice, just acknowledgment.

Notes of cherries and chocolate greeted her as she reached the ground floor. She smiled. Luke couldn't help himself when it came to the kitchen. Everyone had a hobby that served as therapy. Cooking was his. And honestly, she was reaping the benefits.

Sure enough, she found him at the stovetop, stirring something in a saucepan. He looked up and gave her an odd look.

"Is that a T-shirt?"

She touched the fabric on her head. "It's called plopping. Better for protecting my curls."

"We're locked in a sentient Victorian mansion, and you're worried about your hair."

"Not much I can do otherwise. But I can at least avoid looking like a lion."

"Eh, probably more like a poodle. Yippy little things."

"Again with the dog comparisons," she groaned. "What are you working on?"

He held up a wooden spoon, melted chocolate dripping from it. "Figured I'd try to make something you'd actually like with wine in it. Chocolate panna cotta with cherries and a balsamic port glaze."

She frowned. "Balsamic? That doesn't sound very dessert-like."

"Trust me. The mix of acid and chocolate will work."

"We'll see."

A sharp tap on the window made them both jump. Lovely. More shared trauma. Sephie looked up and spotted Thalia outside, a smug grin plastered on her face.

"Why are you back so soon, and what are you so happy about?"

Thalia cocked a brow. "Had to come back for my car. Isiah drove us to brunch." She gave another dreamy smile. Sephie rolled her eyes. Apparently, the house's matchmaking worked.

Luke chuckled. "Hey, at least she picked the Ghostie Geek."

"I suppose," Sephie muttered.

"I'm standing right here," Thalia called.

"And?" Sephie shot back.

"You're just jealous."

"Am not."

"Ladies," Luke cut in, "come on."

Sephie gestured toward him. "I have a himbo twirling around the kitchen making me Italian desserts. I think I'm good."

"Hey! We talked about the himbo thing!"

Thalia's jaw dropped. "Are you two together?"

"No!" Sephie and Luke shouted in unison.

Thalia smirked. "But you want to be."

Heat crept up Sephie's neck. She couldn't deny that if something happened to Luke in the ballroom, she would've been devastated. Maybe they were just close after all they'd been through.

Thankfully, Thalia switched topics.

"Is that wine?"

Sephie nodded. "Yeah, it was hiding downstairs."

Thalia squinted. "Let me see it."

Sephie shot her a look but motioned for Luke to bring it over. He held it up to the window. Thalia leaned in close, her eyes lighting up.

"That's Arden Dell Ales?"

Luke glanced at the label. "Yes?"

"Dude, that's like, stupidly expensive stuff."

"Of course you know that," Sephie muttered.

Thalia rolled her eyes. "No, seriously. Dad saved for ages to get Mom a bottle for their anniversary."

Sephie palmed her face. "Wait, no, you're right. So what the heck is it doing here?"

Luke studied the bottle. "I thought it seemed familiar. I think my Yiayia drinks it."

"Flex, are you just now admitting your family's rich?"

He pulled the cork out with his teeth and spat it onto the windowsill. "Stupidly so. I don't get any of it. I'm supposed to 'learn how to live on my own,' or whatever."

He took a swig, then poured some into a skillet. Thalia looked horrified.

"You found a vintage Arden Dell Ales, and he's making jello out of it???"

"Panna cotta. It's fancier."

"Whatever. You could make serious bank off that."

Sephie shrugged. "There's more in the cellar."

"There's more in the cellar?! Dear lord, what's this house done to you?"

"Just saying."

"Want me to tell Jessica or someone? Maybe there's another owner."

"Sure, good idea."

Thalia pointed to her temple. "Big bwain."

"No, that'd be your new boyfriend."

Giggling, Thalia skipped off to her car. Sephie shook her head, smiling as she wandered back to the kitchen. Luke was multitasking, whisking the port and balsamic in one skillet while pouring custard into ramekins. He nodded toward them.

"Put those in the icebox, would you?"

She arranged them on a baking sheet and carried it over. "Counting on the house to speed up the chill time?"

"That's the hope," he said, dumping cherries into the port. "I can stash this in there too if the house gets fussy."

Sephie picked up the half-full wine bottle and sniffed. Still smelled like rotten fruit. How was this stuff so expensive? She turned the bottle in her hands, eyeing the label.

Arden Dell Ales.

Arden Dell Ales.

"Luke?"

"Hm?"

"Arden Dell Ales."

"Good job, you know how to read."
She groaned. "No, Arden Dell Ales. A, D, A."
Luke nearly dropped his spoon.
"Ada."

Chapter 42

Luke and Sephie moved to the dining room, once again feeling slightly guilty they mainly ate in the kitchen. The dining table, however, had far more room to spread out piles of research.

"Anything?"

"Nope."

They'd been combing through the remaining papers, which turned out to be mostly pre-marriage love letters between the Ashlands and some random business correspondence. Luke held one particularly raunchy note between his fingertips like it was a used tissue.

"I assumed people back then didn't actually follow the whole 'pure till marriage' thing, but dear lord."

Sephie giggled. "Not like they went all the way before marriage."

Luke dropped the letter. "No, but they sure had a lot of practice."

"Sounds like Gus was quite the lover. That piano playing came in handy."

"Okay, stop."

"No wonder this house turned into such a perv."

"Sephie."

She chuckled and turned back to Cora's journal, hoping something she'd missed would stand out.

Wednesday, July 8th, 1835

This summer has been unbearably hot. At least with no staff in the house, I'm free to walk about in my slip and stays without causing scandal. Small comforts.

I suggested to Gus we turn the ballroom into an indoor swimming pool. It is becoming rather fashionable, and it would certainly help with the heat. He said he'd think on it, but his attention is fixed on finishing the new house. It's coming along well. I've had a few peeks, and it's a fine build. I look forward to helping with the furnishings once it's ready.

"Looks like Gus built another house in 1835."

Luke's brow furrowed. "For who? One thing everyone knows is the Ashlands lived here until they died."

Sephie shrugged. "I don't know, but it's the only new detail I didn't notice before. And why mention it if it wasn't important?"

"Very true." He sifted through the pile and held up another paper. He double-checked it, then flipped it toward Sephie. "This one's from the year before. Looks like a full materials order—enough to frame out a pretty big house."

"Vacation home, maybe?"

He scanned the order form. "No, the shipping address was in town." He sipped the ruby-colored liquid from the glass he'd poured. Both he and Sephie had been keeping a close eye on it, but the house didn't appear to be refilling it this time. "This stuff is fantastic, by the way. You sure you don't want to try it?"

Sephie wrinkled her nose. "I'll wait until the dessert's set. The alcohol should be cooked off, right?"

"Oh, mostly," he teased.

She smirked and looked again at the bottle label. "So let's say Arden Dell Ales was started by Ada. Why would the crate be here?"

Luke stroked his chin, feigning deep thought. "Cora and Gus let her and the baby stay here, right? Maybe she started the company here?"

Sephie sighed. "Or maybe… Cora gave her Cora's Folly?"

Luke nodded. "That'd also make sense. Judging from everything we've found, and your dream, it looked like she was days away from launching. It was all ready, and Cora just gave it to Ada?"

"That'd be the most selfless thing I've ever heard if it's true."

Sephie opened the locket and gazed again at the portrait of Ada. She was beautiful but looked so young. Too young to have had a baby out of wedlock and survive on her own. Unless she was some kind of prodigy, Sephie doubted Ada started the business alone.

"Cora did mention she and Gus wanted kids, but there's no evidence that ever happened."

"There'd at least be a nursery around here if they had any," Luke added.

"Maybe this was their way of still having children? Ada looked like she had no one else except the Ashlands." She rested her chin on the table. "I swear, there's a new twist every day."

"That there are." Luke straightened a pile of papers when a folded sheet slipped out. They both stared at it.

"I feel like we should read that," Sephie said quietly.

"Probably."

"Your turn."

"What?!"

"I just went into the cellar crawlspace in the dark. Your turn for spooky crap."

Luke groaned but picked up the paper and carefully unfolded it. He frowned, then read aloud:

"Ashland Properties formally severs all professional and personal ties with Mr. Duncan Flatley due to ongoing misconduct, including inappropriate behavior toward Mrs. Cora Ashland and Ms. Ada Pischner; breaches of workplace ethics; and disturbing allegations of psychological manipulation and torture. Mr. Augustus Ashland has arranged for Mr. Flatley's relocation to Ireland, where he will receive treatment at Greensburrow Sanitarium. Legal action will not be pursued provided Mr. Flatley makes no attempts to contact any member of the Ashland or Pischner families."

"Oh. My. God," was all Sephie could say.

"Well," Luke said flatly, "they took care of Duncan. And that confirms Ada is the Pischner Jessica found. I wonder if the surname stuck around."

"I'm sorry, you just glazed over something insane," Sephie sputtered. "Psychological torture?"

He cringed. "I'm going to guess that's related to the creepy green book upstairs."

Sephie shuddered. "Duncan was a bad guy."

Luke reread the notice. "He might not have started out that way, but getting mixed up with the dark arts can do things to a person."

"I thought you said it was all a bunch of crap?"

He nodded. "It is. But that doesn't mean just believing in it can't make someone go crazy. I mean, how do you think cults get started?"

Sephie pulled the T-shirt from her hair. Her curls tumbled down, still a mess. It felt like every time they figured something out, another random piece of the puzzle dropped into their laps, giving them more questions than answers. She wasn't trying to start a detective agency, but it sure felt like one.

She glanced at Luke. "You're not gonna like what I say next."

Luke groaned. "I know. We need to look at Duncan's stupid book."

Chapter 43

Sephie dragged the little side table to the library entrance and propped the door open. She wasn't sure it would do anything, but it had become habit at this point. Luke grimaced as he joined her.

"I don't feel good about this."

"We've been in here tons. What's the problem?"

"Oh, I almost died, you heard two loud bangs from in here, Duncan was apparently loony tunes, and there's a creepy book that nearly made me vomit. You know, normal day at the old grind."

Sephie nodded. "Fair point. Stay here, my turn."

"Scoob?"

"Yeah?"

"Please be careful."

She nodded again and headed to the shelf. An unnatural chill ran up her spine, and her lower lip trembled. Just in case, she pulled her shirt over her nose and mouth. There hadn't been any gas or muck when they initially found the book, but she wasn't taking chances.

She approached the shelf where she'd thrown the book and cautiously reached behind the other volumes. Her fingertips brushed the cloth cover, and she exhaled sharply. Nothing bad. Yet. She pulled the book out and glared at it. Duncan had clearly gotten what he deserved in life. But what happened when he died?

"Everything okay in there?" Luke called.

"For the moment."

She could hear her own voice waver. Things were okay. She took one more deep breath, held it, and slowly opened the cover.

Nothing.

Until—

"UGH!"

"Luke?!"

"I'm assuming you opened that stupid book?"

"Yes," she said through gritted teeth.

"There's something really, really bad in there, Sephie. Not as bad as when I was right behind you, but it felt like someone stabbed behind my eyeballs."

"Jeez. Sit down or something."

"Already did. Just hurry up and read."

"What could possibly be connected to this that's making you feel so horrible?"

"I honestly don't want to know."

Waiting another few seconds for assurance, Sephie pulled her shirt down and flipped through the first few pages. The subtopics were scrawled in Duncan's terrible handwriting: souls, spirituality, psychic talents… the occult. She turned to a new page and found a crudely drawn diagram of a naked man, arms outstretched like a crucifix. An orb and pillars surrounded the figure.

"Flex?"

"Hm?"

"You play *Amnesia?*"

"The heck?"

"As in *The Dark Descent.*"

"I know what it is, Scoob. What does that have to do with anything? I'm assuming I'd know if a Grunt popped up."

She chuckled. He had good taste. "No, there's a really badly drawn picture of Alexander in here."

Luke let out a deep belly laugh. "That's from the Liber Divinorum Operum. Hildegard of Bingen wrote it."

"Hildegard of Bing-what? And why is a poorly drawn replica in here?"

"Hildegard was a nun, mystic, and theologian. Pretty phenomenal for a woman. Wouldn't surprise me if Duncan thought he was her second coming or something."

"Gross."

She kept flipping through the pages, noticing the handwriting grew increasingly erratic. She stopped at a page featuring a pentagram in the center. Underneath, in thick black letters: "Ritual Sacrifice."

Grimacing, she slammed the book shut. Another folded paper slipped from beneath the cover, fluttering to the floor. Sephie arched a brow and bent to pick it up.

"What's that?"

She squeaked and bumped her head into Luke's chest.

"How were you so quiet?"

He smirked. "I can be sneaky when I need to be. Now, what is that?"

Sephie unfolded the paper. A child's drawing. Three figures, labeled: "Mama," "Me," and "Aunt Cora."

Luke smiled. "I think that confirms Ada and her baby were well cared for."

Sephie held up Duncan's book. "Then why was it in here?"

He shrugged. "I came over because you got too quiet. What spooked you?"

"Ritual Sacrifice."

"I'm SORRY?"

"Yeah. That was written in there."

Luke took the book from her, eyeing the cover but not daring to open it. "Black magic is a bunch of bull. It gives Satanism a bad name. The closest real witches get to 'dark stuff' is cord-cutting—helping someone move past toxicity. Stuff like that."

"I guess Duncan didn't get the memo."

"Or didn't care, then went nuts." He looked at the drawing again, and the color drained from his face. "Oh god…"

Sephie blinked at him, confused. She glanced at the drawing, at the green book, back at Luke…

Oh god.

"You don't think—"

"I do think, unfortunately. Really wish I was a himbo right now."

Sephie snatched the book and stomped toward the library exit.

"Scoob?"

She ignored him, marching straight to her bedroom. Her nails dug into the cloth cover like she wanted Duncan to feel it, wherever the hell he was. He'd been a vile, disgusting man, and she wanted to erase every trace of him. The house slammed the bedroom door open for her, and the fireplace burst to life. Grinning, she stood in front of it.

"Scoob!" Luke caught up and reached for her shoulder, then thought better and gave it a gentle tap. "What are you doing?"

Sephie turned around, eyes blazing. "Burning this wannabe baby murderer's beloved death book to a crisp."

Luke held up his hands, palms out, then placed them gently on her shoulders. His thumbs rested lightly against her collarbones. She relaxed slightly under the pressure.

"Sephie, the guy was scum. Dirt. I wouldn't compare him to gum under a shoe. But if that book is giving off this kind of toxic energy, throwing it into fire might be the worst idea."

She slumped. He was probably right. The last thing she wanted was to unleash more toxic fumes. Or something worse.

"He was going to kill a baby, Luke. His own baby. Oh god, what if he did?" She wiggled out of his grasp and began pacing, tossing the book back and forth between her palms. "What if he did a ritual in the ballroom? That would explain why it transformed and why you ended up in the middle of it. I just—"

"Sephie!"

She froze, breathing quick and shallow. She squeezed her eyes shut.

In through the nose, out through the mouth. Ten, nine, eight…

Her eyes cracked open. "Sorry."

"Don't apologize for freaking out over something worth freaking out over. Now —" he took the book from her hands, "I don't think Duncan did anything. If he murdered a child, it would've been in Cora's journal. Or police reports. Or news articles. And that drawing made by a toddler wouldn't exist."

She took a few more deep breaths.

"Okay."

Luke bit his bottom lip. "We probably need to get this thing professionally cleansed once we're out of here. Until then, shove it in Gus's desk?"

"No. It needs to be way out of the way," she said. "The attic?"

"That should work. Kept the rest of the stuff safe. And it's filthy, which is fitting."

She headed back into the hallway. "Come on then, stepstool."

Luke groaned. "Could we maybe find an actual ladder? I don't feel like catching you again."

"As you've said, I'm tiny."

"Not the point, pipsqueak."

Chapter 44

"Three, two, one—"

Sephie carefully stepped off Luke's shoulders and grabbed the attic door pull chain. He grabbed her waist easily and placed her gently on her feet. She grinned up at him.

"We make a good team."

"I still wish you'd have let me get a ladder."

"Waste of time," she waved dismissively before picking Duncan's book off the floor. "I'll just run this up there real quick."

Luke watched her disappear into the ceiling. "Find a super dusty area."

He listened to her duck-waddling above him, clearly trying to find the grossest corner to store Duncan's cursed relic. He'd been wracking his brain to figure out if any of his contacts could help cleanse an object like this, but nothing came to mind. There was also the fear the book might mess with someone else the same way it had messed with him.

"Sephie?" he called up.

"I found an absolutely disgusting corner, don't worry."

He chuckled. "You wouldn't happen to know any witches, would you?"

"Flex. You know who you're talking to, right?"

"Oh right, you came in here a skeptic."

"Exactly. So, no. No clue."

There went that idea. He'd probably have to dig through the library again. Not that he expected to find a how-to guide on magical artifact detox wedged between Cora's journal and 19th-century grocery lists.

A loud crack from above.

"LUKE, MOVE!"

He dove just in time as the attic stairs exploded into a mess of splinters. In less than ten seconds, what used to be a staircase was now a pile of sawdust.

Sephie's head appeared from the attic entrance, her eyes wide. "Are you okay?"

He winced, rubbing the back of his neck. "Gonna have a couple new bruises, but yeah, I'm fine."

They both stared at the mess.

"What caused that?!"

"I don't know! The whole house has been functional, why now?"

She tapped on the attic floor under her. "The rest of it seems solid. Dirty, but still standing."

"This is really the only spot the house hasn't cleaned up, right?"

"If you don't count the ballroom, yeah."

He wasn't counting the ballroom. That was its own disaster.

"Maybe the house just... forgot about the attic?"

"Maybe. But why forget this one spot?"

"Hey, nothing with a mind is perfect," Luke said, smirking. "You caused that hole in the front steps, remember?"

Sephie grunted.

"Okay, well," she shifted so her legs dangled out of the ceiling. "Help me down."

"Please let me get a ladder now."

"Nope."

And with that, she slipped out of the attic. Luke caught her easily, bridal-style. He rolled his eyes.

"Have I told you that you're insane?"

"Eh, probably. But I knew you'd catch me."

She wasn't wrong.

He was reminded again how small she was in his arms. Fragile wasn't the word, seeing that Sephie could break someone's nose with a good elbow. But still. Holding her like this flipped some kind of switch in his brain. The very primal "protect at all costs" part. And the longer he held her, the less he wanted to let go.

She wasn't rushing to get away either. Arms looped around his neck, that trademark smirk tugging at her lips. And she was staring right back up at him like she saw something worth staying for.

This was nice.

"You're adorable."

Sephie blinked at him.

Crap. Had he said that out loud?

He tensed, halfway ready for her to punch him. But she didn't. She just looked at him. Wide eyes, lips parted like she couldn't decide what to say. A flush crept into her cheeks.

"...Thanks, Luke."

Still, neither of them moved.

His hands had unconsciously curled tighter at her waist. She was fisting his shirt now, like if she let go she might float off. And he could feel her heartbeat. Not just hear it, but feel it. Racing against his chest like it was trying to sync up with his.

He leaned forward, just slightly. Their faces were so close now. Breath mingling.

Her eyes flicked to his lips, then back up.

And then she cleared her throat.

Luke swallowed and eased her down, letting her slide out of his arms. She stepped back, suddenly fidgeting like she wasn't sure what to do with her hands.

"Um," he muttered. "Sorry."

Her arms dropped, but she didn't look mad. If anything, she looked a little dazed.

"You don't have to apologize," she said, softer this time. "It's nice being complimented by a hot guy."

He blinked. "You think I'm hot?"

She genuinely laughed. "Don't let it go to your head."

"Too late," he shot back, grinning despite the tension still thrumming in the air.

Oh, what the hell?

He leaned in again, slow this time, testing the waters. One inch. Two.

Knock knock knock.

The loud banging from downstairs could not have been timed worse.

Sephie groaned. "Come on," she said, spinning on her heel and storming for the stairs. "Let's go update whoever it is."

Luke followed, cursing under his breath and trying not to stomp. She liked him. Like-liked him. This tiny, stubborn, gremlin of a woman liked him. And he was finally about to kiss her.

Of course, *Dead Serious* had to show up and ruin it.

Xavier and Rob were waiting at the front window. Sephie was glaring daggers, and Luke couldn't help but grin. She was genuinely mad—hopefully because they weren't upstairs making out right now.

Rob raised an eyebrow. "You two hook up yet?"

"Not yet," Sephie deadpanned.

Luke went bright red.

Xavier ignored the jab. "Nothing came out of the Pischner lead. Looks like the family line's completely dead."

"Actually," Luke said, stepping forward, "we think we've figured it out. There was an Ada Pischner who got pregnant by Gus's business partner."

"Who was a freak, by the way," Sephie added.

"That he was. The Ashlands took her in to help her out."

"And?" Rob asked.

"We think Cora gave Ada her wine business and helped her start over. You ever hear of Arden Dell Ales?"

"The fancy rich people booze?" Xavier asked.

Luke nodded.

"Pretty sure that company was owned by the Melks for the longest time, not the

Pischners. A family friend took over when the CEO passed away a few years ago." Rob added.

Sephie narrowed her eyes. "How do you know that?"

Rob shrugged. "I can be cultured."

"We can dig into the company records if you want," Xavier offered.

"Yes, please," Sephie said. Luke nodded in agreement.

Xavier glanced between the two of them. "You guys need anything else?"

Rob smirked. "They've got wine and unresolved tension. They're good."

"Hey!" Sephie and Luke said at the same time.

Xavier laughed. "Luke, keep that idea in mind."

Before Sephie could question it, Luke gently grabbed her wrist and pulled her away from the window as the guys turned to leave, chuckling.

"What idea?" Sephie hissed.

"I'll tell you later."

No, he absolutely would not.

Chapter 45

He was about to kiss her.

The Greek lumberjack Flexorcist had been about to kiss her.

And Sephie would have let him if Xavier and Rob hadn't shown up.

She liked him. Really liked him. And it kind of scared her. She'd wondered for the longest time if she were actually asexual. She hadn't come anywhere near kissing a guy since she dumped Brandon all those years ago, and honestly, she hadn't missed the more sexual parts. But the fact she was now openly thirsting for attention from a beautiful man pretty much put the asexuality theory to rest.

She needed to pull herself together. It had only been three days. Three. Days. Surely that wasn't enough time to fall for a guy, right? Gran would've thoroughly disagreed. Thalia too, if she were being honest. They both would've told her to go play tonsil hockey with Luke and stop overthinking it.

It'd just be a kiss, not like they'd be pronounced husband and wife or anything. The sexual tension was becoming unbearable, and there were only so many ways to take the edge off. They'd smooch, probably get a little handsy, then get back to solving the mysteries of Ashland Manor. Easy.

Except Sephie didn't want it to be easy. She was pretty sure Luke didn't either.

They'd already agreed to be friends if—no, when—they made it out of the house. But she wanted more. She wanted to taste his recipes, go on more investigations, hear stories about his absurd family, and wake up cuddling him because she chose to.

She wanted more than just a paranormal fling.

A ramekin sliding in front of her made her jump.

"Sorry," Luke said. "It's ready."

Panna cotta. Right.

Luke sat across from her with his own ramekin, waiting for her to try it first. They were back in the dining room, the paperwork now stacked off to the side. The house had replaced the clutter with a vase of carnations and two candlesticks. The light bounced off the flowers, casting flecks of pink and red across Luke's face.

"Scoob, you good?"

She blinked. "I don't know, honestly."

"Did you get hurt coming down from the attic?"

She shook her head.

He frowned. "Maybe you just need to eat. Please try it."

She picked up a spoon and eyed the dessert. It looked both rich and delicate, the chilled chocolate jelly somehow creamy. Glossy red cherries in glaze crowned the top. She scooped a bite with a little of everything and lifted it to her mouth.

The mix of chocolate, fruit, and acid jolted her taste buds awake. Luke was right—the flavors absolutely worked. And the texture practically dissolved on her tongue, the glaze coating every corner of her mouth.

A loud, feral moan escaped her throat before she could stop it. She slapped a hand over her mouth, horrified. Luke grinned.

"I'll take that as it's good?"

"It's probably the best thing I've ever put in my mouth."

"That's what she said."

She groaned. "Flex."

He took a spoonful of his own. "Sorry, but you practically handed that one to me."

God, was he dumb. And it was so cute.

She kept eating. "So you think Ada ended up getting married?" she asked between bites.

Luke frowned. "Highly unlikely. You could be the prettiest, kindest, most amazing woman back then, and no guy would give you a chance if you were a single mother."

Sephie sighed. "That's messed up."

"Agreed. But it's not a dead end. Ada might not have gotten married, but I bet her kid did." He took another bite and grinned. "Damn, I'm good."

He sure was.

Focus.

"So at some point, a Pischner married a Melk, and the wine company stayed under that surname ever since."

She managed to swallow another moan with her next bite.

"It had to be early on," he said, already scraping the last of the chocolate from his ramekin. "Pischner would've been more memorable if it stuck around."

Sephie tapped her teeth with her spoon. Why did Melk sound so familiar?

Luke gently reached across the table and lowered her hand. "Don't do that. You'll mess your teeth up." His hand lingered. Her breath hitched.

"Scoob, listen—"

The memory struck her out of nowhere.

"Oh my god," she dropped her spoon. Luke pulled his hand back, and she immediately missed the warmth.

"Sorry, I just remembered something. Melk."

"What about it?"

"Lucy Melk."

He thought for a moment, and his mouth fell open. "As in our client Lucy? I never got her last name."

Sephie nodded. "It makes sense. Rich family full of assholes, matriarch hands over her company to a business partner and leaves the house to the only grandkid with a soul."

Luke jumped up and grabbed the stack of papers, flipping through quickly. He pulled out the order form and scanned it.

"You remember the address from Lucy's investigation?"

Sephie ground her teeth. "Maybe?"

"Willow Street ring a bell?"

Her eyes lit up. "That it does." She stood and moved closer.

"Gus built Ada a house," Luke said.

"And that's why there's no sign of children here," she added. "Good lord, it seriously must be nice to be rich, just being able to build someone a house."

His grin widened. "Did we just solve a mystery?"

Energy buzzed between them. "I think we did."

"Warning, I'm picking you up."

"Wha—"

He scooped her up and twirled her around like he had days ago. But this time it wasn't a stunt, it was pure joy. She laughed and clung to him.

"Stop! I'm getting dizzy!"

He stopped, but held her tight. Her feet dangled, and she didn't care. Their faces were inches apart, and before she knew it, her gaze drifted to his mouth.

And then, she was leaning in and pressing her lips to his.

Her kiss was a question—gentle, soft and exploratory, barely more than a breath between them. Hesitant but hopeful, the kind you ask with your whole body. She brushed her lips against his again, a shiver running down her spine. God, what if she'd misread this?

His kiss was the answer she was hoping for—solid, sure, deliciously slow. A low, involuntary sound escaped him as he deepened it, like he'd been holding his breath too. One of his hands slid up to cradle the back of her head, fingers sinking into her curls, while the other settled at her waist, obviously trying to avoid gripping her hipbones.

Her lips parted with his, just slightly, and his breath met hers. It came out in hot, short puffs, nearly crackling between them. When he finally pulled away, their foreheads touched. Both of them were panting, but neither moved to create space.

"You need to shave," she whispered.

He gave a low, rough laugh. "Apologies for the whiskers. But you didn't seem to mind."

She stroked a finger along the edge of his jaw, his beard moving softly beneath her touch. He leaned into it with a quiet sigh, and something in her melted. *How could someone be this big and this tender?*

"Have you seriously not kissed a guy since your twat of an ex?" he murmured. She smirked and nodded.

Something changed in Luke then. His hands suddenly gripped under her thighs, flipping her around in one fluid motion. She gasped as her back hit the tabletop, papers scattering like leaves around them. Luke hovered over her, arms braced on either side of her, gaze fixed on hers. He had a sweet yet wicked look on his face.

She'd been afraid of whenever this might happen. That being caged in like this, even by someone she trusted, might snap her back to that cold, sharp memory on the forest floor. Dr. Alias warned it might come without warning.

But Luke didn't press. He didn't move. He just waited, all that energy in his body held still for her. He leaned in just an inch, expression softening.

"Is this okay?" he asked, voice barely above a whisper.

Sephie took a breath. Her skin was tingling and heart racing, but not from fear. From a fiery need.

"Yes," she said.

He traced his thumb along her bottom lip, then down to her chin, along the edge of her jaw, and finally to the delicate curve of her ear. Her entire body shook under ohis touch.

He kissed the corner of her mouth, the edge of her jaw, the soft slope of her neck. His lips were warm and welcoming. His breath brushed hot trails against her skin.

There was no flashback of cold metal at her neck. Just Luke.

She couldn't help but moan softly when he swept his tongue across the hollow of her throat, then up to the base of her ear, where he paused.

"Still okay?" he asked.

He let out a surprised yelp as she wrapped her legs around his waist and pulled him closer until there was no space left between them. He gave her a surprised but delighted grin.

"More than okay," she breathed.

And just like that, every single light in the dining room flickered out as she dragged his mouth back to hers.

Chapter 46

They could have been kissing for five minutes or five hours, Luke had no idea. All he knew was Sephie's mouth was on his, and he never wanted it to end. Her sweet taste clung to his lips, their bodies practically sparking from the tension. Whether it was the chemistry that had been building since day one or just a shared, aching need for closeness, he didn't care.

He was kissing Sephie Blake. And she was kissing him back.

"Luke?" she breathed.

"Yesss?" he teased, gently grazing his teeth along the curve of her throat.

She gasped and fisted his shirt. "What... what time is it?"

He bit lightly, making her shiver. "Does it matter?"

"You a vampire now?" she giggled.

He licked the spot he'd just bitten and kissed her again. "Maybe."

"I see any glitter, I'm running."

He pressed into her just a little more. "I'd love to see you try."

He paused, just in case he'd pushed too far, but then her hands slid lower across his back—dangerously low—and that concern evaporated.

"The sun's going down," she whispered into his neck.

"So?"

She let out a low chuckle. "Do you... want to go to bed?"

He froze. His face was still buried in her hair, which smelled like soap, old books, and vanilla. He took a long breath and pulled back enough to look her in the eyes.

"Sephie, I—"

"I don't mean we need to do anything!" she said quickly, loosening her grip. "I just... mean... like literally sleep together? No, wait, like—"

He kissed her forehead. "You're utterly adorable when you're flustered."

She turned the color of a ripe strawberry.

"I know what you meant. It's not like we haven't ended up sleeping in the same room since this whole ordeal started."

Luke started to pull away, and she whined. She actually whined. Something deep in his gut twisted deliciously.

"Come baaack," she pouted, reaching for him.

This woman was going to destroy him.

He scooped her up again, cradling her with ease. She looped her arms around his neck and tangled her fingers in his hair. He groaned when she began massaging his scalp.

"Careful," he said, his voice raspy.

She gave him a wicked look but withdrew her fingers. He tried not to look too disappointed.

Sephie leaned her head against his chest, letting out a soft sigh. Luke smiled and carried her through the foyer, up two flights of stairs, and down the hallway. Her room was closer, though the bed was smaller. It didn't matter, he just wanted to be as near to her as possible.

"You think Gus did this on his and Cora's wedding night?" she asked.

Luke laughed. "She was a full head taller than him."

"She was a twig."

"Gus did have that construction-worker build."

She pulled his head down for a kiss. Gentle, fleeting, and so stupidly perfect. He rubbed his nose against hers as they reached her room. The house opened the door for them with an audible creak, and he was sure he heard a chandelier tinkling somewhere as if it were giggling.

The fire was low. The window was cracked, letting the scent of the garden drift in. The bed was turned down, with two more recently fluffed pillows added. A maroon silk chemise hung on the closet door.

"What, I don't get fun PJs?" Luke called.

A pair of silk boxer shorts smacked him in the face.

Sephie burst out laughing and slid down from his arms. Her absence caused him to throw his own tantrum.

"Hey, come back here."

"Nah," she said, already walking off. "Let me change. No peeking."

He turned around obediently, pulling the boxers off his face. He imagined her boots coming off, then her pants, her shirt... his stomach flipped.

He undressed quickly, figuring he might as well appease the house's hard-on for his and Sephie's blossoming relationship. Button-down. Pants. Boots. Boxers. He held up the silk shorts and grimaced. Barely anything there. He slipped them on.

"Nice butt."

He spun around to see Sephie, arms crossed, eyes full of mischief. The maroon silk hugged her frame in a way that should've been illegal.

Her gaze traveled slowly down his body. She licked her lips completely unashamed.

Luke yelped and covered himself. "HEY! You said no peeking!"

"Didn't think you'd actually wear them," she said, smirking. "I turned around to a whole new muscle group."

His face definitely matched the color of the silk shorts now.

She stalked toward him, confident and feral. Her fingers slid up his hips, across his stomach, over his chest. She played with his chest hair before giving both pecs a squeeze.

Then she pushed.

His knees hit the bed, and he dropped backward with a surprised gasp. Sephie straddled him, her fingers roaming his skin like she had every right to. He gripped her hips, thumbs pressing into the soft dip above her thighs. Her lips grazed his neck.

"You're remarkable," he mumbled.

She rested her head against his chest. "How so?"

His hands kept exploring— her waist, hips, thighs.

"You're strong. Fierce. You don't need anyone. But I just want to take care of you."

She smiled and twirled his chest hair. "Never get rid of this."

He chuckled. "Was expecting another Sasquatch joke."

"Nah. The more scruff, the better. It's stupid, but it makes you seem so much manlier to me."

He flipped her onto her back, careful but deliberate, settling beside her on the pillows. There was something molten in her eyes as he pulled the covers over them.

Sephie snuggled up against him, arms looped around his back. He tossed a leg over her, refusing to leave any distance between them. She pressed her face against his chest.

"Is it too early to ask what we are?" she mumbled.

Luke ran his fingers through her curls. "Right now? Two nerds being held hostage by a house who need comfort."

"I'm cool with that," she whispered.

He kissed her temple. "Me too. For now."

"For now?"

He took a breath. "Sephie, I like you. A lot. I want to keep liking you when we're not stuck in a haunted house. I've dreamed up like a dozen recipes just thinking about you trying them."

She looked up at him and grinned. "I won't complain about having a himbo who cooks for me."

"Not a himbo."

She kissed him again. "No, you're not. But you're definitely my Flexorcist."

He grinned. "Whatever you say, Scooby-Doo."

The fireplace flickered low and finally died out. Beneath the covers, the room filled with soft laughter, hushed words, and the quiet sound of skin and silk brushing against each other. Fingers traced new paths, lips wandered, and little gasps echoed with each new discovery.

Nothing was rushed. Nothing forced. Just two people finding each other in the dark—one kiss, one sigh, one lingering touch at a time.

Eventually, the world outside faded. Limbs tangled. Hearts slowed. Breaths synced.

And just before sleep claimed them, Sephie's hand tentatively slipped under the hem of Luke's waistband. He felt her hold her breath, waiting for a sign that this was okay. That it was right. He simply murmured her name against her hair.

She smiled.

Then finally, wrapped in each other, they drifted off, completely at peace.

Chapter 47

Like most mornings at Ashland Manor, Sephie drifted awake snuggled tightly against Luke. The difference this time? They'd done it of their own accord. A lazy smile pulled at her lips when she realized her hand was still tucked in his waistband. He wasn't chiseled, but the V-cut of his abs was unfairly prominent. Then again, she was the one with her hand down his pants—maybe it was fair after all.

They hadn't gone too wild the night before. Everything stayed over the clothes, aside from that last moment before sleep took them. Luke treated her like something precious, his hands exploring gently. Every brush of his fingers, every kiss, made her tremble. And he couldn't seem to stop threading his fingers through her curls, which turned her into mush.

She almost wished Brandon could see her now—cuddled up with a mountain of a man who'd spent most of the night kissing her senseless. Brandon never wanted to take care of her. He'd dismissed her independence like it meant she didn't need affection. But Luke? Luke could reduce Brandon to pulp and still have the energy to scoop her up and kiss her stupid right in front of him.

Thalia was going to lose it. She'd say something like, *"You were just complaining about him, and now you're all over him?"* Or, *"Should've known you needed a man who could actually manhandle you."* And definitely, *"I thought you said abs weren't paranormal!"* She'd probably start plotting double dates with her and Isiah and planning two weddings in secret.

Oh god. Gran. Did she know what was going on? Luke said spirits could only pass through when invited, but Gran had been toeing that line for a while now. She couldn't have been watching… right? Surely Luke would've said something if Flo had been hanging around while he was trying to get handsy with his new kissing partner.

And what would Dr. Alias think? Her love life, or lack thereof, had never been a big topic during their sessions. She'd always insisted she was going to be alone forever, so what was the point in trying? But Alias repeatedly told her she needed to let people in. To accept help. He and Luke would probably get along just swimmingly.

Beside her, Luke shifted and rolled onto his side. Her hand slipped farther into his boxers before she could stop it, brushing against a whole lot more than she intended.

She froze, holding her breath, bracing for the awkward aftermath. But his eyes fluttered open slowly, still heavy with sleep.

"Mmm. Well, good morning," he murmured with a smirk, pulling her in closer and dropping a hand to her backside.

"Should've known you play dirty," he whispered.

"I didn't do it on purpose!" she hissed.

He gave her butt a gentle squeeze, and she let out a small yelp.

"No, but you were the one who put your hand in my waistband to begin with." Her ears burned.

"You let me."

"Duh," he said, kissing her cheek. "Why wouldn't I?"

She sighed happily and closed her eyes again, fingers brushing against his skin. He was so warm. His hand resumed its slow tracing, and she giggled.

"I take it you're a butt man?"

"I'm a you man."

"Good answer."

She whimpered when his hand left her bottom, but sighed as he trailed a finger up her stomach and gently palmed her breast. He'd done it the night before, but he was still being cautious. She could tell. The way his hand hesitated, how his movements slowed.

She withdrew her hand from his boxers, and he let out a groan of protest.

Then she gripped his hand and pulled it away from her chest.

"Crap, sorry. Too much?" he asked, voice low and sincere.

She smiled softly, then guided his hand beneath the chemise and placed it back on her breast, skin to skin.

"No," she whispered. "Not too much. Just right."

Luke inhaled sharply but didn't move away. The sun started to pour through the window, catching his hair and making it gleam copper. Sephie smiled up at the bright blue sky.

Wait.

"Luke."

He lazily drew his thumb over her nipple. She shivered.

"Luke, the window's open."

He groaned. "Dammit."

"We'll get back to that later."

"Oh, will we?"

She gave him a smug smile and climbed out of bed. Wandering to the window, she placed her hands on her hips. It wasn't just cracked, it was wide open. A robin zipped past and chirped at her. A breeze carried the garden's scent inside. It was like waking from a dream.

Luke wrapped his arms around her from behind and rested his chin on her head.

"Okay, now you're being the cute one."

"Can't help it. You just fit perfectly."

And she really did. The size difference between them only made things better. Luke enveloped her like a human-sized heated blanket. Being in his arms made her feel safe. It was terrifying how much she wanted that to continue. How much she wanted him.

"Do you think the house intends to let us go?" Luke asked.

She hummed. "Hard to say. We're on the top floor. It's not exactly easy to climb down."

"We could ask the crew to bring a ladder?"

"You and ladders."

"Hey, it's well known I'm a klutz. I'm sure you could shimmy down, but there's no way I'm letting you do that."

"Aw," she said, turning to face him, hands on his stomach. "You ruin all the fun."

He booped her nose. "I just got you. I'm not risking you getting hurt."

She melted. Again.

"Okay, you win. You'll get your ladder."

The window slammed shut. They both flinched.

"Oof," Luke muttered. "It did not like that."

To prove the point further, the window creaked open again, loudly and dramatically. Sephie winced and covered her ears.

"Fine! Sorry! I guess barely clothed spit-swapping only gets us an open window!"

The floorboards groaned in protest.

Luke chuckled and kissed the top of her head.

"Hey, we're getting there. And maybe the window opened because we figured out the Melk/Pischner mystery? Maybe there's something else we're supposed to discover."

She nodded. There was also that. Maybe the house wasn't forcing them into anything, it was just delighted to see warmth and affection again, and not quite ready to let it slip away.

Luke headed for the half bath. "Got any breakfast cravings?"

A familiar warmth bloomed low in her belly. "Waffles?"

He gave an exaggerated bow. "Of course, m'lady."

"And maybe throw on some actual clothes."

"What, maroon not my color?"

She pointed at his groin. "Something down there's trying to prove how macho you are."

He yelped and slammed the door behind him. "I have to pee!"

Shaking her head, Sephie turned back to the window and paused. A mourning dove perched on the sill, calmly preening its feathers. She rubbed her eyes. No way it was real.

But it was still there. The dove puffed up, cooed once at her, and flew away. Mourning doves stood for hope, love, and freedom.

Because of course they did.

Chapter 48

Sephie had to settle for French toast, seeing as they were thirty-ish years away from the invention of the waffle iron. It was fine, though. Luke had added blueberries and strawberries to the glaze from the night before, creating a fruity syrup that more than made up for the menu change.

She watched him dance around the kitchen, barely sipping her coffee because she was too distracted. He wore a simple white T-shirt and brown corduroy pants and somehow looked handsome as hell. The muscles in his arms rippled as he stirred various mixes, and Sephie couldn't help but ogle him.

"Like what you see?"

"Hm?" She shook her head, dazed.

"Scoob, you're drooling."

Sure enough, a bead of saliva threatened to drip from her bottom lip into her mug. Embarrassed, she wiped it away with a finger. Apparently, she'd been thirstier than she realized.

Luke gave her a coy smile and sauntered over, holding the bowl of berries. He dipped a finger in the syrup and held it up.

"Want a taste?"

She scrunched up her nose. "Really?"

"Yes."

"I'm not that kind of girl," she smirked, crossing her arms.

"Humor me."

She couldn't help but smile. He'd been so sweet and kind, even when she'd broken his toe. Since they'd finally given in to their connection, he seemed to carry a confidence he hadn't had before. It was sexy.

Sephie leaned in and parted her lips, just barely taking his finger into her mouth. She swirled her tongue around it, savoring every bit of the deep purple syrup. Then, with a little pop, she pulled away.

Luke stood there completely frozen, mouth agape.

Sephie laughed and took a long sip of coffee. Like he'd said before, she played dirty.

"That was completely unfair," he muttered.

"I got moves."

"I did not need to see that."

They both turned toward the window, mortified. Sephie's jaw dropped at the man standing next to Jessica.

"Dr. Alias?!"

The man narrowed his eyes behind clear-framed spectacles. "Well," he huffed, "I assume you've put your asexuality theory to rest."

Sephie shrank into herself while Luke scrambled back to his pancakes. She hadn't planned for her moment of gusto to be witnessed by her employer and her goddamn therapist.

"Great, I owe Rob fifty bucks," Jessica muttered.

"What?!" Sephie squawked.

"Don't worry about it. You two are cute," Jessica said, holding up a binder. "Seeing as you're one step ahead of us, I'm assuming you traced the Melk family?"

"Sort of," Sephie replied. "We know the most recent member was a shared client."

"Lucy?" Jessica asked, flipping through papers.

Sephie nodded. "She moved when…"

"When a very traumatic experience happened that we don't need to talk about," Dr. Alias finished for her.

"Sephie, could I talk to you privately? Thalia was worried."

Of course Thalia was worried. Sephie had been seeing Dr. Alias weekly. She'd probably assumed Sephie was a few seconds from a breakdown after missing her appointment that week. And she had been until Luke.

"Yeah. Meet me around back. The living room has a window."

Luke appeared with two plates stacked high with pancakes. "Want me to meet you there after?"

She nodded, and he kissed her forehead before she walked out of the room.

"Awwww," Jessica cooed.

Sephie rolled her eyes. Most of the *Dead Serious* crew was clearly rooting for them, even if Rob had bet on it.

Still, it was kind of sweet.

Dr. Alias wore a smug smile on his face when Sephie met him at the back window.

"You were right," she said, arms crossed.

He cupped a hand around his ear. "I'm sorry, what was that?"

"You were right!" she huffed, throwing up her hands. "I'm too closed off. I hate letting people in. I usually hate people in general. I treat others like crap because I've been hurt. Blah blah blah."

He laughed. "Lovely. Self-awareness is always a good start. But that's not why I needed to talk to you."

"You could've led with that."

"Hey, you came in all guns blazing. I wasn't about to waste it." He flipped open a small notebook. "Now, is that giant you were macking on named Luke Mavros?"

She frowned. "Yes? How do you know that?"

He didn't answer. "Has your grandmother tried to connect with you at all?"

"I… well, yes, but—"

He pocketed the notebook and gave her a gentler smile. "Follow your instincts, Sephie. Listen to the house."

"Oh, don't you go all woo-woo on me. I don't pay you for that."

"That one's for free," he said, walking away. "Remember, you just said I was right."

She blinked after him, wondering how her reliable, science-loving therapist had turned into a cryptic weirdo.

"Knock-knock?" Luke called behind her.

She turned and crossed her arms. "He's gone. Feed me."

He chuckled as he handed her a plate, and she immediately started shoveling pancakes into her mouth. They were light, fluffy, and soaked with just the right amount of syrup. Not quite as fun as suckling it off his finger—but still delicious.

"Sheesh, slow down, you'll get the hiccups." Luke nudged her toward the sofa and sat beside her. "What was that about?"

"Oh," she said, mouth full, "my therapist just went all Tangina on me."

"... Tangina?"

"Do not tell me you haven't seen *Poltergeist*."

He gave her a sheepish smile.

"We are fixing that once we're out. Movie date."

"Date?" he grinned.

"Yes, date! Focus, Luke."

He leaned back. "I'm going on a date with Scooby-Doo."

She rolled her eyes. "As I was saying, my therapist was acting like a horror-movie psychic. Telling me to follow my instincts and crap. If he'd said that from the start, there'd be a few people walking around severely disfigured."

Luke raised an eyebrow. "What's this guy's name again?"

"Dr. Samir Alias."

Silence.

"What?" Sephie laughed nervously. "You were all for me being in therapy."

He burst out laughing. Sephie smacked his chest, and he grunted. "Oh please, like that hurt."

"You caught me off guard," he chuckled, rubbing his chest. "Sorry, it's just that your therapist is a medium."

"What?!"

"Yeah. We've done a couple events together. He taught me how to put up mental walls. The good kind." He crossed his legs. "Wow. You hate mediums, and one of them's been one of the best people in your life. Who would've thought?"

Luke polished off his pancakes while Sephie stared, dumbstruck.

"You gonna finish that?"

She covered her plate. "Yes, they're fabulous. I just… need a minute. What if he's been reading my mind this whole time?! I don't need my therapist literally in my head!"

"Sephie, chill. Mediums don't read minds. That's telepaths."

"Still! He knew I hated mediums. If I'd known he was one, I would've scared him off ages ago—"

Luke reached out, grabbed her face, and kissed her. A good, long, firm kiss that left her breathless and blinking.

His voice softened. "Hey. Deep breath. He clearly wanted to help you. And he did. You're okay."

Sephie blinked again, breath slowly steadying. "That was manipulative."

He smirked. " I'm sorry, but it worked."

She smacked him again.

"Still worth it," he said, grinning.

She couldn't argue with that either.

Chapter 49

Sephie had gone into full-blown investigation mode, determined to figure out what the house was trying to tell them. She'd spent two hours rereading every single word in Cora's journal. Luke had been tasked with going through the love letters, order forms, and receipts. He'd pretended to read them, not especially keen on having more mental images of Cora and Gus doing the naughty burned into his brain. Instead, he watched Sephie over the edge of the pages, though she seemed too absorbed in the journal to notice.

"Luke, I don't see you reading."

Or maybe she wasn't.

"There's nothing of substance in here. Just the Ashlands seeing how far they could go without going all the way."

Sephie frowned and closed the journal. "I guess you're right. I'm on my second read and nothing's stood out."

"We need a break," Luke huffed.

"This is the only 'work' we've done. What do you mean, a break?"

He stood and walked around the dining room table to stand next to her. She looked up at him, lips pursed. He grinned and leaned down for a quick kiss.

"I mean, maybe we can just talk?"

"About?"

He pulled her to her feet, took her hand, and began leading her out of the room.

"Scoob, you do realize that even though our chemistry is off the charts, we've only known each other for, like, four days?"

She smiled at their hands clasped, his engulfing hers. "True. So what do you propose we do about that?"

"We get a snack, play twenty questions, and maybe cuddle?"

"Luke Mavros, are you asking me out?"

"Yup."

A clanking sound echoed from the stairwell. They looked up to find a picnic basket waiting on the bottom step. They grinned at each other.

"Well," she said, "I can't turn that down."

Soft piano music floated through the air. Down the hallway, the candelabras lining the path to the ballroom had returned.

"Hell to the no," Luke scowled.

"Agreed," Sephie scoffed, grabbing the basket. "I'm guessing there's something in there the house wants us to find, but I'd prefer you not almost die again."

He took her other hand and started up the stairs. "The house can chill for a bit. We're going on a date, it should be thrilled."

On the second floor, a trail of flower petals lined the runner. Sephie sighed audibly but followed the romantic path, pulling Luke behind her. It led to a guest room.

"Why here?" Luke asked.

Sephie shrugged and reached for the doorknob. Locked.

"I'm sorry," she called out, "what on earth do you want now?!"

Luke groaned. "Should we just have the date in the hallway?"

Sephie set the basket down and suddenly jumped up onto Luke, wrapping her arms around his neck. He got an instant flashback to their awkward bathroom incident. But this kiss was sweet and delicate, nowhere near the wet slap she'd planted on him before.

She hopped down and tried the knob again. Still locked.

"Maybe we are supposed to stay out here," she mumbled.

Luke looked at the flower petals again. Sure enough, they led to this door and were even going underneath it. A soft pinkish glow was peeking out from the bottom. No, the house wanted them in there. It just was going to make them work for it.

"Incoming."

Sephie squeaked as Luke picked her up, her legs instinctively locking around his waist. He pressed her hard against the door, and his mouth was on her neck before she could even catch her breath. She made the most delightful little sounds as he ran his tongue along her throat.

"Luke…" she gasped.

He crushed his mouth to hers with a raw, burning need. One of his hands slid up her side, fingers splaying across her ribs before fisting her hair. Her hands clawed at his shoulders, then tangled behind his neck, desperate to keep him close. Their tongues tangled, wanting to taste every inch of each other. He growled low in his throat when she bit his bottom lip, and his grip on her thigh tightened. He could have melted into her right then.

The door clicked and opened behind them.

Sephie shrieked as they toppled backward. Luke managed to flip at the last second, taking the brunt of the fall onto a pile of waiting cushions.

Sephie landed sprawled across his chest like a bug on a windshield.

"I said the house was a perv," she muttered into his neck.

He laughed and looked around.

"Whoa."

She rolled off him and stared at the room. "Whoa."

The bedroom had been transformed into a cozy, romantic haven. The bed was gone, replaced by a massive pile of floor pillows. Soft, glowing pink lanterns hung from the ceiling. Vases of fresh flowers sat on every surface. It was like the room had been plucked from a dream.

Luke pulled the picnic basket closer and opened it. Inside was a pitcher of lemonade, ham and cheese sandwiches, and a plate of chocolate chip cookies.

"Well, this is sweet," Sephie murmured.

She stood and wandered through the room, the glowing latterns making her radiate light while her wild curls haloed around her face. Her lips swollen from kissing, eyes bright; just the sight of her made Luke melt a little more.

"It recreated their second wedding anniversary."

"Oh?"

"Yeah, Cora wrote about it. Gus planned the first one; she planned this. They switched every year."

"Stupid perfect couple stuff," Luke teased.

"I'm fine when I'm reaping the benefits," she said, settling beside him and resting her head on his shoulder.

He wrapped an arm around her waist, tugging her close. He half-expected to wake up from a long dream. But she was right there, and definitely real.

"So," she said, grabbing a sandwich, "twenty questions?"

"We already covered upbringing and family. What do you want to know? I'm an open book." He shoved an entire cookie into his mouth.

"You know about mine, but when was your last relationship?"

He almost choked. She patted his back while he coughed up crumbs.

"Flex, I'm going on seven years. It can't be that bad."

"The fact that you're still that good of a kisser is impressive," he croaked.

She giggled and handed him lemonade. He gratefully gulped it down.

"It was about a year ago," he finally said. "One of the biggest mistakes of my life."

"Why?"

"Word of advice: don't date a client."

She winced.

"Oh, it gets worse."

"I fail to see how."

He rubbed his forehead. "She came to me grieving her dead fiancé. I tried to help, but he wouldn't come through. She kept coming back, desperate. I... broke my own boundaries."

She kissed his shoulder. "You thought she was cute."

"Guilty. One thing led to another. She thought I could help bring him back. Like, literally."

Sephie shuddered. "Ew."

"Yeah. Total Craft-wannabe witch vibes. I dumped her after three months. She checked herself into a hospital, thank god. That whole situation kinda put a damper on dating."

There was a pause.

"I don't know if it means anything," Sephie said, blushing, "but you're definitely the best kisser I've ever experienced."

Luke grinned. "Scoob, is it too early to ask you to be my girlfriend?"

Her eyes widened. "You were just saying we've only known each other for four days."

He pulled her onto his lap. "I saw you in pink undies with questionable writing on them on day two. I think we're fast-tracking this."

She groaned and buried her face in his neck. "Don't bring that up."

He chuckled. "I won't push anything. But I want to know I get to keep you after all this."

She lifted her head and gave him a look. "Quoting Casper, really?"

"Worth a shot. What I mean is, I want to keep being cuddle buddies. Officially."

She rubbed her nose against his. "Yes, Luke, I'll be your girlfriend."

Eventually, their sandwiches were gone, and the cookies were nothing but crumbs. Luke leaned back into the cushions, pulling Sephie down with him. They lay there, shoulder to shoulder, eyes drifting up to the softly swaying lanterns above them. The light danced across the ceiling, casting flickering patterns like petals in the wind.

Sephie reached out and linked her fingers with his. "Pretty sure we're in a Sarah Dessen adaptation."

"Hey," he said. "I was promised a horror movie."

She snorted. "Fine. But you plan the date after that."

His eyes lit up. "You really are taking lessons from Gus and Cora."

She smacked his chest and nestled closer.

Above them, the lanterns were blossoms of light, suspended in their own private sky.

Chapter 50

Sephie woke from the nap they'd accidentally slipped into, a fuzzy blanket now draped over them. Luke was curled against her, using her chest as a makeshift pillow. She smiled, fingers slipping through his hair. He was back in teddy bear mode.

She blinked. The pink glow had shifted into a misty cloud. Sephie narrowed her eyes. Was the ceiling... a hardwood floor?

"Luke?"

He just nuzzled in closer, his breath warm against her skin.

"Luke." She poked the back of his neck.

"Ouch," he grumbled, blinking awake. "I thought we weren't doing that anymore."

She pointed upward. "Can you see that?"

He rubbed his eyes. "Um. Where'd the ceiling go?"

"Okay, good, you see it too."

They both sat up and instantly flopped back down in confusion. The floor beneath them had turned to smooth white marble. The lanterns had vanished, replaced with towering white pillars.

"Are we on the ceiling?!" Sephie hissed.

"I think?" Luke said. "Are we dreaming?"

"Can you share dreams?"

Sephie stared upward—or downward?, trying to make sense of the warped reality. Floating above them was what looked suspiciously like an upside-down piano.

"Is that the ballroom?!"

"Jesus," Luke muttered, waving away more pink fog.

"Yeah, it is."

"I don't like this," Sephie said, gripping his hand.

"Me neither."

"DUNCAN, NO!"

Luke clutched her hand so hard she thought something might snap. A flash of curly red hair darted across the ceiling—or rather, floor. They were seeing everything from some creepy, detached bird's-eye view. Another figure came into view, hunched over a book.

"She said Duncan, right?" Sephie whispered.

Luke nodded. They watched the redhead, who had to be Ada, rush to the ballroom doors, pounding on them. Duncan remained planted in the center, muttering under his breath.

"Can we do anything?" Sephie asked.

"I don't think so," Luke replied. "The house is showing us something that's already happened. We're just spectators."

"When I said horror movie, I didn't mean this."

A child's cry rang out.

Sephie looked closer. Ada was holding a toddler.

"No..." she whispered.

Luke pulled her in, rubbing her arm in slow, soothing strokes. "We know it ends okay. We just have to watch."

"But why is it showing us at all?"

"I don't know."

"Ada," Duncan called out, eerily calm. "Bring me our child."

His voice was smooth. Too smooth.

"Our child?" Ada spat. "You've wanted nothing to do with her since you found out she existed!"

"That was before I realized how valuable she could be." He approached her slowly. She clutched her daughter tighter, trembling. "It's necessary. Together, we can reach the peak of enlightenment. Give her here."

"I'm guessing this is the spiritualist cult crap you were talking about?" Sephie muttered.

"Yup. And I hope something happens soon. I don't feel great."

Sephie hoped so too. She didn't want to find out if Luke's impending puke would hover or fall.

Duncan grabbed Ada by the back of the neck and dragged her to the center of the room. The toddler wailed. Ada struggled, clutching her daughter to her chest. Duncan forced her to the ground.

"This is your last chance."

"Duncan, please. Just… just think about what you're doing."

"Two's better than one, anyway."

Sephie clutched Luke tighter. His face was pale, his breathing shallow.

"Hey, house?" she called. "We get the point."

A loud **CRASH** echoed as the ballroom doors blew off their hinges. Gus charged in, wielding a log like a battering ram.

"Holy cow," Sephie breathed.

"Duncan! Let them go!" Gus thundered.

"This doesn't concern you," Duncan snapped, still gripping Ada.

"Gus better destroy him," Luke muttered, gagging slightly.

"Last warning, Duncan," Gus growled.

A low chuckle rumbled from Duncan—until Cora flew into the room like a missile, tackling him mid-sentence. Ada scrambled away, rocking her daughter.

Duncan tried to rise, but Cora had him locked in a chokehold between her thighs. A wet gurgling echoed.

"Cora, I told you to wait," Gus sighed, dropping the log.

"Sorry, honey," she panted. "I knew you wouldn't do anything."

"Talk about a toxic man," Luke murmured.

"I think he gets the point, dear," Gus said. "Let go."

Cora released her grip, and Duncan coughed violently. He looked up, seething.

"You pathetic, demonic bitch!"

Cora's fist met his jaw with a crunch. He hit the floor, silent. She shook out her hand, wincing.

"Might've broken something. Worth it."

Ada approached and Cora wrapped her and the baby in a protective hug.

"Shhh, it's okay. Aunt Cora dealt with the bad man."

The pink cloud thickened. Sephie could barely make out the green book glowing in the center of the ballroom. Then she felt a sort of weightlessness washed over her.

"Uh, Sephie?"

Luke was rising, not of his own volition, drifting upward toward the ceiling. He was heading for the book. Pink mist coiled around his limbs like ropes.

She managed to get to her knees, catching his wrist. "What the hell?!"

"I don't know! Don't let go!"

It felt like the house was playing tug-of-war. Her nails dug into his skin. The book flashed again, a sickly green, like it was trying to take something from him.

"Stop!" she yelled.

The pull loosened.

"Let. Him. Go."

In a heartbeat, the vision vanished. The pink cloud dissipated. The lanterns returned.

And Luke dropped.

He landed with a thud, fortunately cushioned by pillows. And, unfortunately, Sephie.

He scrambled off her, trying not to crush her further. "Sorry."

"Not your fault," she coughed. "Payback for the broken toe."

"Bruised ribs are worse than a toe."

"Kiss it and make it better."

He leaned down and kissed her cheek with exaggerated care.

She groaned. "What a way to end a date."

He lay back down and pulled her against him, holding her in the curve of his body like he was trying to steady her himself. One hand came up to cradle her face, his thumb brushing over her cheek in slow strokes. Her pulse was still racing under his touch, and the faint taste of copper coated her tongue.

Luke pressed his forehead to hers, murmuring reassurances. He breathed with her, slow and even, until she started to match his rhythm. The tightness in her shoulders eased and she relaxed into him. When her breathing finally evened out, he pulled back enough to look at her, looking grave.

"I think we need to get rid of that book."

"Great. When I said I wanted to do more investigations with you, I didn't mean we'd end up doing *Dead Serious: Couple's Edition.*"

Chapter 51

"Ladder."

Sephie rolled her eyes. Again with the ladder. They just needed to get back up into the attic and figure out what to do with Duncan's cursed book. But after that encounter they'd just had, she was more willing to compromise.

"La. Dder."

"Fine."

"What?"

"I said fine."

He blinked. "I'm amazed."

"Oh, stop." She took his hand and led him toward the stairwell. "It can wait until tomorrow, though. That's the only reason I'm agreeing. Maybe the house will have magically rebuilt the pull-down by then."

"Doubtful," he shrugged. "It didn't even bother cleaning the attic."

They wandered down to the foyer, still hand in hand. A breeze passed through, shifting the chandelier slightly, and Cora's lavender soap scent wafted through the air. Sephie glared and raised their clasped hands.

"We're together, for real. You didn't have to pull that stunt on our first date."

Nothing.

"It's ashamed," Luke quipped.

"It should be."

"Well," he said, gathering her into his arms, "we're together. Isn't that what really matters?"

She couldn't help but grin. He was her boyfriend. Her boyfriend. She'd gone from wanting to strangle Luke every two seconds, to tolerating him, to crushing on him, to making out with him up against a haunted door. Pretty amazing progress for less than a week.

"Hey, Lovebirds! You still alive?"

Rob's voice echoed from outside the front door. They moved to the front window and found him, Dr. Alias, and Thalia standing there.

"What a ragtag group," Sephie muttered.

Thalia was bouncing like a kid. "You're holding hands!"

Luke lifted their intertwined hands proudly. Sephie flushed.

Thalia squealed. "You're so perfect together. You really just needed a big strong man to manhandle you, huh?"

Sephie had called it.

Desperate to change the subject, she turned to Dr. Alias. "Any reason you didn't tell me you were a hack?"

He gave a half-hearted shrug. "Because I'm not."

"Semantics."

He chuckled. "I had paperwork from your past therapists and did my own research, Sephie. I knew you were a skeptic and didn't want it to interfere with helping you."

She exhaled.

Luke gave a small wave. "Hi, Samir."

"You are not on a first-name basis with my therapist."

He kissed her knuckles. Thalia cooed.

"Shut up," Sephie grumbled.

"Nope. You've got a giant beefcake for a boyfriend. I'm allowed to be happy for you."

"I do find it amusing you got the geek, and I got the lumberjack," Sephie mused.

Rob's smug grin appeared. "You two won me fifty bucks, so thanks."

Sephie's eyes nearly rolled out of her head.

"I guess I should actually give you updates," Rob continued. "We looked up that Flatley dude."

Luke dropped Sephie's hand and crossed his arms. She had to fight the urge to whine. "And?"

"He got checked into that Ireland sanitarium for a few months. Then they realized there was a whole lot more wrong with him than just physical issues. He was transferred to a mental institution."

Sephie flinched. Mental institutions in the 1800s weren't exactly known for being humane. Duncan might've been better off in a prison cell.

"I take it he died in there?" Luke asked.

Rob nodded. "Probably would've been lobotomized if that had been invented earlier on."

"Lobotomized?" Thalia asked.

"Shoved an ice pick into the eye socket and scrambled the brain a bit," Dr. Alias answered.

Thalia gagged.

"Speaking of Duncan," Luke said, "Samir, do you know any witches?"

Dr. Alias arched a brow. "Why?"

"Duncan left behind one of the most cursed books I've ever seen. We've stored it in the attic for now, but it'll need cleansing if we want to put a stop to the house's issues."

A smirk spread across Dr. Alias's face. "You're in luck. I do know a witch. So do you, Luke."

Luke frowned. "Not personally, I'd remember that."

Dr. Alias grinned. "It's Sephie."

Four pairs of eyes whipped to her. Her mouth opened and closed like a fish. No sound came out.

"I am not," she finally sputtered.

"You are," he said calmly. "Your grandmother was, and you've definitely inherited some of her talents."

Luke wrapped an arm around her waist. "Hey, it could be worse."

She was still processing.

"Wait, how do you know Gran was a witch?"

"I told you," he said, brushing a hand through his jet-black hair. "I did my research."

"Damn," Luke muttered. "Samir, you should be in the FBI or something."

"They tried to recruit me once. It's not my style."

"Of course they did," Sephie groaned. This was too much.

Thalia stuck out her bottom lip. "Why didn't I get the witch DNA?"

"Thalia, really?" Sephie deadpanned.

"You've got a hot guy and powers. Not fair!"

"Uh, not powers," Rob corrected. "More like abilities. Sensing things."

The group turned to Rob.

He shrugged. "Told you. I'm cultured."

"That isn't just culture," Luke said.

"Back to the task at hand," Dr. Alias cut in. "Sephie's a witch. Trust me. You should be able to figure out what to do with that book."

"But—" Sephie started.

"Follow your instincts," he interrupted. "Now, I'll see you in my office next week."

Rob and Thalia both shrugged and followed him, not before Rob gave Luke a thumbs-up and Thalia winked.

"Glad you're so sure we'll be out of here by then!" Sephie shouted.

Luke rubbed her arm. "Maybe we will be. If not, it's not so bad."

"You just got almost sucked into a Pink Elephant Parade."

He laughed. "But I didn't. And have you noticed? Whenever you're super firm with the house, it doesn't push back."

She bit her bottom lip. He was right. The house had pulled some dramatic moves, but once she stood her ground, it mostly gave her what she wanted.

"I suppose," she mumbled.

"Seems like something only someone with a paranormal-ish background could pull off."

She frowned. "Can we just say it's because I'm a mean little ball of anger?"

He laughed—hard. Then grabbed her face and kissed her so thoroughly she saw stars. Her knees buckled, and he held her upright.

"Yes, my little gremlin. You are just so mean."

"Shut up."

"Make me."

She jumped onto him and gave him a soul-shattering kiss of her own. His eyes were glazed when she pulled away, still clinging to his neck.

Then his expression shifted.

Sephie touched his cheek. "What's wrong?"

He winced and gently set her down. "Flo's back."

Of course she was. "Why now???"

Luke rubbed his temple. "She's being persistent. I can throw up a wall if you want, but it'll drain me."

Sephie planned to distract herself from the whole "being a witch" thing with a nice cuddle session, but Gran apparently had other ideas. She probably wanted to gloat. Sephie sighed. She'd survived two decades of nagging; she could endure a little victory lap.

"Gran, please behave."

Chapter 52

Of course Flo had to make another appearance the second he finally had his beautiful new girlfriend all to himself again. The last thing Luke needed was to be mid-makeout when an eighty-something spitfire decided to nag him from the beyond.

Come on, handsome. Gotta give my granddaughter some grandmotherly advice.

She had definitely been a witch when she was alive—there was no other explanation for how clearly she got into his head like this. Luke could practically picture her cupping a hand around her mouth, whispering her demands right up against the veil.

Luke!

"She's being persistent," he muttered. "I can throw up a wall if you want, but it'll tire me out."

Don't you dare, young man.

"Gran, please behave."

Luke took that as her okay to let Flow through, and let out a sigh of relief as she did. He closed his eyes and massaged his brow bone. God, his head hurt. Whatever dark magic that book of Duncan's was laced with had done a number on him. Then there was the whole almost dying in the ballroom thing. And the dream he and Sephie had shared, complete with ceilings becoming floors and nearly being sucked up into nothing. Now there was another version of Sephie in his ear, like the cherry on top of a very cursed sundae.

"…Luke?"

Sephie's voice was barely a whisper.

He opened his eyes. The color drained from her face, leaving her somehow paler than usual. Her eyes were wide, focused on something just over his shoulder.

He turned slowly.

And there it was: the transparent outline of a very small human.

"Oh," the figure said, voice echoing and hollow. "Well, this is new."

Luke stared, mouth agape. He was absolutely certain this was Flo. She was even shorter than Sephie, which was saying something. Her features were indistinct, like watching an old movie underwater, behind frosted glass.

But she was here, floating in front of them, not just the voice.

"Gran?" Sephie finally squeaked.

"Hi, sweetie!"

The figure zipped right through Luke on her way to Sephie, making him shiver from head to toe. Yep, apparition. Great. Just another thing to add to the running list of weird stuff he'd never dealt with before. Why couldn't this happen when he was in his tiny kitchen and able to call his mommy for help?

Luke blinked up at the two of them, Sephie and her ghost grandma, as the latter kept floating her limbs straight through the former.

"I can't even give you a hug? Dammit, that's not fair."

"Gran!" Sephie flailed her arms. "Stop, that's cold!"

"Oh, sorry!" Flo stopped, hovering in place. "I'm just excited, that's all."

Sephie looked back at Luke, utterly flabbergasted.

"*Fine*. I believe in ghosts!"

"Hey, let's not be drastic," he said.

Her eyes narrowed. "Drastic? You're the one who talks to the dead!"

"I know, I know! I guess I'm just thrown that we've been through all this and now you're admitting it."

She raised a brow. "I mean, I could go back to being the bullheaded little chihuahua, but I don't think you liked me as much."

He chuckled and stepped closer. "I just… I'm going through a lot lately, and I keep thinking I'm gonna wake up. All of this feels borderline absurd."

Sephie reached out and took his hand. "I'm real. This is real." She gestured to the ghost. "She is also apparently very real. I'm pretty sure I stopped being a skeptic as soon as we got locked in. Gran's just the final nail in the coffin."

He smiled. "You bullheaded little thing."

Flo began to float in circles around them, making a sound halfway between a giggle and a gust of wind.

"Oh my goodness, oh my goodness, oh my goodness! Did he woo you? Win you over?"

Sephie chewed her cheek. "Gran, I know you've been eavesdropping in his head, but meet Luke Mavros… my boyfriend."

Flo floated next to Luke, giving him a once-over. "He's a striking young man, Sephie. Good choice."

"She didn't exactly choose me," Luke said, pulling Sephie in. "But I'm glad I crashed into her life the way I did."

"Oh, give her a kiss."

"Gran, I said behave."

"What? Let me live vicariously for a minute." Flo zipped around them again.

"He's a lot bigger when I can see him. I'm amazed he hasn't torn you in half."

"GRAN!"

Luke had blushed more in the past few days than in his entire life.

"I'm just glad she agreed to be my girlfriend," he mumbled. "There's so much more I want to learn about Sephie before we… you know. Stuff."

"Yeah, that's sweet and all," Flo said, "but come on, she's gotta be aching for you to show her a good time."

"Gran, *quiet*."

Silence dropped over the room like a curtain. The apparition zipped in frantic circles, waving her translucent limbs and miming frustration.

Luke looked at Sephie. "Scoob?"

"Flex?"

"Didn't we just talk about how the house listens when you get firm with it?"

She nodded slowly.

"I'm starting to think ghosts are included in that."

"Well, hot damn."

Flo hovered back in front of them, arms crossed, clearly sulking. Sephie straightened and put her hands on her hips.

"Gran. I love you. I'm glad I can talk to you again. But damn, your constant nagging and pushing me into stuff got real old." The ghost flickered slightly. "I need to move at my own pace. This thing with Luke may be going fast, but I feel good about it."

Luke grinned. "You do?"

She gave his hand a squeeze. "Yes."

He kissed the top of her head.

Flo swirled around them, humming happily. Sephie sighed.

"If you behave, then you can speak."

"I'm sorry!" Flo burst out. "You know it got harder when I couldn't leave the house anymore."

Sephie nodded. "I know. Thank you for saying that."

"Damn, I wish I could give you a hug."

"I know."

Flo flickered and pulsed with light. "Alright, now the important stuff." She settled in front of them. "That therapist finally tell you what's up?"

"That I'm dating a witch? Yeah," Luke said. "And I don't need more motivation to treat her right. She could go full *Mortal Kombat* on me and I'd thank her."

Flo laughed so hard the floor beneath them actually trembled.

"Oh, good man. Sephie, he's worth the wait."

"I think so too," Sephie whispered.

"Okay, witch stuff," Flo went on. "I didn't brew potions or anything, but I was good at cleansing bad energy. You probably will be too. If you take care of that book, you'll be out of here soon."

Luke frowned. "Could you be a little more specific?"

"Sadly, no. It was all instinct for me."

Sephie rolled her eyes. "Everyone keeps saying instinct. Can't I just chant a few words and burn some sage?"

Flo chuckled. "You'll figure it out."

As she spoke, her image became clearer, much sharper around the edges. Luke could finally make out the finer details: a tiny elderly woman with Sephie's angular cheekbones, long white curls drifting like smoke around her face. There was a softness to her now, one that hadn't come through when she was just a voice in his head.

Flo looked down at herself and smiled.

"Oh goody, that means I'm ready to go."

"Go?" Sephie asked, her voice barely above a whisper.

Luke slid an arm around her shoulders. "She stuck around for a reason, Scoob. Now that the witch stuff's out in the open, she can move on." He gave Flo a soft smile. "Unless you've got unfinished business with Satan?"

"Watch it. I will stay just to haunt your ass."

Sephie let out a watery laugh, her eyes shining. "I'm glad you approve," she said quietly. "I think I'd already come to terms with losing you. But this… getting to say goodbye like this, it means more than I can explain."

Flo reached out and brushed her ghostly fingers across Sephie's cheek, just a shimmer of sensation.

"I'm proud of you. Therapy's been good for you. So has he, and let's hope he continues to be." Her gaze turned to Luke. "You take care of her, you hear me?"

"I will," Luke said, holding Sephie a little tighter. "I promise."

"Now go kick some ass."

She smiled at them one last time, eyes twinkling.

And then, in a blink, she was gone.

Sephie didn't move at first. Then she turned, tucked her face into Luke's chest, and let out a quiet sob. He held her there in silence. Not trying to fix it, but offering her comfort by just being with her.

Eventually, she pulled back and looked up at him. "Guess it's really just us now."

Luke smiled softly. "Good thing we make a hell of a team."

Chapter 53

Luke and Sephie found themselves aimlessly wandering around the house, both of them very done with anything paranormal for the day.

"Do you want dinner?" Luke asked.

Sephie shook her head. "The date food filled me up. Do you just want to go to bed?"

Luke shrugged. "I'm honestly not tired."

She wasn't either. That nap had lasted longer than they thought. They'd even checked to see if the house built a new pull down for the attic just for the heck of it, but it hadn't. Now, Luke was swinging their joined hands absentmindedly as they roamed the second-floor hallway.

"Careful," she teased, "You're gonna end up tossing me across the hall."

"Oh, sorry." He immediately relaxed. "I never thought I'd be bored in a haunted mansion."

"Sentient house," she corrected. "But yeah."

"Wanna make out?"

"Flex!"

"What? We've got nothing else to do."

She smirked and pressed a kiss to the back of his hand.

Suddenly, a sound like rushing water echoed from the other end of the hallway. Luke looked at Sephie, whose eyes had gone wide again. They stood frozen for a beat.

"I guess that's what we get for being bored," Sephie drawled.

"I mean," Luke replied, "not like we have to go investigate whatever that was."

The sounds of raindrops falling disagreed.

They sighed and began walking slowly toward the source. A soft yellow glow spilled from under the master bathroom door, now humming with what sounded like an indoor rainforest.

"Lovely. The famous master bathroom," Luke muttered.

"Well, I'm curious, so—" Sephie reached for the knob and found it turned easily. She arched a brow at Luke before opening the door, and they both stepped into the softly lit room. The bathroom had changed again. The tub had doubled in size, a new credenza stood against the far wall, and, most notably, a new door had appeared.

Luke walked over to the tub and rolled his eyes.

"It filled itself."

"Oh?" Sephie asked.

"Scoob, it wants us to take a bath together."

Oh.

She huffed. "Kind of a messed up way to make up for the bathroom incident."

The scent of lavender wafted into their noses again. Sephie took a deep breath, calming slightly. There'd been a hint of vanilla added to this batch. She couldn't deny how intoxicating it was. Luke was already eyeing the steaming water with longing.

"I won't lie," he said, "This looks tempting after being beat up by a house for a few days."

"Hey, I'm not stopping you."

Luke brazenly ripped his shirt off and started undoing his pants. He glanced at Sephie as his bulky limbs became more and more exposed, and he smirked.

"Yes, I'm drooling over my handsome boyfriend, what of it?" she quipped.

His smirk turned into a grin. "Not complaining."

She grinned back as he shimmied out of his boxers, stepped into the tub, and let out a loud, satisfied moan. Now *that* was tempting. She licked her lips and walked toward him. He opened his eyes and leaned against the edge.

"Gonna join me?"

She bit her lip and nodded.

"Can't get in with your clothes on."

Slowly, teasingly, she pulled up the hem of her shirt, revealing the pale skin of her stomach. This wasn't like their previous frantic encounters. This was slower, sultrier, almost agonizing. Luke let out another low moan as her shirt hit the floor and she began to untie the stays.

She felt oddly comfortable undressing in front of him now. This was safe. She could feel that it was safe. Luke's glazed over eyes cleared as soon as her stays joined the shirt.

"Sephie…"

She looked down. Purple bruises crawled from her ribs to beneath her left breast. She pressed on them gently and winced.

"It looks a lot worse than it feels."

Luke moved to the edge of the tub and pulled her in closer. His fingers traced from her hip to her sternum, over one nipple, then up to her bottom lip. She shivered under his touch. He looked up at her, eyes glossy.

"Is this from when I fell on you?" he asked.

"Probably. Like I said, it's okay. Bruised is better than broken."

"I'm still sorry," he murmured, kissing the lowest rib before unzipping her pants.

She grinned and stepped out of the rest of her clothes in one move. Luke's hands roamed freely now, skin on skin, warm and appreciative.

"Damn, you're stunning."

She felt the pink glow creep behind her ears. He wrapped one large hand around her forearm and tugged her gently to him.

"Get in here."

She slid into the tub, the hot water curling around her calves and thighs like a welcome. She turned and positioned herself between his legs. The man had the balls to press a quick peck to her butt cheek as she sunk into the water. She giggled and leaned back against his chest.

"Did you literally just kiss my ass?"

His laugh rumbled behind her. "Yup."

"Well I'll be damned."

"I know who's in charge in this relationship."

She laughed too, then melted into him. The combination of the hot water and his solid frame behind her was everything she didn't know she needed. Peaceful. Comforting. Intimate, but not overtly sexual.

After what felt like forever, Luke's hands crept to her shoulders and began to massage. She let out a moan of her own. His touch was firm but careful, easing the tension from her muscles. Once her upper body had softened, he traced down her arms, then back up her ribs, finally cupping her breasts.

She inhaled deeply. There was lavender, vanilla, and a musky note that was all Luke. When his hands slipped away, she pouted—until he cupped water in his palm and gently drizzled it over her head.

He lathered her hair with the soap and massaged her scalp, and she all but melted.

"I could get used to this," she muttered.

"Me too," Luke replied.

He cradled her head and dipped it back, rinsing the soap as she looked up at him. He looked ridiculously happy, grinning like a kid in a candy store with unlimited funds.

Licking her lips, she pulled herself off his chest and turned to straddle him. Her hands roamed his chest, pausing to play with the soap bubbles caught in his hair.

She kissed one collarbone, then the other.

"Promise me something?" She whispered.

He looked down at her.

"Promise me this'll still be real when we get out of here."

He smiled and pressed his mouth to hers. The kiss was soft and steady, allowing them to simply enjoy the gentle contact.

When he pulled back, she exhaled a breath she hadn't realized she'd been holding.

"Sephie," he whispered. "You're not getting rid of me."

"Well, good," she replied. "I don't know what I'd do without you pissing me off."

"I'd miss that snarky mouth of yours."

She smiled and turned, resting her cheek on his chest. That's when she noticed the new door again, visible from their spot in the bath.

"Where do you think that leads?"

Luke followed her gaze. "You're the architecture expert."

"More like historian. Still, it'd make sense if it were a bedroom, right?"

"Probably. Weird that it's just showed up now."

She smirked, gesturing to their very naked selves.

Luke laughed. "Okay, yeah." He ran his hands along her thighs and gave her hips a squeeze. "Should we explore?"

"Each other? Yes," she teased. "But let's save that for after we cleanse the book. Hopefully, that door leads to the most perfect bedroom ever, and we can use it as a reward."

Luke nodded, eyes twinkling. "Now… back to that exploring each other part?"

Chapter 54

They'd decided on Luke's room that night since the bed was so much bigger. While they both proved to be pretty decent sleep partners, neither of them wanted to risk flying limbs or tumbling off the mattress. They were already sore and bruised enough.

The house, for once, seemed to be on their good side. The credenza had creaked open with a dramatic flourish, revealing two fluffy towels and adult-sized bathrobes that felt like they'd been warmed in an invisible dryer. They dried off, slipped into the robes, and made their way back to the bedroom, where a fire was already crackling in the hearth. Cozy didn't even begin to cover it.

So naturally, the robes came off, and they slipped under the covers completely nude.

Just a few hours later, Luke jolted awake, very much not in the king-sized bed where he'd fallen asleep with Sephie snuggled against his back like a baby koala. That had been warm, cute, and peaceful. This was none of those things.

The bed was gone. The fire, the window, the room. Gone.

He was flat on his back in a surreal dreamscape, trapped beneath a harsh spotlight that lit only the small circle around him. Beyond that, nothing but pitch-black nothingness. He tried to move, to call out, but his body was heavy. He was completely paralyzed. His throat locked up. Everything about this place felt off. Wrong.

The spotlight reminded him of a UFO beam, and honestly, if a crew of bug-eyed aliens appeared next, he wouldn't be surprised. At this point, ghosts and sentient houses had set the bar pretty high for weird.

Above him, Duncan's green book spun slowly in midair like a haunted ceiling fan, the pages fluttering as sickly green smoke began to pour from its center. Behind it, he could just barely make out the wooden floor of the ballroom. The dream (vision?) was grounding itself in something familiar, which somehow made it worse.

Thicker plumes of mist spiraled toward him, creeping lower, curling like vines around his arms and legs. This was feeling way too *Pit and the Pendulum*. And Luke was no Edgar Allan Poe fan.

Sephie…

He couldn't get the name past his lips, but he poured everything he had into the thought, hoping somehow it would reach her. He closed his eyes and focused on real things. Her soft skin glowing in candlelight, the way her curls twisted around his fingers, her smirk that always turned into that wide, gorgeous smile.

Then something shifted.

A soft weight moved beside him.

"Luke?" Sephie's voice, groggy and questioning.

More movement.

"Luke!"

A sharp little jab landed at the base of his neck, dragging him out of the dream like a fishhook. He groaned as he was yanked back to reality. A warm arm snaked around his chest, and Sephie twirled a patch of his chest hair between two fingers.

"Morning?" he murmured.

"Nah, nearly," came her sleepy reply.

Luke stretched with a groan, his shoulders popping in protest. "Seriously, are you gonna need a bigger bed?"

He rolled toward her, pulling her against his chest like he had that first night the house put them together. She nestled in easily.

"You and your thing for chest hair."

"It's rugged as hell."

"I'm glad you think so. But maybe don't burrow in for the winter."

She tilted her head to look up at him, eyes heavy with sleep but still sharp. "You okay? You said my name in your sleep. Sounded kinda panicked."

Luke stroked her lower back. "Let's just say the book's decided to haunt me in my dreams now."

A beat.

"Well," Sephie said, "we either cleanse that book today, or we find a way out of the manor."

"Aside from sleeping together, I don't think we've appeased the house enough to let us go."

She waggled her eyebrows.

"Scoob..."

"I'm kidding," she added quickly. "We're already speedrunning this. No need to jinx it." She kissed his chest, her lips warm against his skin. "So, book-cleansing it is."

Luke traced his fingers along the line of her spine. "You know I lied when I said I wasn't interested before, right?"

"I know." Her voice was already drifting. "We can talk about it later. I need more sleep."

Luke grinned and settled into the pillows, watching the first hints of sunlight peek over the horizon. Sephie was already lightly snoring, her breath soft against his chest.

He blinked—

And suddenly, the spotlight was back.

Only this time, the world around them had a soft, glowing periwinkle hue. Luke wasn't alone in the circle of light. He was back on the mattress, Sephie still wrapped in his arms, sleeping peacefully. He looked up.

The green book hovered above them again, but this time it looked different, duller in fact. A thick coat of dust clung to its cover, like it hadn't been opened in decades. Luke narrowed his eyes.

Then Sephie shifted against him and muttered, "Oh, piss off."

To his astonishment, the book wobbled, dimmed… and vanished. The periwinkle mist around them swallowed it whole, dissolving the scene into soft, spinning light.

Was it her dream now?

"Too light," Sephie mumbled again. Instantly, the mist collapsed, and they were back in Luke's bedroom. The fire flickered, the silk sheets clung to their skin, and the familiar weight of the house settled around them once more.

Everything felt grounded. Solid. Normal.

Well… as normal as anything could be in a magic house.

Luke smiled and shut his eyes again, drawing Sephie closer.

Yup, definitely a witch.

And he wouldn't have it any other way.

Chapter 55

"Either the house wants to make this as difficult as possible," Sephie muttered, "or it's genuinely concerned for our well-being when it comes to this book."

Bright sunlight from the hall window streamed in, making Sephie want to get outside even more. She and Luke were standing beneath the attic opening once again. The pull-down staircase still hadn't returned. They'd searched high and low for a ladder, but the house was either hiding one exceptionally well, or simply hadn't let one materialize.

"I mean," Luke said, "it seemed to be in a good mood last night. I'd hope it's concerned."

"Well, it'll have to get over it." Sephie crossed her arms.

Aside from denying them a ladder, the manor had introduced a handful of minor inconveniences. All of their clothes had mysteriously disappeared, last night's bathrobes included. After a very firm talking-to from Sephie, the house eventually relented and tossed them some basics. The pieces were completely mismatched with clashing patterns, but at least they weren't naked.

The kitchen decided to hide the French press, prompting a near caffeineless-fueled meltdown on her end. Luke saved the day with a makeshift pour-over using cheesecloth. Somehow, the coffee still turned out amazing.

When he went to make breakfast, none of the cookware was in the cabinets. Luke pouted for a while, muttering about the "incredible" steak and eggs he'd planned to make. Instead, they foraged through the pantry, collecting every fruit they could find and cobbled together giant fruit-and-granola bowls. Not fancy, but good enough.

At least the manor hadn't locked them in anywhere. Sephie was grateful she didn't have to go full Wrath Mode again. Glares and scoldings were working just fine. For now.

Except when it came to ladders.

"You're gonna have to toss me up there," she declared.

Luke rubbed a hand down his face. "I suppose I don't have a choice?"

"Nope." She reached her arms toward him. "Up, please."

"Please don't say it like that."

She stuck her tongue out. He grabbed her waist and lifted her onto his shoulders with practiced ease.

"Try not to pull my hair this time?" he asked.

"Not into that? Got it."

"Seph."

She paused. He'd called her Seph. Only Gran and Thalia had ever gotten away with that before. No exes. It usually made her skin crawl. But with Luke, it felt completely right.

Somehow, she managed to stand on his shoulders. Luke rose on his tiptoes, giving her just enough height to scramble into the attic. It wasn't graceful—Luke gave her a final shove by the hipbone—but she made it.

"Please be careful," he called up.

She sneezed in response. The attic had gathered even more dust and grime since her last visit. Not surprising. Duncan's book was practically a magnet for filth. She spotted it right where she'd left it, now nestled under a thick cobweb in a particularly musty corner.

"Greeeat."

"Something wrong?"

"No, just more cobwebs. I just washed my hair."

"Don't you mean *I* just washed your hair?"

She smirked, brushed off the cobweb, and grabbed the book. A spider scurried away to a safer corner. Smart.

"Look out," she called, crawling back to the opening.

Luke backed up as far as he could. "Try not to torque it. I don't need it popping open and sucking me into a green vortex."

With one last look at him, Sephie dropped the book. It hit the rug with a thud and a puff of dust.

She peeked out to find Luke practically plastered against the opposite wall. "Maybe we should've rethought this," he muttered.

"It's closed. Even if it makes you sick, catch me first, then you can throw up."

"Oh yeah, that'll make the house real happy."

"You're being annoying again, Flex."

"I'm allowed to have concerns."

"Good lord." She rolled her eyes. "Just get over here and catch me before I break both my ankles."

She dangled her legs through the opening for effect. Luke groaned and walked over, carefully avoiding the book, before holding out his arms. She dropped into them easily, cradled just the way she liked.

"My big strong man takes such good care of me," she cooed.

Luke's cheeks flushed pink. "That's not fair."

She traced her fingertips along the back of his neck. "What isn't?"

"Shut up."

"Make me."

He kissed her so hard she briefly forgot how to breathe. When he pulled away, she was grinning like an idiot. He set her down gently, making sure her legs were steady after being smooched senseless.

But the warmth quickly faded as her eyes drifted back to the book.

Scowling, she leaned down and picked it up. The cloth cover was now clammy and damp with mildew. She turned it over in her hands.

"You good?" she asked, glancing at Luke.

He nodded. "So far."

The book didn't feel evil, just heavy and wrong. She wished Gran had given her something more than a vague "use your instincts." Sephie could barely trust herself to get through the day without having a mental breakdown, let alone cleanse haunted objects.

"Um…" she passed the book from one hand to the other. "I… don't know."

Luke stood behind her, his fingers barely ghosting over her shoulders, before settling into a steadier, grounding touch.

"Maybe just ask it to leave?"

"It can't be that easy."

"You never know unless you try."

She sighed, holding the book in front of her. "Hey, Duncan? If you're still around, do you think you could just… move on?"

Nothing.

She and Luke exchanged a look.

Cautiously, she lifted the cover. Duncan's scratchy handwriting glared back at her. She flipped a page. Still fine.

"Oh my god," she whispered. "I think I did it."

Luke wrapped his arms around her waist and squeezed. "I think you d—"

She shrieked and dropped the book. Her palms were already bright red and she had to hold back a gag as the smell of burnt flesh hit her nose.

"That bastard burned you," Luke muttered, grabbing her wrists for a closer look. Then he reached for the book, only to recoil instantly, clapping a hand over his eyes.

"AGH! Okay, it burned you and somehow twisted my optic nerves into a knot!"

Sephie gritted her teeth and glared at the book like it had personally insulted her lineage. It had landed open at that diagram. A faint wisp of green smoke leaked from the pages.

She growled and stomped on it. A small puff of smoke escaped, like a dying breath.

"DUNCAN," she snapped. "You need to get the hell out of here. You tried to kill your own baby, you nearly killed my boyfriend, and now you burn me on the most inconvenient part of my body?!"

She stomped again.

"GET. OUT!"

A wheezing whistle slipped from the book's spine. One final, curling tendril of green smoke twisted upward and vanished into thin air.

Luke lowered his hands and blinked rapidly.

A beat.

"Okay… I think that worked."

Sephie glanced down at her hands. The redness, peeling skin, and the forming blisters were gone. Completely healed.

She stared. "I had to *yell* at him?"

Luke rushed over and scooped her up in one motion. She laughed and kicked her legs.

"See?" he grinned. "That smart mouth of yours is actually good for something."

She kissed him. "Damn right."

Chapter 56

Sephie finally got the chance to toss what was left of the book into one of the house's fireplaces. She chucked it into the one in Luke's room. She could admit it—she was a little too gleeful as she watched the flames consume the last of Duncan's horrors.

"Well, that explains why your parents thought you were an arsonist," Luke said beside her. "Remind me to never get on your bad side."

"I thought you would have realized that already," she replied.

He kissed the top of her head. "Oh, I did. Just reiterating."

They watched the last of the paper burn into ash and left the room, hand in hand. A calm pulse now moved through the house; the sentience still lingered, but it felt as if the manor had finally exhaled. Candles burned brighter, the floorboards no longer creaked randomly, and every door remained unlocked.

Sephie looked down at their clasped hands and sighed softly.

"What's up, Scoob?"

"It just feels weird that we're about to see if we can get out of here or not."

He chewed his lip. That was answer enough. She knew what he was thinking. If the door stayed locked, what would they have to do next? And if they could leave, what then? Would they go their separate ways? Would reality pull them apart?

Luke stopped as they stepped into the foyer, turning to face her and taking both her hands. It was around eleven a.m., and sunlight streamed in through the front windows. The chandelier cast tiny rainbows across his face, and in that moment, he looked nothing short of divine.

"Sephie, look," he said, voice soft. "I meant what I said. I like you a whole heck of a lot. If we'd met outside all this, I still would've done everything in my power to win you over."

She smiled up at him. "You mean it?"

"Absolutely." He kissed her forehead, then leaned down until their noses touched. "And I know you're stubborn as a mule. Which is why I trust you'll do whatever it takes to make this work."

They stood like that, wrapped in quiet and colored light. That familiar hint of musk clung to Luke's skin, calming her nerves. Somehow, he wasn't just someone who respected and protected her. He genuinely liked her, enough to stay.

"Okay," she breathed. "Let's do this."

They turned to the front door together. Sephie squeezed his hand.

"You want to do it?"

"I don't know."

She reached for the knob. Luke gripped her hand just a little too tightly, but she barely noticed. The silence held as she turned it—and the knob gave way.

Sephie let out a sigh of relief as the door swung open. They stared out at a clear blue sky, the sweet scent of wildflowers drifting in. A dove cooed nearby. It was a stunning contrast to the gloom of their first day. Luke reached over and gently closed her dropped jaw.

"Shall we see if we can walk through?"

She nodded. Luke offered his arm like a proper gentleman, and she took it, giving his bicep a playful squeeze. He exhaled with a dramatic sigh, then led her out the door.

It hadn't been that long, really. But it felt like they'd lived a dozen lives in those few days. Sephie didn't flinch when Luke caught her before she stepped into the same hole she'd stomped on day one.

"First thing we do? Fix that," she muttered.

"It's the least we can do."

They drifted toward the gardens without thinking. The wisteria arch hung heavy with blooms, and the makeup tent had been disassembled and folded neatly to one side.

"You think the house did that or the crew?"

"Who knows," Luke said.

"Is this... awkward?"

He guided her to a fountain rimmed with lily pads. They gazed at their reflections: a pair that couldn't have looked more different. But still, they worked.

"I think it feels weird because we went from coworkers who hated each other to this in a matter of days. It shifted so fast. But as long as you want to try, so do I."

She smiled. "I'm more than willing."

His hand slid into her curls, and she suppressed a moan. He chuckled low, kissed her neck, and she melted.

"Careful," she whispered.

"I don't think I want to be," he replied.

"SEPHIE?!"

They groaned. Thalia.

"Goddammit," Luke muttered.

Sephie sighed. "We should probably let them know the house didn't eat us."

They walked back to the front, where Thalia was knocking frantically on the glass. Jessica, Samantha, and Jace hovered behind her.

"Where are they?!"

"They're out," Sephie called.

The group turned. Thalia sprinted to them and wrapped both Sephie and Luke in a hug.

"You're safe! Welcome to the family, Luke!"

"Thalia! Jesus Christ."

Luke ruffled Thalia's hair, and she shrieked. "Watch the hair!"

"How are you two already like this?" Sephie rolled her eyes.

She headed toward Jessica, but Jace blocked her path. His face somehow looked worse with his nose still bandaged and eyes dark.

"Hold it, missy."

He grabbed her shoulder. Her vision didn't go white like before, but her breath hitched. She grabbed his wrist, twisted, and yanked his arm out of joint. He howled.

"You twisted my arm out of the socket!"

Luke stormed in, grabbed Jace's shoulder, and with a sharp motion popped it back into place. Jace yelped.

"There. Don't want my girlfriend to get in too much trouble," Luke muttered, then unceremoniously pushed him into the dirt.

"Well," Thalia said, "he keeps getting more pathetic."

Jessica nudged him with her foot. "Go home. I told you we didn't need you anymore."

"But the house is open! We can finish the episode! Without them."

"I think you'll find that isn't the case. It's the exact opposite, in fact," Jessica said smugly. "I negotiated new terms. We're going to continue without you, Jace."

He staggered to his feet, red-faced. "*Dead Serious* is nothing without me!"

"Hey, pretty boy," Samantha added, "your screen presence isn't exactly trending."

Jessica pulled out a folder and handed it over. "Amended contracts. You're on indefinite medical leave. If ratings stay stable or improve, we'll revisit your status."

Jace sputtered, then ran toward the house—and slammed into an invisible wall. He landed on the ground, hard.

"THIS ISN'T FAIR!"

Jessica sighed. "Sam, help me get him to the car?"

Luke walked over and lifted Jace like luggage. "Point me in the direction and pop the trunk."

As Samantha led him away, Thalia draped an arm around Sephie.

"Jessica's got an offer for you."

"I figured as much. What are the details?"

Jessica smiled. "You and Luke did amazing research under extreme conditions.

We want to make you the focal point for the remainder of the episode. We'll highlight the Ashland legacy, the house's history, and its unique properties. Whether you share the supernatural side is up to you."

"And we'd be paid standard regular salaries, not guest rates?"

"Correct," Jessica said, pulling out another binder. "Here's your amended contracts. Review them, and let me know by tomorrow."

"Let you know what by tomorrow?" Luke returned, slipping his hand into Sephie's. Thalia bounced on her toes.

"They want us to be the focus of the episode," Sephie said, handing him the folder.

Luke nodded. "We'll tell you tomorrow. We have plans."

Sephie squinted. "What plans?"

Jessica grinned. "Do you need a ride?"

"Nope," Luke said. "We're staying one more night. We still have some unfinished business."

Thalia smirked. "Unfinished business, huh?"

Sephie nudged her with her shoulder.

Jessica nodded. "Got it. Hope it goes well."

"Have fun, lovebirds!" Thalia cooed.

"Oh, go suck on Isiah's face," Sephie retorted.

Once the others were off the property, she turned to Luke.

"You're bad."

He kissed her neck, right out in the open.

"And?"

Sephie tilted her head, letting herself bask in the glow of him, of them, of the house that had gone quiet for the first time.

"So what now?"

Luke pulled her toward the steps, that grin she was quickly becoming addicted to spreading across his face.

"Like I said, we have unfinished business," he quipped, "it just so happens to do with that master bedroom."

And with that, they disappeared back inside. Not trapped this time, but choosing to stay.

Chapter 57

Luke couldn't keep his hands off Sephie as soon as they were back in the house. Something about knowing they could come and go as they pleased just heightened his need to have her close. His mouth stayed pressed to hers, their tongues tangling amidst hot breath. Her skin was smooth, her curls thick enough to easily fist, her mouth just perfect in every way.

"Luke?" Sephie gasped softly as she pulled her mouth away.

He gave a small whine and dipped to her neck. She let out a low chuckle.

"As much as I'd love to keep doing this until tomorrow, we actually do need to look over those contracts."

He pulled back and gave her a look. "You actually want to keep filming?"

She smirked and nodded.

"I mean, I'm glad to, I just figured you'd want to be done with everything."

"It sounds like it'd be even more money than before. I feel like we could both use it."

There was that.

He nipped at her neck again. "Surely, not much could be changed. Can't we just sign it in the morning and enjoy our last night here?"

She giggled but grabbed his face and pulled him away. "I just want to make sure."

Luke gave an exaggerated frown.

"Oh stop. We'll have some fun later, don't worry. Why don't you see if the house gave you any ingredients for a celebration meal?"

He grumbled, but he'd probably want to take advantage of the manor's hospitality while he still could. There was no telling when he'd next have access to this kind of bounty.

"You just want me to feed you."

"Duh," she teased, "but I also know how much you've liked cooking in here."

He kissed the top of her head.

"Fine, I'll cook you a nice feast."

Sephie grinned. "I'm going to go see if our phones work again."

He'd completely forgotten about modern technology. Between exploring the house, inventing new recipes, and making out with his girlfriend, he'd been more than occupied. Maybe it was time to finally delete Candy Crush...

Luke watched her until she was out of sight, then headed to the kitchen. Like the rest of the house, the kitchen now carried a peaceful air about it. He glanced at the windows and noticed they now had locks. Curious, he unlocked the middle one and pulled it wide open. Cooking with the windows open always made him feel a little more grounded. A bird chirped nearby and he grinned. If only they could stay here forever.

"Alright," Luke turned to the pantry, "let's see what you've got for me."

The icebox creaked in response. He arched a brow and leaned over to open it.

"Holy..."

Inside, a giant brisket took up nearly the entire space. He glanced around and spotted a glass baking dish already set out. He pulled the meat from the box and dropped it into the dish, ideas for rubs and seasoning flashing through his mind.

"What's that?"

Sephie had returned, both their phones in hand.

"Hope you like brisket."

"I do, but that thing's huge."

A clank sounded from a nearby cabinet.

Sephie walked over and opened it, laughing as she pulled out four miniature glass dishes with lids.

"I guess giving us to-go boxes just proves it's okay with us leaving."

"Kind of bittersweet," Luke hummed.

"I know," she said. "Side track, our phones work again. Your mom's been blowing yours up. No, I didn't open it."

Luke laughed. Classic Mom. His family couldn't visit in person—both his parents were CEOs of huge companies—but that didn't mean his mother wouldn't try to find a way to check in.

"Come here," he said, pulling Sephie to his side and grabbing his phone.

"You think now is the time for the whole meet-the-parents thing?" she muttered.

"Oh, don't worry, I'm just texting her to let her know I'm alive." He held the phone out and snapped a quick selfie.

Sephie yelped. "Hey! Warn a person!"

He studied the photo. He was grinning, arm around Sephie. She had her trademark smirk, eyes almost glaring. She looked exactly like herself. Perfect.

"You look like my adorable gremlin of a girlfriend. Don't worry."

She rolled her eyes, but he saw the smile pulling at the corner of her mouth.

Whitney Houston's *I Wanna Dance With Somebody* started blaring from his phone. Sephie burst into laughter.

"Why am I not surprised?"

He waggled his eyebrows and answered the call. "Hey, Mom."

"Luke Oisín Mavros, you don't even call, and then you just drop a girl on me out of nowhere?"

"I was gonna say put her on speaker, but I can hear every word," Sephie teased.

"Told you, Boston," Luke replied, then tapped the speaker button. "Be nice, Mom. You're on speaker."

"Sephie, is it? Hello, dear. I hope my dipshit son is treating you right."

Luke rolled his eyes. "Great to talk to you too."

"He is," Sephie said brightly. "But he's also really good at keeping me in line. I definitely needed that."

"You're both okay?" his mom asked, her voice softening.

"Yeah, Mom. We're fine. The house was intense, to say the least, but it's all good now. We're leaving tomorrow."

There was a pause—just long enough for Luke to glance at the screen.

"I was relieved when the crew checked in. But I was still worried, especially since you couldn't call or text. You know your dad and I couldn't get away from work to come see for ourselves."

Luke shrugged, rubbing the back of his neck. "We were just… stuck without technology, it was really like being transported back in time."

"I'm just glad to hear your voice. And to know you're with someone who makes you laugh again. You haven't smiled like the way your are in that photo in a long time."

Luke blinked at that. Sephie gave his hand a small squeeze.

"Promise me you'll stop by when you get back. I worry, you know."

Luke smiled softly. "Yeah, Mom. I'll come by."

"Good. Bring Sephie. She looks like a little moonbeam with a sharp edge. I like her already."

"Thanks, Mom," he said, a smile tugging at his mouth. "Love you."

"Love you too, sweetheart. Now go feed that girl."

"Working on it."

He hung up, and Sephie burst out laughing again. He loved her laugh. He loved it more than he knew what to do with.

"I like your mom."

"Of course you do."

"Isn't that a good thing?"

He pulled her into another kiss, shutting her up in his favorite way. She didn't seem to mind; her hands roamed his back, neck, then tangled in his hair. He let out a low growl, picked her up, and set her on the counter, stepping between her thighs. Who needed brisket when he had her?

Her legs wrapped around his waist automatically, pulling him in until there was no space left. He felt her smile against his mouth and kissed her harder. Her lips were soft, but the way she kissed him back was fierce. Sephie didn't kiss like a girl in a romance movie, she kissed like she was winning a battle that didn't exist.

His hands slipped under her shirt, thumbs brushing just below the stays she still wore. Her breath hitched, skin warm under his fingers. Her hands slid up into his hair again, tugging him closer. He trailed his mouth down her jaw, finding the spot that made her sigh.

She arched into him, her hips shifting in a way that made his head spin. He kissed her collarbone and murmured something against her skin that made her shiver and dig her nails into his shoulders.

And then the oven *dinged*.

They both froze.

That was... new. It was way too modern for a haunted Victorian manor.

"Is that—?" Sephie started.

"It somehow updated the oven to ding?" Luke muttered against her neck. "Of course."

As if on cue, something rustled in the pantry, followed by a thump. A bag of brown sugar had landed dramatically just inside the doorway.

Sephie groaned and leaned back against the cabinets, her head thunking lightly. "Unbelievable. It spent almost a week trying to play matchmaker, and now it's trying to stop us from desecrating the brisket."

"Technically," Luke said, sighing as he kissed her forehead, "I think it just wants to make sure dinner gets made."

"Rude."

"We did say have fun later. Maybe it thinks it's owed something happening in the master bedroom."

She smirked. "Are you still up for that?"

"Hell yeah." He kissed her nose and bent to grab the brown sugar. "Now, I'm thinking brown sugar rub and some root veggies..."

Chapter 58

"Okay, fine, it was definitely worth waiting six hours for this."

Of all times to not speed up cooking, Ashland Manor had picked today. It forced Luke to slow roast the brisket, brushing on more of the drippings and rub every hour. While they waited, they spent time revisiting the entire house, noticing that the sweet, settled calm had spread everywhere, even the ballroom.

Luke still refused to step foot inside. Sephie didn't blame him. She understood all too well what happened when you tried to face trauma too soon. They stood just outside the entrance, gazing at the beautiful hardwood floors and cream flourishes, grateful not to see any more green smog.

The library was somehow even more magical than before. A heavenly glow seemed to cascade through the room. One of the windows had been thrown open, and the scent of roses wafted in, mixing beautifully with the smell of old paper. Sephie could've sworn she heard violin music playing from somewhere, but she didn't question it.

She grabbed a copy of *War and Peace* and headed back into the garden, planting a kiss on Luke on the way. He'd tried to keep her in the kitchen, but she danced away, teasing that if she had to wait for dinner, he'd have to wait for cuddles.

After a few chapters, she turned to reviewing their updated contracts. Thankfully, there wasn't much to worry about: no tricks or fine print. The biggest changes were Jace's removal and a pay increase, both of which only worked in their favor. Luke signed his copy when he came out to let her know dinner was finally ready.

They were back in the dining room now, and the manor had gone all out. Bouquets of roses and geraniums lined the table, matching flower garlands draped from the ceiling. New china, silverware, and crisp white napkins gleamed beneath the glow of bright sconces. The wallpaper sparkled faintly again. It all looked like something straight out of a *Home & Gardens* feature spread.

To Luke's amusement, Sephie didn't even try to suppress her moans after the first few bites.

"Well damn."

"Shut up and take it as a compliment."

He grinned, taking a bite of his own. "Trust me, I am."

Sephie let him gloat. He deserved it. She savored her meal, letting the warmth of the room and the food wrap around her. She knew they'd have to leave the next day and return to the outside world. She'd probably get coffee with Thalia and debrief everything. Luke would want to dive straight back into his restaurant. Hopefully, they'd continue to enjoy this strange, beautiful thing between them.

"You think the city will let us visit again?" she asked.

"I'm not sure," he said. "That's more your department."

"Maybe I can work out something with them. Like a caretaker arrangement. We'd check in every now and then."

Luke grinned. "I'd like that."

"Me too."

He wiped his mouth with a napkin. "Didn't think to make dessert. Sorry."

Showtime.

Sephie wiped her mouth and smiled. "Oh, I have that covered."

Luke blankly stared at her.

"Flex. Master bedroom."

His eyes widened.

"Oh. OH."

Laughing, she stood and sauntered over to him, licking her lips in mock seduction. He gazed up at her, pupils already darkening. She took his hand and tugged him toward the stairs.

"You're making it hard not to call you a himbo."

"My brain short-circuits when you talk like that."

"Sure it does."

They reached the master bedroom faster than expected. It was the last room they hadn't explored. A soft glow spilled from under the door. Though the house had been quiet since the book was destroyed, something about the silence now felt absolute.

They stood there, fingers laced, just breathing. Sephie could hear her pulse in her ears—and judging by Luke's, he felt the same.

With one last squeeze of her hand, he turned the knob. The door opened to reveal an enormous room. A grand four-poster bed draped in a canopy stood in the center. Two arched windows, veiled in sheer chiffon, allowed moonlight to spill in, casting everything in soft silver. No candles needed.

Sephie whispered, "Whoa."

Luke stepped behind her, wrapping his arms around her waist. "This... this is definitely a bedroom."

"I'm guessing it belonged to Gus and Cora."

"Seems likely."

She turned to face him. "We don't have to do anything. We can just sleep."

He kissed her gently. "We'll do whatever you want."

She smiled and slid her hands under the hem of his shirt. He shivered, and she pressed her nose to his chest, her hands roaming upward. He lifted his arms, and she pulled his shirt off before tossing it aside.

"Quit objectifying me," he teased.

She leaned forward and licked between his pecs. He groaned.

"I do what I want."

Their next kiss was slow. No rush, no curses or danger looming. Just mouths, skin, and moonlight. They fumbled toward the bed, Sephie hitting it first. She flopped back as Luke leaned over her, one hand pulling off her shirt, the other undoing the ties of her stays.

"Still rocking the corset, huh?"

"Not a corset, this is far more breatheable. Victorians knew how to make underwear."

He loosened the knots and peeled the stays away, his gaze darkening.

"Tell me if you want to stop."

She nodded.

He kissed along her collarbone as the stays slipped away. His fingers traced gently over her ribs, then upward. Her breath hitched as he brushed her nipples. She trembled.

"You're going to be the death of me," he muttered.

"Please haunt me if so."

She flipped him over and straddled him, grinning as her hands mapped his chest.

"Always need the upper hand," he said.

"More like you were about to ruin my plan."

He laughed until she kissed his throat, trailing her tongue along his neck up to his ear. She kissed, licked, and nipped her way down until she reached the waistband of his pants.

"Sephie..." Her name on his lips almost sounded like a warning. But she was ready to play with fire.

"Shhh," she murmured.

He rested his head back on the pillows as she continued her journey down his body, planting kisses along his chest and stomach in a slow, purposeful manner. She let her hands creep up along his sides as she followed a very deliberate path downward. When she finally dipped lower, he sucked in a quick, sharp breath.

There wasn't much talking after that. Just his fingers curling tight in the blankets, the occasional shaky curse, and the sound of her name falling from his lips. She kept it steady, focused, aware of every shift in his breathing, every time his hips jerked without permission. Being able to bring this giant of a man to a quivering state like this was an incredible thing.

And when he finally came apart beneath her, it was like the moment just before a storm breaks—quiet, trembling, and then everything at once.

She kissed his hip before crawling back up beside him, unable to hide the smug look on her face.

"Did I actually kill you?"

"Almost."

"Well, good. I'd miss you."

"Woman, I can't feel my legs."

"Sorry, not sorry."

He pulled her up and kissed her until she couldn't form full thoughts. His hands found the waistband of her leggings.

"Your turn."

She gasped as he flipped her onto her back, tugging away her remaining clothes. They took a moment, drinking each other in. Open. Bare. No games.

"Still okay?"

She nodded.

He didn't need words. His kisses started slow, burning hotter with each one. Her hands tangled in his hair as his mouth traveled lower. Her hips lifted, and he rested her legs over his shoulders.

And then…

Her voice broke into moans she couldn't stop. Luke moved with purpose, adjusting pressure, finding every spot that made her gasp. It didn't feel new. It felt remembered, like his body had known hers long before this moment. Her back arched. Her thighs trembled.

She tried to speak, but couldn't. Her body jolted out of nowhere as everything snapped. It felt as if the moon had come crashing down into the ocean, a burst of light exploding into the cosmos.

For a second, she couldn't move, could barely breathe.

Luke flopped beside her, looking infuriatingly proud of himself. He pulled the covers over them.

"You good?"

"I think I blacked out."

"Excellent."

She elbowed him lightly and curled close. Her skin tingled. Her brain hadn't caught up.

The house, amazingly, had stayed quiet.

After a long pause, Sephie murmured into his chest, "So. How was your dessert?"

Luke snorted. "Best damn thing I've ever tasted."

Chapter 59

Luke woke from one of the best night's sleep he'd ever had just as the sun began to rise. Bright pink and deep orange replaced the moonlight, casting a warm glow through the room. Sephie was still snoring, wrapped up in sleep. Her fair skin flushed under the dawn, and Luke marveled at how she glowed, whether it was sun or moonlight. She was his own little celestial being. Sometimes, he swore the freckles on her cheeks twinkled like stars.

He wanted to stay there forever. But his bladder had other plans.

To his relief, the bed didn't shift as he slipped from under the covers. A black silk robe hung neatly on the master bathroom door, making Luke chuckle.

"Don't want me walking around in my birthday suit?" he whispered to the house.

One of the sconces flickered in response.

He took the hint and slipped the robe on. It was surprisingly cool and comfortable. After relieving himself, he caught his reflection in the mirror and grinned. He looked so stupidly happy, and somehow that made him even happier.

The bottom of the blanket flipped as he returned to the bedroom, revealing something beneath the bed. Brows raised, Luke crouched and reached under, fingers closing around a metal handle. He pulled out a slim, well-kept briefcase. The pink sunlight flashed off a small inscription on the front: Ashland.

Flipping the clasps open with care, he lifted the lid.

Inside, nestled in black velvet, was a single stack of paperwork tied with twine. He lifted it out and double-checked the case. There were no hidden compartments. Sephie made an adorable snorting sound and rolled to her side. Her leg stretched out under the covers, her foot flexing like she was waking it up from a nap.

"Luke?" she mumbled sleepily.

He walked to the bed, papers in hand. Her eyes were barely open, but she reached out anyway. He set the papers at the foot of the bed and slid back under the covers. She burrowed into him immediately, her face pressed to his neck. Luke sighed, content, fingers trailing lightly along her ribs.

"Where'd the robe come from?" She muttered.

"I had to pee, so the house gave it to me," he said.

"Take it back off."

He smirked. "But that means you have to let go of me again."

"Fine."

"Fine, I can move, or fine, leave it be?"

She squeezed him tighter. That answered that. He kept tracing her skin, memorizing every soft, warm inch.

"You gonna make me breakfast one last time?" she murmured.

Luke sighed, torn. He wanted to. But...

"What do you think about coming to the restaurant instead? It wouldn't be a last time, it'd be another first."

She pulled away to look up at him. Her smile was so radiant it made his insides melt.

"I'd love that."

"Okay then."

She planted a few kisses on his chest before sinking back into sleep, her snores gentle against his skin. Luke smiled, stroked her hair, and let himself drift off again.

He wasn't sure how long they slept, but he found himself back in one of the first peaceful, normal, dreams he'd had in ages. The bedroom filled with clouds, glowing in the soft hues of the sunrise. Doves flew in slow, graceful loops around the ceiling, cooing. The air smelled like flowers and fresh rain. Somewhere, a couple laughed gently.

Luke turned his head to see Cora and Gus, standing hand in hand among the clouds. Cora gave him a warm smile; Gus nodded. Then they faded.

"Flex?"

He stirred. Morning sunlight now filled the room. Sephie looked at him, eyes wide.

"Did you see them too?"

He nodded. "I think they were giving us their blessing."

She snorted. "We don't need a blessing from a random couple."

"Scoob, we're literally together because the power of their love made this house sentient."

She huffed and jostled the bed, sending the stack of papers sliding.

"Oh shoot," Luke said, remembering. He slid out again and spotted another black robe draped over a bedpost. He held it up with a grin.

"M'lady."

Sephie giggled, then slipped out of bed and into the robe. Luke kissed both her cheeks, then grabbed the papers.

"These were in a briefcase under the bed. I figured we could go through them together."

He pulled off the twine and unfolded the top page.

Luke flipped through the stack, his eyebrows climbing higher with every page. "This is... everything. The deed to the house, transfer records for the winery, even savings accounts set aside for Ada. They didn't miss a single detail."

Sephie leaned over his shoulder, eyes wide. "It's like they prepped this for whoever came next."

"Not whoever," he said. "Us."

She smiled. "You still think they might've been spies?"

He tapped the edge of the page against her nose. "If they were, they were extremely organized spies."

"Sentimental ones too," she added, pointing to a page labeled *For the Garden.* "These are handwritten notes on how to care for every single plant out there."

"They weren't hiding anything," Luke murmured. "They were waiting."

Sephie looked up at him. "Waiting for someone to understand it."

He kissed her temple. "Well, I guess that's us."

A low piano melody drifted through the hallway, no longer bashful or mysterious, but clear and bright.

Sephie tilted her head. "What is that?"

"*Les Ogives*," Luke said, smiling. "Inspired by Notre Dame."

The melody deepened, swelling as it shifted into an echoing organ arrangement that filled the space like stained glass sunlight.

Sephie snorted. "Just gotta be dramatic, don't you?"

They hadn't initially brought much, so they grabbed their things quickly, but in a comfortable rhythm, letting the music guide their movements. Just as they stepped off the stairwell, Sephie glanced over her shoulder. The house stood quiet, dignified, as if it were watching them with pride.

She stepped back and whispered, "Thanks for everything."

A breeze stirred in the foyer, brushing against their cheeks like a kiss.

Luke reached for her hand and looked back at the house one last time. The place had been a curveball. Just like *Dead Serious*. Just like Sephie. He hadn't come here looking for closure or romance or some big emotional breakthrough. He came for a paycheck and a chance to finally get the restaurant really going.

But somehow, he'd ended up with more than he planned. A lot more.

The house, the ghosts, the locked-in-room talks—it had all worked out. And now he was walking away with someone who, for whatever reason, decided she liked him enough to kiss him.

Not bad for a detour.

Sephie brushed her thumb along the back of his hand. "You ready?"

He turned toward her and grinned. "Yeah. Just taking a mental picture."

"Of the house?"

"Of you. But the house is a close second."

She rolled her eyes and tugged him forward.

"Hungry?" he asked, shutting the front door behind them.

"For food or for dessert?" she teased.

He smirked. "Let's start with brunch. Dessert can come later."

She beamed. "Good, because I've got ideas."

Seven Months Later

"I'm so sorry, are you Sephie Blake?"

Sephie wanted to sink right into the floor. She'd tried to hide in one of the restaurant booths with her book, but it obviously hadn't worked. She peered over the pages and found a terrified-looking teenage girl, clutching a book of her own to her chest. Sephie relaxed; the kid was more nervous than she was. Forcing what she hoped was a gentle smile, she set her book down.

"I am. What's your name?"

The girl's shoulders relaxed. "Morgan."

"What can I do for you, Morgan?"

The girl gently held out a pen and her book, revealing the familiar blue cover.

"Would you sign my book?"

Sephie genuinely smiled and held out her hand. "Sure."

She took the book, opened the front cover, and saw her own headshot smiling back at her. Sephie would never get used to this. She quickly wrote, "To Morgan, thanks for your support," followed by her signature, and handed the book back. Morgan gave a quick nod of thanks and scurried away. Sephie had to hand it to Thalia—she'd managed to market the book to an audience that looked a lot like the author herself.

"Who was that?"

Speaking of Thalia.

Sephie glanced up to find her sister leaning on the booth, cell phone in one hand, dinner plate in the other. She'd worked her tail off the past couple months and had become queen of multitasking.

"Another fan of the book. She wanted me to sign her copy."

"Awww," Thalia cooed. "I never thought something like *There's Plasma in the Walls* would reach such a wide audience. But look at you—we're going to have to get you a bodyguard." She held up the dinner plate and snapped a photo. "Sorry, collaboration with the pottery house down the road."

Sephie grinned. "Thalia, you do realize a huge part of both my book's and the restaurant's success is because of you, right?"

Thalia rolled her eyes but let a cheeky grin slip. "What, little ole me? Nah." She leaned over and planted a kiss on Sephie's cheek. "Isiah's taking me to a winery tonight, but I got all my work done—don't worry."

Sephie had to bite back a knowing smile. "Got it. Have fun."

Thalia practically floated away. It was so nice to see her genuinely happy. Luke patted Sephie's shoulder in passing as he wandered out of the kitchen. He was wearing a goddamn apron and somehow making it look sexy. He slipped into the booth across from her and took her hand.

"Hey, Scoob."

She leaned over the table and gave him a quick peck. "Hey, Flex."

"Thalia have any clue she's getting proposed to tonight?" he waggled his eyebrows.

Sephie smiled. "Nope, thankfully. Isiah's been trying so hard to keep it a surprise."

Luke shook his head. "Those two are so inseparable, I'm amazed she didn't catch on."

Sephie wasn't surprised. Thalia had wanted to prove herself when it came to marketing. Since Luke hired her, she'd worked tirelessly until the restaurant was packed most nights. Sephie hadn't even asked for help with the book launch—Thalia had just taken it on. She'd been so busy diving back into her career, Sephie was amazed she got any sleep.

Luke lifted Sephie's hand to his mouth and kissed her knuckles. She cocked a brow.

"What do you want?"

"What, I can't love on my girlfriend?"

"You usually only do the knuckle kiss when you're trying to butter me up. So go right ahead."

Luke smirked. "Fine. Xavier reached out again."

Sephie pulled her hand back and groaned loudly. "Luuuke."

"I didn't agree to anything! He just had another pitch."

She rolled her eyes. Their *Dead Serious* episode had ended up being a roaring success. The couple's chemistry wasn't just real—it lit up the screen. Just as Xavier had predicted, Sephie's snarky wit and Luke's lovable lumberjack energy had captivated viewers. Producers had been chasing them ever since, begging them to star in a show of their own.

But Sephie was content with the little life she and Luke were building together. Luke had brought on a full team at the restaurant and even set up benefits. She'd taken time off from investigations to focus on writing, and with Luke's support, her debut had come together fast—and found an enthusiastic audience.

It was the move-in that surprised everyone: Luke was living with Sephie two weeks after Ashland Manor. But after growing so used to each other's presence, even a short separation had felt off. Sephie worried it was too fast, but Luke kept reminding her that nothing about their relationship was typical. And if it was working, that's what mattered.

And granted, Luke's mom was confused that Thalia was the one getting engaged first.

Sephie sighed. "So what exactly is Xavier suggesting this time?"

Luke perked up. "I think you'll actually like this one."

"Doubtful."

"He wants to research Lucy's house, to glean more information on Ada and all that."

Her jaw dropped. Luke reached over and gently closed it, making her playfully bare her teeth.

"Lucy's legit willing to come back, just as long as you're on the research team. And since we're kind of a matched set, it'd be a duo investigation."

She smirked. "I hate group projects."

"But you love me."

"Yeah, yeah, whatever."

He leaned over and kissed her nose. She couldn't help but smile.

"You know I love my Flex."

"So, you'll do the show?"

She huffed. "I will seriously consider it."

He stood up and headed back to the kitchen. "That's a yes."

"Is not."

"I know you, Scoob. Now, I've got eclairs to tend to."

Sephie crossed her arms and stared ahead, smiling to herself. It was wild how much could change in just seven months. Things she thought she was done with—men, investigating, honoring Gran, even a real relationship with Thalia—were now huge parts of her life.

And she wouldn't have it any other way.

She twirled the chain of Ada's locket, still resting against her chest, and whispered with a soft smile,

"Thanks again."